AF241244

Contractually MINE

A BEST FRIENDS BOOK CLUB NOVEL

JENNIFER CHIPMAN

also by jennifer chipman

Best Friends Book Club

Academically Yours - Noelle & Matthew

Famously Mine - Tessa & Oliver

Disrespectfully Yours - Angelina & Benjamin

Contractually Mine - Zofia & Nicolas

Fearlessly Yours - Gabrielle & Hunter

Merrily Mine - Emily & Mason

Gracefully Yours - Charlotte & Daniel

Cousins Coffee Club

(Best Friends Book Club Second Generation)

Uniquely in Love - Ellie & Owen

For the girlies who love a blond, golden retriever book husband who says "my wife" like it's going out of style. 💍

playlist

- fake smile - Ariana Grande
- champagne problems - Taylor Swift
- Older Than I Am - Lennon Stella
- Nothing New - Taylor Swift
- Camouflage - Selena Gomez
- I'm Not That Girl - Stephen Schwartz, Idina Menzel
- Gravity - John Mayer
- Gorgeous - Taylor Swift
- Glamorous - Fergie
- Mastermind - Taylor Swift
- Everything Has Changed - Taylor Swift, Ed Sheeran
- You Belong With Me - Taylor Swift
- I Wanna Be Yours - Arctic Monkeys
- I Believe in You - Michael Bublé
- Line Without A Hook - Ricky Montgomery
- This Side of Paradise - Coyote Theory
- Something Just Like This - The Chainsmokers
- Close to You - Gracie Abrams
- I Believe - Jonas Brothers
- Somewhere Only We Know - Keane

- Check Yes, Juliet - We The Kings
- bad idea - Ariana Grande
- Guilty as Sin? - Taylor Swift
- Tears - Sabrina Carpenter
- Love Me Like You Do - Ellie Goulding
- Perfect - Ed Sheeran
- Dress - Taylor Swift
- Juno - Sabrina Carpenter
- invisible string - Taylor Swift
- Fall - Jonas Brothers
- Two Is Better Than One - BOYS LIKE GIRLS, Taylor Swift
- Call It What You Want - Taylor Swift
- Hestitate - Jonas Brothers
- peace - Taylor Swift
- Gravity - Sara Bareilles
- Someone to Stay - Vancouver Sleep Clinic
- Help Me Make It Through the Night - Michael Bublé, Loren Allred
- Need You Now - Lady A
- Stay With Me - Sam Smith
- Close Your Eyes - Michael Bublé
- You & I - One Direction
- Stay Stay Stay - Taylor Swift
- Heart Like Yours - Willamette Stone
- Everything - Michael Bublé
- To Love Somebody - Michael Bublé
- This Love - Taylor Swift
- Love Her - Jonas Brothers
- Ours - Taylor Swift
- Everyday - High School Musical 2 Soundtrack
- Paper Rings - Taylor Swift
- Best of Me - Michael Bublé
- King Of My Heart - Taylor Swift

prologue

Nicolas

Walking into the lobby of Willamette Tech always gave me a sense of immense satisfaction. Maybe it was because I knew that one day, it would be *mine*.

In two years, when I graduated from college, I'd be joining the ranks, working my way up in the company and learning the ropes from my father, the current CEO. I couldn't wait. Everyone kept telling me the last two years in school would go buy so fast, and not to blink because it would be over.

Though, fuck, part of me would miss college. The parties, the friends, the girls. My life was perfect.

The lobby was pristine—glossy tiled floors and large glass windows that the sun shined through on a rare sunny day in Portland, the large reception desk a slab of white quartz. It was sleek and high end—exactly what you'd expect from a tech company making their mark on the world. We were one of the fastest growing tech companies outside of Silicon Valley, a badge of pride for everyone who worked here.

I was here to visit my father to finalize my internship for the summer, the one my university required I complete to finish my degree. It seemed completely unnecessary to me, considering I already had a job offer post college, but it meant I got to spend more time here, and so I couldn't complain about that.

Heading towards the elevators, I rolled my shoulders back, walking like I owned the place. It was a mantra my dad had instilled in me since I was young. I'd always tried to absorb his lessons. To be the perfect heir he'd taught me to be.

It was only when I'd started college that I'd realized how much more there was to life. How much I'd been missing. Now I was determined to live life to the fullest, never letting anything —or anyone—hold me back.

The doors in front of me started to close, and I slipped my hand in between them, holding the elevator open.

"Sorry." I slid in, the only other person inside a girl. She looked to be around my age, maybe a few years older, from her blouse and a tight skirt.

I pushed the button for the top floor—the one my father's office was in—before leaning against against the wall, I watched the numbers increase as we went up, up, up.

She looked straight forward at the doors, reaching into her bag to grab a small red tube, but her grip slip, and it clattered to the ground, rolling away from her. "Oh!" The girl exclaimed, her dark brown curls bouncing as she lunged for it. Still, I was faster, picking it up. I held it out to her and she turned to look at me— giving me a full view of her face for the first time.

Holy fuck. She was *hot*.

Grinning at her, I held out my hand, offering her the red lipstick. My eyes darted down to her lips, and I felt captivated by them. Which was fucking *weird*, because no matter how hot a girl was, I'd never looked at them and wanted to know if they were as soft as they looked.

She frowned at me, grabbing it quickly. "I could have grabbed that."

I shrugged my shoulders. "No big deal, really." The girl stared at me, and I opened my mouth again, hating the silence.

"I'm Nicolas, by the way. Nicolas *Larsen*." I emphasized my last name.

"Zofia," she said, blinking at me with no recognition. "Nice to meet you. Do you work here?"

She really had no clue who I was, did she?

"I'm Alexander Larsen's son," I told her. "The CEO?"

"Oh." She looked unimpressed, and it felt a breath of fresh air. So many people only saw dollar signs when they found out who I was.

The elevator door dinged open, and she stepped off, turning back to me. "Bye." She brushed her hair back over her shoulder, her eyes holding mine one last time as the door slid close.

"Damn," I said to myself once I was all alone.

There was something different about her, and I wanted to know more.

Wanted to know *her*.

No matter what it took.

1
zofia

"Come work for me."

My fingers stilled on the keyboard as I took in the man standing in front of me. "What?" I asked, as if I hadn't heard him right.

"Come work for me," he said again. It was late, and the rest of the office was empty. I was working overtime, trying to finish the project I was currently working on.

"Huh. That's what I thought you said the first time." Furrowing my brow, I cocked my head at him. "I *do* work for you," I reminded him, waving my hand around the room as if that answered his point. "Head of HR, remember?"

Nicolas Larsen, the CEO's son—and the current chief financial officer of Willamette Tech—ran his fingers through his silky blond locks. I'd noticed from our company meetings that he had a habit of doing that whenever he was nervous. "I mean, be my assistant. Work for *me*."

Sometimes it was strange, how much he had changed since we'd first met, my first week at the company. He'd transformed from the flirty college student into a charismatic businessman.

Still confident, slightly cocky, and a little too sure of himself, but enough to make me actually consider what it would be like to work under him.

I thought about going backwards. Being just the girl who went to fetch coffee and perform mundane tasks once again. That hadn't been me in years, and I had no desire to go be just someone's assistant ever again.

"No."

"Please?" he asked. Like *that* would make a difference. As if a simple plea could change my mind. But the pout on his face, combined with his pleading eyes, was almost too much to ignore. *Almost.*

I tapped my manicured fingernails on my desk. "Why?"

"What do you mean, *why?*" Nicolas frowned, letting out a sigh. "I need a new assistant."

What happened with the old one? I wanted to ask. *Did you sleep with this one, too?* The ones who he'd had as his assistants in the past had all been the same: young, giggling girls who fawned all over him, easily susceptible to his charm. I scrunched up my nose. The rich, playboy type might have done it for some people, but not for me.

Nicolas stepped forward, about to open his mouth to say something else, when I held up a hand. "I just—look." I frowned. "You could have any assistant you wanted. Why *me?*" It wasn't like I had experience in being an executive assistant. And he could find anyone to bring him coffee.

"Because," he responded, like that was any answer at all.

"*Because...?*" I repeated.

He cleared his throat. "Miss Narayan, it's a simple decision, really. You're intelligent and an incredibly fast thinker. I've been watching you." His cheeks flamed, somehow making the freckles on his nose stand out. "Not in a weird way, but just—do you know how organized you are?"

"Well, I—" My fingers ran over the wood of my desk. Currently, I sat in a cubicle, surrounded by the other HR team members. I'd been working for Willamette Technology—a medium-sized software company—for the last few years. Even though I didn't have some big, fancy corner office, I didn't mind. After all, I liked my job and the people I worked with. After my last promotion, I was content.

"You're bright. Witty. Got the entire human resources department to run more efficiently than I've ever seen it within less than one quarter after taking over the team. I need someone like you."

"Thank you?" I was glad my achievements were being noticed, but I still didn't know why he'd come to me.

I'd heard the rumors about Nicolas Larsen and his stream of assistants. They were out the door faster than you could snap your fingers. I tried my best not to listen to the gossip at work, but I'd heard it. The rumors definitely didn't paint a pretty picture, and I had no desire of being one of the next who didn't quite line up for the task. No matter how well he thought I did my job.

In theory, he was a catch. At twenty-seven years old, he'd worked his way from the bottom of his dad's company to sitting on the Executive Team. He was set to inherit hundreds of millions of dollars from his father one day. There was no doubt in my mind about any of that.

Luckily for him, I had no interest in sleeping with my boss.

Unfortunately for him, I had no intention of having him *be* my boss. "I'm sorry, but it's still a no."

His shoulders drooped, and I wondered if anyone had ever told him no before.

"What can I do to make you change your mind?"

I snorted. "Marry me."

He blinked. "Really?"

"*No.*" I crossed my arms over my chest. Sure, my family had been pressuring me to get married for the last few years. But there was no way I was marrying *him*. "Why would I marry you?" I snorted. "Please." I went back to typing on my computer, hoping if I ignored him, that he'd go away.

Nicolas shrugged. "Not to beat a dead horse, but I really need your help. *Please*, just consider being my assistant. I'll do anything. Seriously."

"*Anything*?" I crossed my arms over my chest. What kinds of things could I extort from this man by agreeing to do his bidding?

"Come on, we're friends, right?"

I looked up at him, surprised. *Were we?* Sure, we'd worked together on a few projects, and I always smiled at him when I saw him around the office, but *friends?* "We are?"

"Come on, Zofia," he pouted, looking like a dejected puppy. It was strange to hear my first name from his lips for the first time. He'd always called me *Miss Narayan* before. Never Zofia. Not with that smooth, warm voice, and that tone... "Give me something to work with here."

I rubbed the bridge of my nose with my thumb and pointer finger. "You're relentless."

"Yes." He popped a smile, those pearly white teeth poking through the perfect set of lips.

No. Ugh. What was I thinking? I didn't *like* Nicolas Larsen, let alone find him attractive.

Sighing, he slumped down onto the chair next to me. The cubicle where my friend Gabbi normally sat, although she was visiting her family in Boston this week. "Can I tell you a secret?"

"Probably a bad idea." I swiveled my chair towards him, crossing my legs. Maybe if I gave him my full attention, he'd leave faster. "But sure."

He looked around the room, like he was making sure no one

was around. "My father is planning on retiring at the end of the year. Which means I only have a few months to prepare."

"Prepare for what?" A few months? It was July—he had plenty of time.

"To take over." That blond brow raised again. "Becoming CEO. Of course."

Oh. Right. Well, that made sense. "Sure, but what does that have to do with needing *me*?"

"I told you—you're exceptional at your job." Only, he hadn't used those exact words before, and I ignored the way they made me feel. *Exceptional.* I could feel my cheeks heat, and I was glad my blush wouldn't be evident with my brown skin. Nicolas looked around the department. "I've read your resume. This can't be all you've ever dreamed about, can it? Plus, the benefits are pretty great." I raised an eyebrow, and his cheeks went a little pink. He waved his hands. "Not *those* kind of benefits, I promise."

"I know," I reassured him.

The worst part was—he wasn't wrong. I *had* set my sights higher before. Before my life had fallen apart. I was turning thirty soon, and sometimes I felt like I'd given up on my dreams for financial security.

Sure, I had an apartment I loved, and a cat. I had a few good friends. I was still close with my family, even if I saw them less these days. But something was missing. Passion. Drive. *Fulfillment.*

The spark that made me want to keep going.

Would I find it working under Nicolas? I didn't think so.

I traced the lace pattern on my pencil skirt. "What kinds of duties would we be talking about?"

"Nothing too unusual. Managing my schedule, making travel arrangements, organizing reports and documents… helping me plan events for the company. A bit of everything. Overseeing employees like you are now, only on a larger scale."

"Events?" I perked up. *Shit.* I didn't mean to sound interested.

"Yes." Nicolas grinned—excited to have interested me in something. "Including the company retreat my father wants to host in two months."

"Two months?" I couldn't believe what I was hearing. "Is he crazy?"

Nicolas laughed. "Yes."

"That's not enough time."

"I know." He rolled his eyes. They were beautiful, a shade of blue I'd never noticed on anyone before, that almost felt like the color of the ocean. A deep aquamarine that perfectly complimented his blond hair and freckled complexion. "But my father…" He shook his head. "He's got this idea in his mind, and he will not let it go. So I've decided to just indulge him on the matter. Now I have to plan it, and I don't know the first thing about planning an event, especially one of this scale, and—"

"Okay." *No!* Why had I said that? The answer was supposed to be *no.* Why was I caving to this man?

Why did the idea of planning a work retreat make my heart race? It wasn't anything huge, but I'd always loved event planning. Organizing, managing, and figuring out all the details. At one point, I'd almost gone into wedding planning.

Before I'd lost everything.

"Okay, what?" He repeated, sounding shocked.

"Okay. Yes." I couldn't believe the words were actually coming out of my mouth. "I'll be your assistant." Plucking a non-existent hair from my skirt, I pretended to be unaffected. "Suppose I can help with all that."

"*Yes!*" Nicolas practically cheered, pumping his fist into the air. "This is going to be great. You'll see."

"But I have a few conditions." I wouldn't accept without negotiating my salary and other benefits. Might as well get a raise with this *promotion*. An office of my own would be nice, too.

"Anything."

I grinned. Definitely an office.

Okay—maybe this would be fun.

Maybe I'd like being Nicolas Larsen's executive assistant after all.

2
nicolas

june

Zofia wandered outside, finding me standing on the balcony. Our friends were inside, celebrating with dessert and laughter, but I was content to stay right here, enjoying the summer night.

"Hey, gorgeous," I said, flashing a grin at her.

"Hey, you." She gave me a warm smile, her skin a lovely golden hue after some time in the sun. Zo was beautiful no matter what the time of year, but she looked like she was glowing today. The look suited her.

Or maybe it was just this place, this trip, that made her come alive. I'd never seen her so free.

Our friends Benjamin and Angelina were getting married this summer, and had decided to have a joint bachelor and bachelorette party in Napa, California. They met at our work retreat last year and had quickly fallen in love, despite hating each other at first. Thanks to some meddling on my part, they were forced together, and the rest is history. Now, Angelina was my chief marketing officer, while Benjamin served as the chief financial officer. They'd both assumed their positions around the same time that I had, all three of us working on developing and growing the company together.

Angelina and I had met in college, where we'd lived in the same dorm. Even though I'd been a year above her, we'd become close friends. Or as close as we could be. It had become clear to me early on that she kept everyone at an emotional arm's length, like she was trying to protect herself.

I'd majored in Finance, and she'd been in Marketing, so we'd ended up in multiple classes together before I graduated. When she and her best friend, Gabbi, were graduating, I'd sent them information on job openings within Willamette Tech. Ang had ended up in the marketing department, while Gabbi worked in HR—same as Zofia. I'd spent many nights at the bar after work with the two of them, though now our gatherings had included Benjamin—and more recently, his brother Hunter.

And now we were all sharing one large house in Napa together.

I tipped my head up, looking at the night sky. It was magnificent here—stars visible in a way that they weren't in Portland. I was used to living in a city where it was gray and drizzling ten months out of the year, that I appreciated seeing the stars on a clear night.

"The view is incredible," I said, taking another sip from my glass of wine. I'd had a few over the course of dinner, and felt more relaxed than I had in months.

"It's beautiful out tonight," Zo observed.

You're beautiful, I wanted to say. But she wasn't *mine* to compliment, and she never would be. I had to remind myself of that. No matter how attractive I'd always found her.

I leaned forward, draping my arm over the railing, and ran my hands through my shaggy blond hair. It was probably time I got a haircut, but I liked it at this length. As long as it wasn't poking my eyes, we were golden.

"You excited for tomorrow?" Zofia asked me, drinking from her own glass. She didn't drink often—just on special occasions —but it was good to see her letting loose a little. She'd changed into a new dress for dinner, something shorter than I'd ever seen her wear around the office.

Maybe that was why all these thoughts were flooding my brain. Feelings I'd kept at bay over the last year. It was impossible not to notice how stunning she was. Ignoring the spark between Zofia and me felt like a monumental struggle today. The longing had only festered, feeling like a simmering flame.

Seeing her like this—relaxed, unburdened, *happy*—felt like I was looking at a completely different woman than the independent, strong-willed assistant I saw every day.

"Yes," I finally answered, remembering she'd asked me a question. "It'll be fun. I've never gone on a wine train before."

She made a noise of agreement.

"They look happy," I mused, looking at Angelina and Benjamin, who were swaying slowly in front of the large windows we could see into from the deck. She was lit up with happiness, laughing in her fiancé's arms.

Zofia smiled. "They really do."

Looking at my friend now—in love, about to marry a man she'd insisted she hated a year ago—I hardly recognized her. It was so different from a year ago, when they'd been in an email feud. Gabbi and I had finally had enough of hearing them complain about each other, and after our scheming, they'd ended up stuck together for the week last fall—at the retreat I'd begged Zo to help me plan.

"I feel a little responsible," I said with a smirk.

"For getting them together?"

"Of course. Without me, who knows how long it would have taken them? And I couldn't take the fighting anymore."

She laughed. "Who do you think got all of the HR reports?"

I shook my head, holding back a chuckle. "Now they're getting married."

"Feels like everyone is, these days."

"Everyone but us, huh?" I nudged her with my elbow.

"What do you think is going on with Gabs and Hunter?" Zofia asked, looking over to where the pair stood, a heated gaze passing between them. Was it obvious to everyone but them how much they wanted each other?

"Not sure yet. Gabbi perks up whenever he's mentioned though, so I think it's safe to say she likes him. And apparently they're planning a trip together for after the wedding."

"He looks at her like she's a breath of fresh air. Like he can't imagine life without her." Zofia looked away.

Not that he was the only one. I couldn't imagine my life without *her*. I hummed, the sound rumbling in my chest.

She'd been the best damn assistant I could have ever asked for. I was pretty sure she kept my head screwed on straight. Which meant I needed to make it through this weekend being this close to her *without* touching her.

"There's no way they don't end up hooking up this summer," I murmured.

She laughed. "Maybe. Who else do you think is going to end up coupling up?"

"Those two." I gestured with my chin at Charlotte and Daniel, who were in the kitchen, laughing as she stole a cookie from his hand. Daniel was Angelina's brother, and he'd been best friends with Charlotte since college. "It's written all over their faces."

She hummed in appreciation. "I was talking with Charlotte about that earlier, actually."

"And?"

"She doesn't want to risk their friendship. Says he's too important to her and she can't lose him." Zofia's eyes met mine.

"Well, I guess I can understand that," I whispered, resisting the urge to reach out and brush my hand across her forehead, pushing back the strand of hair that had sprung free.

We were close. Too close. Maybe closer than we'd ever been, even when she was bending over my desk to fix something on my computer. Even when we sat side by side in meetings.

If I turned my head, and she turned hers…

"Fuck," I muttered, pushing myself off the railing, putting a few feet between us.

"Nic?" she asked, clearly surprised by my sudden outburst.

"Sorry. I just…" *Am having a hard time holding back right now. Want to tell you how beautiful you are, but that would be inappropriate. Because I'm your boss.* All things I wanted to say, but no words made it out of my lips. I just stared at her. With the warmth of her skin, those dark brown curls spilling over her shoulders, and that dress emphasizing her sensual curves, I'd never found her more stunning.

Shaking my head, I tried to rid myself of those thoughts. Stuffing them down deep so I wouldn't betray her trust and confidence. It wasn't right, harboring these thoughts. Wanting her.

"What's wrong?" She stepped closer to me, her hand landing on my biceps.

Touching me. I sucked in a breath. "I shouldn't." My words were barely more than a breath.

I brushed that strand of hair from her forehead, mesmerized by her. It was intoxicating, this level of closeness. The smell of her perfume drifted up, alluring, making me want to bury my face against her skin.

Everything I wanted—everything I couldn't have. My biggest temptation.

"Nicolas…" Zofia's gaze dropped to my lips. Hers looked so soft, and I wanted to know what they'd feel like against mine.

Had always wanted to, really, from the first day I'd met her in the elevator, when she'd had no idea who I was.

"We *can't*," I said, though it was a weak protest. "I'm your boss." A reminder neither of us needed, I was sure. And yet.

And *yet*. There was no way she couldn't feel the rapid beating of my heart. All for her. Just for her.

"Not here," she told me, her hand sliding up my arm. "Here, you're just Nicolas, and I'm just Zofia. And our friends are getting married this summer. That's it."

"*Just* Zofia, huh? You make it sound so simple." But there was nothing simple or *just* about her. She was so much more than I ever could have imagined.

"Exactly." She took another gulp, finishing her wine before setting the glass down on a patio table. "It doesn't have to mean anything. So you shouldn't hold back."

"Maybe we've both had too much to drink," I groaned.

"No." Zo shook her head with a smile, the action lighting up her face. "Only the two glasses. *Perfectly* sober."

It would have been easier if we were drunk to deny how much we both wanted this. To use it as an excuse to put distance between us, to back away from my gorgeous assistant. But I couldn't. Not when her hands were on me, and her lips were so close to mine, and all I wanted to know was how they felt against mine.

"You know what they say," I said, wanting to kiss her so damn bad. "What happens in Napa stays in Napa."

She giggled. Actually *giggled*. I'd never heard that sound from her before, but suddenly I wanted to hear it a thousand more times. Tonight, preferably. "I don't think that's how the saying goes."

I shrugged. "Maybe it can for tonight."

This was insane. Wasn't it? That I was staring into her beautiful brown eyes, wondering if it was possible for them to fucking sparkle, and neither of us was moving away. That I was flirting with Zofia.

Over the past year, we'd both been strictly professional. Maybe this was both of us finally snapping. Giving into our baseline needs. My dick was on board, even though I knew it was such a bad idea.

"You're so beautiful," I said, running my thumb over her cheekbone. "So beautiful I don't quite know what to do with myself." Her eyes fluttered shut as I continued to explore her face in all the ways I'd never been able to before.

Zo's lips curved up in a small smile. They were the prettiest shade of maroon, a color that perfectly complemented her warm brown skin tone. "You could tell me all the things you want to do."

I let my forehead rest against hers. "Gorgeous girl." I let it slip out, forgetting all the reasons I shouldn't. "You shouldn't tempt me. You'll find out exactly what terrible thoughts are running through my brain."

She reached up, pushing her fingers into my hair and combing through my blond strands. "Maybe I want to know all of your filthy thoughts, Nicolas."

I grabbed her hand, pressing my lips to her warm skin. "I can assure you, you definitely don't." Not when I had a year of them built up. A year of longing. A year of imagining what I'd do to her if I ever had her body against mine.

"So," she started, "are you going to kiss me?"

"I—" Maybe Zofia could see the panic on my face. "This—*us*—it would change everything."

There was no hiding the longing or desire in hers, because she smoothed her hand over my chest, and I was surprised at how quickly it calmed me.

"This doesn't have to change anything," she promised. "We'll have this weekend, and then we'll go back to normal. Nothing has to change."

Except *after*, I'd know what Zofia's lips felt like. I'd know what she tasted like, what little sounds she made. But fuck, I had to know. I wouldn't be able to go back, but I didn't want to, either.

Zofia's hands slid up my chest till they were wrapped around my neck, softly playing with the hair at the nape of my neck. "You won't lose me," she murmured. "I promise."

"Fuck it," I murmured, wrapping an arm around her waist and pulling her into me until our bodies were pressed together.

Then I did exactly what she asked. Outside, on the patio, where anyone who was inside could see us, I pressed my lips to hers. Kissing the woman who had starred in all of my dreams for the last year. My every fantasy. *My assistant.*

Not that I cared about that right now. Not when her lips were soft and warm, just like I'd imagined, as I moved mine over hers in light presses. She tasted like cherries and wine, a combination that shouldn't be as alluring as it was.

I ran my tongue over the seam of her mouth, nibbling on her lower lip, pleased when she opened for me. It was sexy as hell when she tightened her fingers in my hair, pulling me down tighter against her mouth. We devoured each other's mouths, like we were making up for all the time we'd lost in the last year by not kissing.

"Why haven't we been doing this all along?" She panted as I kissed down her neck.

"Because I'm your boss," I answered, hands roving down from her waist to squeeze her ass lightly. "And fraternization is frowned upon."

She laughed. "Shut up and kiss me more, Nicolas."

"With pleasure, gorgeous."

And so I gave her my mouth, digging my fingers into her hips until I finally heaved her into my arms, settling her on the railing in front of me so I didn't have to bend down anymore. She was not short—especially when she wore heels—but at this angle, I could take my time properly, getting acquainted with her lips, letting my tongue meet hers over and over and over again. It was even better, especially with how Zofia's hands wandered my body, doing some exploration of her own.

"*Fuck,*" I groaned when she ran her hand down the front of my slacks, letting her palm rest over my cock—already half-hard and standing more at attention by the moment. She made a sound of protest when I lifted her off the railing, setting her back on her feet. When she looked up at me, her eyes dark and her lips swollen from kisses, it took everything in me not to take her mouth again.

"We need to go inside before this goes any further, Zo." She whimpered, and I brushed a hand down her side, squeezing her hip. "Anyone could see us out here," I reminded her. Even though the living room that looked out onto the deck was empty, and all our friends had vanished. "Come to my room."

"Okay," she breathed.

I pulled back, tugging a loose curl. "Really?"

Zofia bit her lip. "Just for tonight."

I knew what this was. Just for tonight—just for this weekend. I didn't want to complicate things with our friends finding out and misunderstanding.

Brushing my lips against her ear, I let them drag over the sensitive skin of her neck. "Meet you in there in a few minutes." *In my room.* Fuck. I wasn't ready for this.

I felt her body shudder as she nodded.

Wordlessly, she slipped inside the house, closing the sliding door behind her. And I stared up at the stars for a moment, wondering if I'd just made the best decision of my life—or the worst.

3
zofia

Standing in front of Nicolas's door felt like the craziest thing I'd ever done.

Even crazier than kissing him, because I *knew* what was going to happen tonight if I went in there. When I went in there.

Still, I didn't give myself another moment to change my mind. Not bothering to knock—why would I, when he was expecting me?—I wrapped my hand around the doorknob and let myself in.

This morning, when we'd all been picking rooms in the large house, Nic had chosen this one, with a large, king-sized bed and an en-suite. No one had fought him for it—maybe because he was Ang and Benjamin's boss. Hunter and Gabbi had given them the master, and the size of their suite was *huge*. Still, I couldn't help but feel jealous when I compared it to the size of the room I was sharing with Emily—Benjamin and Hunter's little sister. *Shit, Emily.* I hoped she wouldn't mention my absence to anyone.

Nicolas was lounging on the bed, his shirt a few buttons undone, staring at me. I'd waited a few minutes before coming to him, not wanting to be caught.

"Hi," I said, leaning against the door.

"Hey." He grinned, looking every bit the suave playboy I'd always known he was. Not that I'd ever experienced it directly as his assistant—we didn't flirt. We kept things professional.

"Are you sure about this?" I was hyperaware that my hand was still wrapped around the doorknob, but I couldn't let go yet. "Just sex?"

Nicolas nodded once. "Never been more sure about anything."

And what was I supposed to say to that? Instead, I rocked back on my heels, wishing I was wearing heels instead of being barefoot.

But right now, I wasn't Zofia from the office, armed with a pencil skirt and red bottomed heels. I was vacation Zofia, and vacation me did crazy things like having a one night stand with the man who signed her paychecks, apparently.

"Come here," he murmured, crooking his finger towards the bed.

When I didn't move, Nicolas was off the bed, crowding me against the door. My heart was pounding in my chest as he ran his hands down my body, settling them on my hips. He leaned forward, and I thought he was going to kiss my lips, but he pressed an open mouth to my neck instead.

"You have no idea, do you?" he asked against my skin.

"About what?" I questioned—or at least I thought I did. It was hard to focus when Nicolas's lips were skimming down the sensitive skin of my throat, his hands bunching my short dress up, exposing the sheer pair of panties I was wearing.

"We'll have to be quiet," he said against my ear as his fingers skimmed the waistband. His knee pushed mine apart, widening my stance for him—giving him better access. "We don't want anyone to know."

I nodded, covering my mouth to hold in my gasp as his hand

slipped down the front of my panties, fingers stroking lightly over my entrance.

Nicolas pushed two fingers inside me at the same time his lips finally found mine, his tongue twining with mine as he kissed me deeply. He tugged at my lower lip with his teeth as he crooked his fingers, rubbing the spot that made a moan slip from my lips.

But I wanted more. I wanted everything he could give me.

Yet pressed against the door by his muscular body, I couldn't move.

"Nicolas," I said against his lips as he pumped his fingers inside me, working me higher and higher.

Was I actually going to come from this? I couldn't remember the last time I'd gotten off so fast. Probably because it had been a long time since I'd had sex, period. And even longer since I'd *enjoyed* it.

I ran my hands down his chest, admiring the definition of his abs. God, he was fit. His body was almost unfair. I struggled to tug his shirt out of his pants, unable to concentrate between the way he was kissing me like a starved man and the way his fingers moved inside me.

Too good. This was too freaking good.

Why hadn't we been doing this for months? I didn't normally do casual sex, but if he could make me orgasm this quickly, I'd have to reconsider my stance.

His thumb found my clit, applying the perfect amount of pressure, and I whimpered as another wave of pleasure burst through me.

Yes. I couldn't cry out—on account of Nicolas's mouth on mine—but I felt the orgasm hit me, my insides spasming around his fingers.

He kept working me through it until I slumped against him, breathing rough. He pulled out his fingers, bringing them up to his mouth, and I watched as he licked them clean. It was way hotter than it should have been.

"Fuck. You taste—" He let out a groan before lifting me up into his arms. Nic's erection pressed against my still sensitive core, fluttering from my climax and I wrapped my legs around his waist, pushing him further against me. When I felt his hard cock brush over my clit, I let out a groan of my own.

Nicolas carried me to the bed, setting me down onto the plush comforter before kneeling in front of me. He looked... *fuck*, he looked nothing like the man I'd grown used to seeing every day.

He looked like a god, a king before his throne, and yet he was kneeling for *me*.

"I want to taste you," he rasped, his eyes dark.

My body heated, and I squeezed my legs together. "You don't... you don't have to do that," I protested.

He frowned, his hands resting on my knees. "Why not?"

"I don't..." I bit my lip. How did I explain that I didn't *enjoy* oral sex? It was fun at first, maybe, but I'd never come from it. Maybe because it often seemed like a chore that my ex acted like he was forced to do versus something he enjoyed doing, and I didn't want some halfhearted attempt at going down on me. Not by the man in front of me. "I just don't like it." I squeezed my eyes shut, mortified.

Nic ran his hand up my inner thigh. When he spoke, his voice was velvety soft. "Hey. Zo. Look at me, gorgeous." When I did, he pressed a kiss to my thigh. "Please, let me taste you, because I've been dying to all night." He kept moving higher until his mouth was pressed over my panties and he sucked my clit through the fabric. The pressure was like pouring gasoline on an already burning fire, and I arched my back, moaning from the burst of pleasure it brought me.

"*Fuck*." His eyes were closed, as if he were savoring the

moment. Hooking his fingers through the waistband of my underwear, he looked up at me. "Yes?"

I nodded, because apparently, I couldn't deny him anything. Had it been like this since he'd begged me to be his assistant? "Please."

"Thank fuck," he muttered as I lifted my hips to help him take them off. My dress was still bunched around my waist, giving him full access to my lower half. I couldn't take my eyes off him as he brought his mouth to my entrance, licking the remnants of my orgasm before burying his tongue inside me. My fingers found the back of his head, digging into his hair as he fucked me with his tongue, groaning as he lapped up my taste.

And oh, fuck, that was hot.

He really *was* into this, wasn't he?

Before I could get close again, he pulled back, smirking at me from between my legs before standing up to put his mouth on mine. Nicolas's hands gripped my hips, keeping me in place as he stroked his tongue over mine, letting me taste myself on him.

"Mmm." I lost myself in the kiss, in whatever *this* was, wanting to live in the now. My fingers scrambled to unbutton his shirt, needing to feel his skin against mine.

God, he was hot, his body toned and *perfect*. I'd never have guessed a CEO who worked in an office all day would have a physique like he did, especially one he hid behind suits every day. But it was glorious and unreal.

"Your body is insane," I mumbled against his mouth as I ran my fingers up his abs.

"You're doing wonders for my ego," he said, giving me that blinding smile I knew so well. "Don't stop." Nic winked and then wrapped his hand around the back of my neck, bringing our lips back together.

I let my eyes flutter shut as we continued to make out, his hands trailing up my skin, exposing more and more of my skin to the air. He peeled the dress off my body, dropping it onto the floor in one smooth motion, and I didn't even stop to ask myself if this was wrong. Was trying not to overthink how good it felt to have his hands on my body, how much I wanted him, and how much that scared me.

Truthfully, I was terrified. How long had I had been attracted to Nicolas Larsen? I wasn't sure when it had started, but I knew it wasn't going to stop. There were so many reasons we shouldn't be doing this, but right now I didn't care. I didn't want him to stop. The way he looked at me tonight? The simmering desire I saw pooled in his eyes must have mirrored my own.

When I opened my eyes, it was to find him standing there, his eyes trailing over every inch of me. Like he couldn't look away.

"*Fuck.*" His voice was reverent. So low, it practically rasped over my skin. "You're beautiful."

Leaning down, he sucked one of my nipples into his mouth through my lace bra.

"Nic," I gasped, throwing my head back as he worshipped them. His hands found the back of my bra, unhooking it as he switched his attention to the opposite breast, and then the garment was on the floor, probably joining my dress and panties.

"Never in my wildest dreams could I have imagined you," he said, flicking his tongue over my hardened nipple.

"*Please,*" I whined, not knowing what I was asking for.

Other than his mouth felt so good, and I was so empty. One orgasm wasn't enough, clearly. What was he doing to me? Turning me into a monster. An orgasm-deprived monster.

He cupped me with both hands, squeezing lightly. "Patience, Zofia. If I only have one night, I want to do it right."

I nodded. But also, I wanted his pants off. Wanted to return the favor. I reached for his pants, unbuttoning the top button before pulling the zipper down, exposing his boxer briefs. Humming in satisfaction, I slipped my hand down them, palming his hard length.

He cursed, pulling off my breasts with a wet pop before pushing his pants and boxers off in one motion, kicking them off.

Nicolas climbed onto the bed, and I scooted backwards so he could settle in between my thighs.

I let my legs drift shut, my hands resting over my stomach as his expression dropped. "Shit," he cursed, dropped a soft kiss to my thigh before sinking back onto his legs.

"What?" I frowned.

"I didn't expect this. I don't have any..." He trailed off.

My eyes widened. "*Oh.*"

Shit was right. I really wanted to feel him inside of me, but I'd never gone without a condom before.

He ran his fingers through his hair. "Let me check my bag. Maybe I have one in there." Nicolas kissed me again, a slow, languid kiss like he was in no hurry at all, before getting off the bed.

I took the moment to admire his tight ass as he rifled through his suitcase—something I could never do in the office.

Finally, he pulled out a small leather case—and after rifling through it, came back victorious. "Thank *God*," he said, ripping it open before joining me back on the bed.

His cock—because there was no other word for it—was hard as steel, the tip looking angry and red with a drip of pre-cum already on its tip. Before I could do anything crazy, like beg him to let me taste *him*, he pumped himself a few times before rolling the condom down his length, fully sheathing himself.

Nicolas positioned himself between my thighs again. This time, his tip pressed against my entrance. "Ready?" he asked, running the tip through my arousal, coating it in my wetness.

I nodded, feeling breathless. "Fuck me, Nicolas." I wrapped my arms around his neck, his stunning blue eyes practically locked on mine as he slipped inside me. Just the tip, at first, but holy *fuck*, did it feel amazing. He was big—bigger than I'd ever had before; the stretch even better than I could have imagined.

Not that I'd imagined what it would be like to have sex with Nicolas before. *Nope.* Because that would have been wrong.

We both moaned as he seated himself fully inside of me, not moving for a moment to let me adjust to his size.

"You good?" He asked, eyes focused on me, like he was making sure I wasn't in pain.

"Better than good," I told him. "I feel—" I shook my head, not having enough words.

"I know." Nicolas sealed his lips over mine.

My eyes drifted shut. "So *full.*"

He pulled out before thrusting in deep, and I let my head hit the pillow, succumbing to the feeling of pleasure every time his hips snapped against mine. Each rock of his body seemed to bring him deeper inside until I was impossibly full, barely holding back my moans.

I knew if we were too loud, we'd be caught. In a house full of our friends, there was no way I wanted to be discovered. The ramifications would be too serious.

Fucking your boss was a bad idea for a reason. Maybe that was why I was so turned on—so wet as he stroked inside me. Because this was *forbidden.* Because knowing I shouldn't made it that much hotter.

"Don't stop," I murmured, wrapping my legs around his waist, forcing him deeper. "I'm so close—"

Like he knew exactly what I needed, his thumb found my clit again, pressing it in rough circles as he dragged a tongue over my nipple.

It was too much, and I was falling apart.

"Nic," I cried out.

"That's it, Zo," he murmured. "Be a good girl and come for me. Come all over my cock. I want to feel that sweet pussy clenching around me."

"Oh my god," I said, my orgasm shattering through me, the filthy words making me burn alive.

It felt like the world had gone white, like every single nerve ending was alive, bursting with pleasure. My insides spasmed around him, and I could feel how hard he was, how each punishing thrust only spurred my orgasm on as he fucked me through it.

I couldn't be sure how loudly I'd cried out, only that I ended with his hand covering my mouth.

He peeled it away, his face intent on mine. "Are you okay? I didn't hurt you, right?"

"Uh-uh." I shook my head.

"Good." His mouth pressed against mine, kissing me softly, then deeply, before trailing kisses down my throat. "You look so goddamn gorgeous when you come."

I knew my cheeks would be darker, feeling the warmth flood to them, but I hoped the after-effects of my orgasm would mitigate my flushed skin. "You still haven't," I murmured, squeezing around him.

He groaned. "Do that again, and I will."

So I did.

Nicolas let out a garbled *"fuck"* before pumping inside me again, returning to his steady rhythm. I watched his face, brushing a loose blond hair back that had fallen onto his forehead. His eyes were dark, pupils practically blown out with pleasure, perspiration dotting his forehead.

It only took a few more strokes for him to come, especially when I ran my hands down his body, squeezing his perfect ass. I watched him in awe as he came, trying to memorize the blissful expression on his face.

I knew this couldn't happen again, and I didn't want to forget any part of it.

When he finished, pulling out of me to take care of the

condom, I pulled the sheet around my body, knowing I should go but not wanting to leave yet.

He came back, leaning against the doorframe, his eyes somehow sparkling with mirth. "You're incredible."

"Thank you," I murmured, letting out a small yawn as I stretched out, naked in his bed.

Nic chuckled as he leaned down, scooping up his boxer briefs and sliding them on before joining me back in bed.

I let out a deep breath. "So… that just happened," I said, biting my lip.

He brushed a hand over my hip, as if he couldn't bear not to touch me. "It did."

"And there was only one condom in there?" I asked, running a finger up his shaft.

He chuckled. "You want to go again, already?"

"If we only have one night…" I said, feeling breathless.

His head dipped down, nipping at my lower lip. "Only had the one." *Damn.* He seemed to see the disappointment on my face, and laughed, squeezing my thigh. "Doesn't mean we can't do other stuff." Nicolas brushed my hair back. "It doesn't mean anything," he affirmed. "Just two people getting it out of their systems."

"Yes." My voice was all breathy. "Just sex."

He cupped my jaw with his hand, his lips moving over mine. "Just sex," he agreed.

And then he kissed me again, and I knew I should regret it— should be worried about how this was going to change our dynamic—but right now all I could think about was his cock, pressing against my thigh, and how I wanted him again.

Maybe because I knew it was only for one night. Knowing this was all we'd ever have. But I didn't want it to end.

There was something hard poking into my back, and a heavy weight draped over my body as I drifted awake the next morning. My body was satisfied—and sore in a way it hadn't been in years.

So I snuggled deeper into his hold, enveloping myself in his warmth and cologne scent—and promptly fell asleep.

I was deliciously warm and comfortable, and I had no desire to open my eyes. Part of me wanted to stay here forever, right in this moment. I snuggled into the feeling, before I realized exactly where I was.

Wrapped in Nicolas Larsen's arms.

Where I'd fallen asleep.

After we'd had *sex*.

I'd lost count of how many times he'd made me come last night, before passing out in his bed, naked and satiated.

Oh God. I needed to get out of here. Needed to sneak back to my room and say—*what?* I could only hope my absence wouldn't be noticed.

Because as good as last night was, there wouldn't be a repeat. Not for us.

I shimmied out from between Nic's arms, looking at his face, still peaceful with sleep.

Fluttering around the room, I found my discarded clothes, pulling them on as quietly as I could, wincing every time the floor creaked under me. After I'd pulled on my dress, I saw Nic frowning at me, sitting up with the sheet covering his lower half.

"Hey." His voice was deep, groggy with sleep, and it made my insides ache.

"Hey. Sorry if I woke you. I should—I should get back to my room. I don't want anyone to find out and—"

Nicolas nodded. "Relax, Zo. I know what this was."

It was a sobering statement. "Do you... regret it?" I almost winced at the question.

"No. Hey." He frowned. "*Never*."

"Okay." I nodded. "Nothing changes, yeah?"

He shook his head. "Nothing." The word was barely audible, but I heard it all the same.

With a terse smile, I grabbed my shoes—and then left without another word.

What else was there to say?

It had been one night. Getting it out of our systems.

And that's all it would ever be.

4
nicolas

THREE MONTHS LATER

september

I'd broken my first rule. I didn't sleep with my assistants.

Except now, I *had*.

We'd said that nothing would change between us, but it felt like everything had. The easy rapport we'd built had turned into awkward silences, and these moments where I felt an impossible divide between us. I hated that. Hated that just because we'd succumbed to the spark between us, neither of us knew how to act around each other.

It had been like a cocktail of poor decisions.

Decisions I couldn't quite bring myself to forget.

Zofia was fiercely independent—always had been, as long as I'd known her. And while I didn't regret it—could never regret *her*—I hated that everything felt different now.

Three months, and yet for me, nothing had changed. Three months, and yet it felt like yesterday when I'd finally felt her skin against mine. I wanted to ask her for a repeat. To feel her skin against mine, once again. But what would it change? We couldn't be together. Besides, I wasn't looking for a relationship anyway.

We'd had one night together—that was exactly what we'd agreed to.

"Son." My father grinned at me from across the table, sipping from a cup of coffee as he sat in my office.

"Yes?" I asked, looking up from my computer monitor. I was reading a report on our current profit margins and wanted to get back to my task at hand.

He hadn't scheduled an appointment. Instead, he showed up unannounced, which he *knew* drove me crazy. I understood, but that didn't mean it made it any less annoying when he hovered like a helicopter parent. The man didn't even check with my assistant to see if I was busy before he barged in as if he owned the place. Which, sure, he sort of *did*. But he'd retired last year, leaving the company in my hands so he could go travel the world with his wife, and still it didn't seem like he could let this place go.

Dad gave me an appraising look. "When are you going to find a nice girl and settle down?"

I almost choked. "*What?*"

"I'm not getting any younger, you know. And I'd like grand-kids while I'm still young enough to enjoy them. Plus, there's the matter of your trust fund."

Ah, yes. I resisted rolling my eyes. He'd been dangling my trust over me like a carrot, just out of reach, for the last few years. I didn't need it—I'd done just fine for myself after graduating college, putting my finance degree to good use even as I learned the ropes for taking over my family's company. My *legacy.*

Never mind that my father's company was now *mine.*

I'd officially taken over as CEO at the beginning of the year. After remarrying, my dad had wanted to retire, and even though

I felt severely out of my depth half the time, it was my birthright. At least I had good friends by my side.

"I'm only twenty-eight," I reminded him, letting out a huff. "I have plenty of time to meet someone and *settle down*." I volleyed his words back at him.

"You say that now, but then you'll blink and suddenly you're fifty and you've wasted the best years of your life."

I scoffed. "Like you did?"

He frowned at me. "I married your mom. Had you."

After which he spent almost all his time working. Yeah, I wasn't touching that conversation with a ten-foot pole.

It was only in the last few years that he'd started dating again. Found a new woman, a new wife. A new family, one I wasn't sure how I fit into anymore. I'd always be my dad's heir, his successor, but things felt different now.

Especially when my new step-mom—closer in age to me than she was to my dad—was pregnant with their first child.

"It's my first year as CEO. You know, the position you recommended me for? I've got enough on my plate without worrying about finding a wife." I was the youngest chief executive officer in the company's history—I had enough to do with proving myself without trying to find a wife to have on my arm at events. Trying to look unfazed, I clicked my pen.

"I know. But the board is worried you're not serious enough about your future and that you have a... how should I put it... *lack of stability*."

"What the fuck? Seriously?" I narrowed my eyes. "That's what they said? Wouldn't they rather I focus on the success and future of the company?" Ever since he'd told me about his plans to leave the company in my hands, I'd been *all in*.

I knew exactly what people thought of me. That I was some cavalier nepo baby who got everything in life handed to him. No part of me wanted to be labeled as a fuckboy or a man took advantage in his position. It was the reason I'd had a string of new assistants in the last few years. Once they'd found out exactly how much I was worth, they'd propositioned me. I'd immediately sent them packing, and yet the rumors persisted.

Yeah, I enjoyed sex. Consensual, no strings attached hook-ups.

When was the last time I'd done that? Over a year ago—around the same time she'd become mine. Well, my assistant. Because she wasn't mine. And she never would be.

Even if I burned for her.

Now, the idea of casual sex felt hollow. There was no meaning.

That didn't mean I was interested in anything deeper, though.

Most of my college friends were settling down, tying the knot and then popping out two point five kids.

I couldn't imagine being in the same boat. I wasn't ready for all of that—a wife, *kids*. I could barely take care of my self, let alone a *baby*. Sure, I had a dog, and I'd had Cooper for the last few years, but that was different. The bachelor life was perfectly fine with me.

He ran his hands through his slicked-back hair. "Honestly, Nic. They think you're a carefree playboy who flirts his way around the city." Maybe I had been that once. I loved to flirt, and I loved women. Besides Zofia, in the last year, I hadn't seen any action besides my own hand.

Though that might have had something to do with the woman sitting outside my door.

The one who occupied almost all of my thoughts. Why had I asked her to be my assistant last year?

Because she was damn good at her job. She had an incredible eye for detail, and she ran her department flawlessly. Reports were always on time, without a single typo or error. Zofia was smart—smart enough to go head to head with me consistently, which was no small feat—and I admired her. Honestly, she scared me sometimes with how brilliant and beautiful she was. She kept my head screwed on tight when I needed it and was so much more than an assistant. She was a confidante. A friend.

But nothing *more*. We both knew the stakes. Who we were to each other. While I would never change it if I had to go back, because I never wanted to forget what it felt like to have her lips against mine, her skin pressed to mine, neither of us had wanted anything serious.

I wasn't built for a relationship—never had been.

"Nicolas."

I jerked up my head, remembering my father in front of me. *"What?"*

"Never mind." He sighed. "I'll see you for dinner this weekend, yes?"

I nodded, holding back my groan. "Of course." Dinner with Dad and his young, pregnant wife. *Fun.*

Dad stood and grabbed his stuff, draping his coat over his arm. He turned towards the door, then looked back at me. "You know, I really am proud of you. I know this job isn't easy."

"I—thank you," I choked out, suddenly overcome with emotion. It wasn't as if my father never told me he was proud of me, but I hadn't expected it.

He opened his mouth, like he was going to say something else, then closed it as if he'd changed his mind before walking out the door.

I went back to the spreadsheet currently open on my computer, overseeing sales projections for our next quarter. We mostly operated in software and did a lot of our business with other companies, though we were also working on expanding into other avenues, which meant I also had the report from the product development team to review, as well as the marketing team's upcoming campaign—and that was all before I had a business dinner tonight with a potential client.

I smoothed a hand down my face. *I could do this.*

So I did what I did best: put on a smile, becoming the guy that everyone loved. And I let everything else—every fear, every worry, every desire—fade out of my mind.

Four hours later, I stood up from my desk, stretching my arms. I hated sitting still all day. Even though I worked out in the gym almost daily, I got restless if I sat in one place for too many hours.

Which meant it was time for a break.

And maybe lunch.

I popped my head out of my office, looking at Zofia's desk, but it was empty. *Damn.* I was going to ask if she wanted to grab a bite to eat with me. Before Napa, we'd shared meals together often—mostly out of necessity, but I enjoyed her company. Now, she spent most days with Angelina and Gabbi, and part of me missed our friendship. How close we were.

My eyes drifted over her desk. There was a photo of her family at her brother's wedding earlier this year, all dressed in traditional Indian attire. Zofia's face was lit up, glowing with happiness. It was a beautiful memory, even though I hadn't witnessed it myself.

She'd worn a similar dress to our company's annual charity gala last year—a beautiful, pale green sari covered in gold embellishments that looked absolutely stunning against her warm brown skin. It had been hard to take my eyes off of her, even when I reminded myself that she was my assistant.

It was hard to ignore the attraction I'd felt to her all these years, but I'd done my best. *Until Napa.* I shut my eyes, trying not to think about that night, how stunning she'd been in her sundress, glowing with happiness. How I hadn't been able to *stop* looking at her, especially with a few glasses of wine in my system.

But Zofia wasn't mine. Not to touch, not to look at, not to *anything*.

Still, I couldn't help but steal a look at the pictures. There was one of her cat, Duchess, and one of her holding her diploma at her college graduation. She had a cup of sparkly gel pens, which I'd long since learned were her favorite, and a vase of pretty white flowers next to a pink candle. It was effortlessly feminine and perfectly *her*.

"Nic." Zofia walked up, her long, curly hair down past her shoulders, wearing a pink pantsuit and a pair of heels with red bottoms. I'd learned rather quickly how much she loved her shoes. "Everything okay?"

"Hey." I flashed her a grin, hoping that if I ignored the fact that I'd had my mouth on her pretty brown nipples a few months ago, I could act normal. "Want to get lunch?"

After a moment, she nodded. "Sure. Angelina is still on her honeymoon, so I don't have plans. Give me a few to grab my things."

Leaning against her desk, I watched as she grabbed her purse and slung it over her shoulder, not bothering to grab her coat. September in Portland was normally still beautiful out—the rain hadn't started yet, and we still had the last bits of summer hanging on. Still, it could get chilly in the office even when it was warm outside, thanks to the air conditioning.

"Where are you thinking?" Zo asked, though she knew there were only a few restaurants I went to regularly, creature of habit that I was. The Willamette Tech offices were in downtown Port-land, which meant we were within walking distance of a ton of different places.

I thought about it for a second. "Thai?" It had been a bit since we'd gone to our favorite Thai restaurant, and I was craving some pad see ew. It was the same place I'd been ordering from since college, which felt nostalgic.

Right now, I needed that. After the conversation with my dad earlier, I felt like I was standing on unsteady ground.

"Perfect." She followed me towards the elevator, and we chatted about general work stuff—what was happening for the rest of the day, the budget reports, the proposals I had yet to approve. Our working relationship was comfortable. *Easy.* I was terrified the day would come when she would leave me. When she realized she was way better than this job—and *me.* What would I do without her? *Suffer.*

Zo kept my head on straight—something I'd definitely needed, because despite being groomed for this position, I hadn't been prepared for the sheer amount of work my father had done every day.

I still couldn't believe she'd agreed to be my assistant in the first place. Of course, her offer package had been incredible, with a whole lot of zeros.

Zofia was staring at me as I turned back to her, walking down the sidewalk. She'd clearly been talking, and I'd been in my head. "Are you even paying attention to me?"

"Fuck. Sorry." I flashed her a grimace, shoving my hands in my pockets. "My dad came by earlier," I said, knowing that was an explanation in and of itself.

Our relationship had always been strained. I knew he loved me, but he had never been the best father.

"I saw. Everything okay?" She tilted her head at me.

"Define *okay*," I muttered. She shot me a look, and I hung my head. "The board is worried I'm not settled. That because I'm unmarried, I'm not taking this seriously. They want *stability*." I put air quotes around the word.

Zofia chuckled. "So you can't do a good job as CEO because you don't have a wife at home? What is this, the fifties?"

I rolled my eyes. "Apparently to them, it is."

We both laughed, and the mood felt lighter.

Lighter than it had in months.

I cleared my throat. "Zofia—"

"My mom called me to tell me another cousin of mine got engaged," she said, interrupting, letting out a huff as she twisted a piece of hair around her finger. "I'm the last single one in our extended family. She asked if I wanted her to set me up with an arranged marriage… *again*." Zofia scrunched her nose in the most adorable way. I found it more endearing than I should have. "I told her no." Her dark brown eyes met mine and there was something deeper there, something I was trying not to read into.

"You did?" I asked, not sure why I was surprised. It satisfied me she wasn't looking for a husband. I hated the thought of her in the arms of anyone else. After that night, it would be hard to watch her be with another man.

It was really hard to remind myself who she was to me when she looked at me like *that*. But I needed her more than I *wanted* her. At least that was what I kept telling myself. That little feeling in my chest—the tightening when I imagined her with someone else—was impossible to ignore.

"After the last time?" She rolled her eyes. "I think it shocks her sometimes that I'm thirty and *not* seeing someone. By this age, she and my dad had already moved our family to the States." Zofia shrugged, the movement causing her dark curly hair to spill over her shoulder. "She had three kids and a dream." A sigh. "But it's hard for her to understand that I want something different for my life. That I'm independent and okay with that."

What's your dream? I wanted to know. I wanted to do whatever I could to make it come true. Wanted to watch her be happy, to see her eyes light up every day.

But I was also a selfish bastard who wanted her by my side.

She was a damn good assistant, and the idea of losing her made my insides uneasy.

Zo quirked her eyebrow as I took her in. "What?"

"I was just thinking… maybe there's a solution to both of our problems."

"Huh?"

"We should get married."

She blinked. "*Married*?" Zo crossed her arms over her chest. "You can't be serious."

"Remember when you asked me to marry you to become my assistant?" I laughed, then realized it was actually perfect. Maybe I'd make good on that request after all. "Think about it, though. If we get married, if it would get your family off your back. The board is up my ass, too, so it would help both of us. And we already know how good we are in bed together." I grinned at her. "I'm just saying. It's a *great* idea. It wouldn't be real. We could just, you know… have a contract marriage."

It would be convenient—and wouldn't that be the best part? I wouldn't need to find an actual wife. Wouldn't need to have someone who expected love or devotion. The board would take me seriously as CEO.

I'd stunned her silent. *Shit.*

Her eyes were wide when she finally responded, "That's ridiculous. We can't just get *married.*"

"Who says?"

"Me." She narrowed her eyes, pointing her long red nail at my face. "And have you forgotten that I'm your assistant, *Mr. CEO*? How would that work?"

I shrugged, shoving my hands into my pockets. "Guess we'd have to figure that out." I had my own motivations for it, but I didn't need to tell her that. The sizable bank account with a lot of zeros at the end being one. Not that having a wife was enough for the clause for my inheritance, but it was a start.

The company didn't have a no fraternization policy, though it was frowned upon being in a relationship with your superior—because there was a power imbalance there.

Would the same thing apply if my assistant were my *wife*? Or would I have to accept the loss of her in one area of my life to have her in another?

Zofia just stared at me. "This is a joke, right? I'm being punked right now?" She pretended to look around us. "Is there someone filming, who's about to jump out and say *gotcha?*"

"Yeah." I laughed. "Never mind. It was a stupid idea." My cheeks burned. "Of course, that would never work. Just forget it." *Even though I knew I wouldn't.* I shot her a curt smile as I opened the door to the Thai place. "Come on, let's eat. I'm starving."

Throughout lunch, I couldn't get the thought of calling her *my wife* out of my head.

5
zofia

The man was absolutely insane. I was pretty sure Nicolas had lost it. *What if we got married?* What was he thinking?

I didn't understand what was going through Nic's mind. A week later, sitting around a table at our favorite bar—*Dusk*—with Angelina, Gabbi, Charlotte and Noelle, I *still* couldn't understand.

There was no way I could marry my *boss*. Even if he'd become a friend over the last year. A good friend, and a good employer. It was a terrible idea, wasn't it? *Yes.* So why couldn't I stop thinking about it?

Maybe because it hadn't felt like a joke.

We already know how good we are in bed together.

The first time either of us had brought up our night together since Napa. I couldn't get that night out of my head. Even now, three months later, I still felt the phantom touch of his hand across my skin, the way he'd given me so many orgasms I'd lost count. My body ached for more, and even my vibrators hadn't been satisfying enough anymore.

I blamed Nicolas for this, damn him.

And then he'd laughed it off afterwards.

After the way my last engagement had ended, I'd decided right then and there that I was content to be alone. Never mind what my family thought.

Luckily, none of the guys were here tonight, because I wasn't sure what I'd say if I had to face Nicolas. That afternoon's conversation had thrown me for a loop. Angelina knew Nicolas best out of anyone; I knew that. Part of me wanted to ask her what she thought about it. And yet… I couldn't bear to bring it up to her. She wouldn't understand.

"Zo?" Gabbi nudged me with her arm. "Are you okay?"

Angelina was telling Charlotte and Noelle about her honeymoon. They'd just gotten back, finally, and I was glad to have everyone home again. The office had been too quiet lately without Angelina and Gabbi, and I looked forward to our lunch dates resuming.

I nodded. "There's just a lot going on with work before we leave for the work conference at the end of the month." Even though it was more than that.

It was everything.

My life was fine. Why didn't my mom see that? I was *happy*. Successful. I had my own place, had a job that paid me more than I'd ever thought possible, and had a closet full of high heels that made me feel like a million bucks.

She squeezed my hand. "If you ever need to talk, I'm here."

"I appreciate you." We'd been friends for a long time, and I knew if I opened up to her, if I confessed what I was feeling, she'd be there for me. "And I'm so glad to have you and Ang both back in the office."

"God, I know," she moaned. "The last week without her has been so boring."

I was jealous that everyone else had been able to take so much time off for the wedding. It had been my first time in Europe—my first time out of the country besides visiting my family in India—but I'd only had a few days to visit Paris since the wedding was held outside of France. Still, I'd loved shopping on the Champs-Élysées, staring at all the luxury goods, and drooling longingly over a gorgeous pair of stiletto heels.

Gabbi and Hunter had gone on a two week trip after the wedding, traveling around Europe, and now the two of them were officially together. Hunter Sullivan was a pediatric doctor, and from everything Gabbi had told me, he was her perfect man —better than any book boyfriends, she said. She'd had a crush on him from the moment they'd met, but it had taken them being best man and maid of honor together to realize they were meant to be.

Was it surreal for her and Angelina that they were now with brothers? That one day, her best friend might end up as her sister-in-law? I knew their bond ran deeper. They already acted more like sisters than friends. Maybe because they'd known each other for more than a decade at this point.

Sometimes I wished I had a best friend like they did—one who had been with me since college.

The four of them had been friends since freshman year, each pair of roommates living across the hall from each other. Even though I felt close to them, it wasn't the same dynamic that they shared with each other. Those bonds ran deep. I was friends with my two brothers, still kept in touch with college friends, and enjoyed spending time with my coworkers, but I didn't have a *person*. Not like they did.

In a lot of ways, the person I was closest to, the one I spent the most time with, was… Nicolas.

What a sobering thought. I clearly needed more friends if my boss was the first person I thought of.

Man, I really needed more friends.

Angelina cleared her throat, looking at me. "How's everything going with you and Nic?"

"What?" I choked on my water. "What do you mean? There's no… *me and Nic*."

Did she know something? Oh, god. I thought I'd been so careful.

Angelina frowned. "I meant with the conference coming up in Vegas."

"Oh. Right. Of course."

She gave me a weird look. "What did you think I meant?"

My cheeks felt warm. "Nothing." It was my turn to look out the window, staring at the street, watching strangers walk by. I couldn't admit that my first thought had been the night we'd slept together. "It's good. Looking forward to it being over, though." I hated those things.

Gabbi gave me a sly smile before she and Angelina made eye contact.

"What?" I frowned at them both.

"*Nothing*," Angelina sang, giving me the same response I'd given her.

I scowled. "Nothing's going on," I insisted, because there *wasn't*. Not anymore. We'd made that clear. It wouldn't happen again.

Neither of them seemed convinced, like they knew I was lying to myself as much as I was to them.

"Boo." Angelina frowned. "I was hoping we could go on double dates."

I laughed, thinking about how very real that possibility was. "Yeah, well." I shrugged. "Keep dreaming. We really aren't anything. He's my *boss*." I gave a forced laugh. "That would be crazy."

Gabbi shrugged. "There are crazier things. Haven't you read any of those billionaire books we recommended?"

"Not yet, no." Because it felt like it hit a little too close to home with my job. And I wasn't sure reading about girls falling in love with CEOs or men who would give them a black American Express card would be very good for my mental sanity. I was already addicted to expensive shoes—I didn't need to give myself a complex. "I'm still working through that fae series, though."

All four of them shared books with each other. I'd slowly started getting recommendations as they included me these last months. Gabbi and I had been friends for years, working closely together in HR, but being a part of the group had made us even closer.

"Oh!" Noelle perked up, clearly listening in to our conversation. "Those are my favorites."

"You're working on a new art piece from the fifth book, right?" Gabbi asked Angelina.

Angelina gave a dreamy sigh—one I'd never have expected from her before she fell in love. It was fun to discover that beneath her sometimes grumpy and rather stubborn exterior; she was a hopeless romantic at heart. "Yes. It's turning out so good."

"I'll report back when I'm done," I told them. "Not that I've had a lot of time this last month, what with your wedding and everything else with work." I let out a breath. "Why is end of summer *so* busy?"

"You're telling me," Angelina said, laughing. "I had a mound of paperwork to go through when I got back to the office, not to mention filing the paperwork to legally change my last name."

"Angelina Sullivan," Gabbi said with a laugh. "I never thought you'd be the first in the group to get married, but somehow, it feels right."

"Cheers to that," Noelle said, and we all clinked our glasses. "Benjamin masterminded his way into your life, and the rest is history."

"I know. It's crazy, right?" Angelina shook her head. "I mean, this time last year, we hadn't even met in person. And now we're *married* and I just…" She blew out a breath. "It feels so real all the sudden. For the longest time, I never planned on getting married. You all know that. I couldn't see myself with anyone, *period*. But Benjamin wormed his way into my heart, dammit, and now I can't imagine life without him."

The two got engaged in Paris this spring after being together for six months—depending on who you asked—and planning the wedding had been a whirlwind.

"And to think, it all started because Nic and I forced you to spend time together at the retreat," Gabbi laughed.

She hadn't been there to witness it—but I had. It was one of my first responsibilities when I'd first become his assistant, and I was proud of how everything had turned out. Even if his father had sprung it on us with less than optimal time for planning.

Sipping my drink, I mused, "It's really a wonder we didn't all see it coming." I thought back to how mad Angelina had been last year. Benjamin had followed her around, clearly already obsessed with her.

Angelina gave Gabbi a small scowl, pointing her finger at her best friend. "You're only off the hook for that because I love him."

"And you love me," Gabbi beamed.

"Yeah, yeah," she huffed.

"Who *did* you think would be the first to get married?" I asked the four of them, curious.

They all looked at turned to their blonde friend, who furrowed her brows. "*Me?*" She pointed at herself. "But I'm the youngest of the four of us!"

"By a few months, maybe. And you like, *love* love, Char," Angelina said. "Plus, you spend an awful lot of time with my brother."

"We're best friends," she insisted, her cheeks turning pink.

Angelina hummed. "Sometimes, I wonder if Daniel's upset that he's not married before me, since he's older."

"I get that," I said. "When my younger brother got married last year, I felt like I had a big target on my face. *Everyone* in the extended family wanted to know when I was settling down and why I didn't have a husband yet." Huffing, I blew a strand of hair out of my face. Of course, they'd all also wanted to know about my failed engagement, something I definitely hadn't wanted to talk about then.

They both gave me sympathetic looks. "You're a catch, Zofia," Angelina said. "I'm sure someone's going to come along soon and snatch you right up."

I shook my head. "Keep dreaming, sister. I'm perfectly fine right now. With this job, I wouldn't have time to date even if I wanted to." I waved her off, because I definitely didn't want to. Wincing, I thought of the conversation with my mom earlier today. "My mother's actually trying to set me up with someone, but I told her no."

"Like an arranged marriage?" Charlotte asked, curiosity evident in her face.

"Yeah. I mean, not quite in the way you're thinking? I'd still meet him and go out with him a few times before we decided if it was the right fit."

Gabbi ran her finger over the rim of her glass. "And you... *don't* want that?"

"Nic keeps me plenty busy. I don't know how I'd have time for a husband at this point in my life." I didn't want to give up the life I'd built for myself. There were still so many things I wanted to do, so many places I wanted to see, foods to try, and things to *experience.* I sighed, looking down at my matte red nails. "I know plenty of people who have arranged marriages who meet their future partner and do fall in love. Don't get me wrong. I just..." I sighed, not knowing how to explain *why* I didn't. Not anymore, at least. Maybe a few years ago I'd dreamed of that—the white picket fence, the husband who loved me, kids running around the back yard.

"Believe me. You don't have to explain the fairytale—that's why we all read romance novels," Charlotte popped in.

"And why I write them," Noelle added with a firm nod.

"Yeah. She just doesn't understand that it's not the end of the world for me to be single at thirty. My brother's new wife just announced they're expecting their first baby." My *younger* brother. I was so happy for them; I really was. Even if it wasn't what I saw for myself anymore. "And another cousin of mine just got engaged. So she's got weddings on the brain."

"She just wants you to be happy," Gabbi offered, her voice soft. She smoothed a hand down her emerald-green cocktail dress, a color I'd seen on her more and more over the last year. It reminded me of Hunter, and the color of his eyes.

"I… was engaged before, actually." I said, shocking the table. It had happened before I started working for Nic—before I was anything more than a coworker to Gabbi. "It was an arranged marriage. He was the son of our family friends, and I'd known him forever."

"What happened?"

What happened. God, where did I start? "He cheated on me."

"No."

I nodded. "Yeah. In my apartment. He moved in with me, because I didn't want to move, and then I caught him with her… in our bed. We were planning the wedding, and both of our families were so happy and then… it was over." I'd been devastated. "I could never bring myself to tell her why we broke up."

"Oh, babe." Angelina placed her hand over mine. "I'm so sorry. I promise, everything's going to work out."

Shrugging, I turned to my drink. "It wasn't meant to be, you know? But I'm happy now. I have a great job, and great friends."

Angelina squeezed my hand. "I'm so happy to call you a friend, Zo." Everyone at the table shared a smile.

"We all are," Noelle offered.

"Thank you," I said, feeling touched.

Who needed a husband when you had people like them in your life?

The bell on my precious baby girl's collar rattled as she ran towards me, and I scooped her up, nuzzling my face into her soft fur. At the end of a long day, there was nothing I loved more than taking my heels off, cuddling my cat, and taking a nice, long bath.

"What am I going to do, Duchess?" I asked her, running my fingers over her coat. She flicked her tail, and I pressed a kiss between her ears, smiling as she let out a happy chirp, nuzzling against my face.

She'd been mine ever since she was a kitten. When I found the tiny rag-doll cat at the shelter, her icy blue eyes had melted my heart, and I'd known she was supposed to be mine. She was mostly white, a total diva, and I adored her. Especially because I seemed to be the only human that she was actually affectionate with.

"Come on, sweet girl," I said, moving towards the kitchen. "Let's figure out dinner."

My cat let out a meow of agreement, and I just smiled, wondering if it was normal to love your pet so much it felt like your heart would explode whenever you looked at them.

Burying my face in Duchess's fur, I inhaled her sweet kitty scent. Somehow, it always calmed me down.

She was my first pet, my gift to myself after I'd moved into my apartment.

My parents had insisted I was welcome to stay living with them, but I'd wanted my own space. My *independence*—not to mention privacy and freedom. Still, family was important to me, and I loved mine. I still went over weekly for dinner with my Amma and Appa. My brothers were my friends, even though we'd tormented and driven each other crazy growing up.

Still, sometimes it felt like I was thirty years old, and I still wasn't an actual adult. Maybe because as a kid, I'd figured I'd already be married with a family of my own by now. My conversation with my mom kept flashing through my mind, how adamant she was at setting me up with someone. And in the abstract, an arranged marriage sounded perfect. I'd get the opportunity to meet him and find out if we were a match before any decisions were made.

After Samir, though, I wasn't sure I'd ever be ready to put myself out there again. I'd been humiliated. Too embarrassed to even tell my family what had really gone down. Luckily, I'd been able to get most of the deposits back for the wedding, but letting all of the extended family know I wouldn't be getting married after all had been mortifying.

I knew Nic had no idea—I'd never told him about my ex. Never told him how close I'd been to getting married to a man who was cheating on me our whole relationship. Because he'd wanted to marry a good Indian girl to make his family happy.

I'd given him my heart, and he'd all but stomped on it.

So I'd vowed never to make the same mistake again.

I wondered what my mother would think about Nic's fake proposal.

A *contract marriage,* he'd called it. Like we were in a Korean drama. In real life, that kind of thing never worked out. Never mind that we'd be lying to everyone.

Could I do that? Pretend that I was in love with him, that I was really his wife? I didn't know. Not to mention that I hated the idea of everyone in the office gossiping about me, or saying I'd only married him to get ahead.

The idea of marrying Nicolas—of having a contractual relationship with him—was completely inane. It could only end one way: in heartbreak.

There was no way I would ever subject myself to that again.

6
nicolas

The more I thought about it, the more I thought Zofia and I getting fake married was an *excellent* idea. We already spent a ton of time together, so no one would think it was strange if we'd said we were secretly in love and decided to get married. We knew we were sexually compatible, which meant we could take care of each other's needs—if she wanted that. Because there was no way either of us would be sleeping with anyone else if we were married.

It seemed impulsive on the surface, a joke, at first. And yet, it was rooted in logic. An easy way to appease the board and her family at the same time.

It was perfect, because there was no way was I going to find someone myself. The idea of spending a few years dating someone before tying the knot? I didn't have that kind of time. Besides, the last time I'd seriously dated a girl was in high school. We'd grown apart, and when we'd decided to go to a different college, she'd broken it off then. Apparently, she didn't see a future for us together. That had hurt, but she'd been right. I'd been ambitious—ready to take over my father's company, to pave a future for myself. She'd wanted something more, and I couldn't give it to her.

Falling in love? I wanted to laugh. Fat chance of that happening.

After my mother had passed away when I was young, dad had shut himself off from the world, his love—and loss—making him blind to what was right in front of him. *His son.*

I even didn't remember her. All I had left of her was the old photos and the baby book she'd made for me. She'd been so excited to have a baby. So excited to watch me grow up. She'd been robbed of that. It wasn't fair. Wasn't fair that we'd both missed out on all of that.

Meanwhile, my dad was about to start all over with his new wife. Give a new baby the childhood I'd never had.

I hated that I was bitter. That there were cracks in my happy, perfect facade. Because while I pretended like nothing was wrong, sometimes it felt like I was slowly dying inside.

The only question was... how did I convince her? Of course, there was the power imbalance. Even after we got hypothetically married, I *was* still her boss. I'd have to figure out how to deal with that.

I had to remind myself that money couldn't buy everything. But my mouth could. And oh, was I *good* with my mouth. Too bad I couldn't put it to use now.

Much to my mouth *and* dick's dismay, because it perked up any time I was around her. After our night together, I'd had to control my reactions a lot more often around the office.

One night together wasn't enough. I hadn't gotten her out of my system—not one bit.

That night together had been *incredible*. Mind-blowing. I wished I'd had more condoms so I could have spent the whole time inside of her. I'd never experienced that level of heat and chemistry before—not with *anyone*. I'd wanted to spend all night tasting every part of her, memorizing each inch of her body, because I couldn't get enough.

But I knew what we'd agreed.

One night. One night as *just* Nicolas and *just* Zofia.

We'd gone back to being boss and assistant, and now, I had to spend the whole day pretending I didn't know what she looked like when she came. That I hadn't had my face buried in her sweet pussy.

Maybe if she was my fake wife, I'd be able to remedy that.

First, I needed to find a way to prove to Zofia that I'd be the best fake husband she could ever want.

Even if she'd never wanted one at all.

I didn't deserve her, but goddamn, I wanted her.

I was so fucked.

7
zofia

"Y ou've *got* to be kidding me," I muttered, looking down at the coffee stain on my brand-new skirt. I'd purchased it last week, when I'd needed some serious retail therapy. Mostly because it was an *excellent* distraction from thinking about my boss's sort-of-proposal. Maybe I'd buy a new pair of shoes this week, too. Or there was a pretty pearl collar I'd been debating getting for Duchess.

Unfortunately, I didn't have time to change, which meant I was stuck wearing it for the rest of the day. *Lovely.* I groaned, trying to clean it up as best as I could while juggling both coffees in my hand—both mine and Nicolas's, which thankfully hadn't spilled—as I headed into the office.

It had been a week since the lunch where Nicolas had suggested we get *married,* and we still hadn't talked about it. I was pretty sure neither of us knew what to say. That, combined with our night together in Napa, and we'd spent our time avoiding any serious conversations.

After dropping my stuff off at my desk, I knocked lightly on the door to Nic's office, finding him on the phone. I set his coffee on the desk, and he caught my eye, his attention dropping to the large stain on my skirt.

You okay? He mouthed, his eyes lingering over me.

"Just a spill," I muttered, tugging on the neckline of my top. "It's fine. I'll survive."

He frowned, but went back to his call, and I let out a breath, slipping out the door.

Neither of us had brought up his proposal since it had happened. Just like we'd still never discussed the night we slept together in Napa. It was driving me a little crazy, because I didn't know how to act around him anymore.

Back at my desk, I grabbed a pack of Tide wipes out of the drawer, hoping I could at least get most of it out of the pretty light blue tweed. It was a damn cute skirt, complete with a matching jacket, and I'd be upset if I could never wear it again.

The women's restroom was empty, so I peeled the skirt off, trying to blot at it with the wipes before rinsing it out. Luckily, I was wearing a pair of spandex shorts underneath, so at least I wasn't running around commando in the bathroom.

"Great," I said, trying not to get more upset. *What a way to start my day.* Now it was going to look like I'd wet myself. *Lovely.* I couldn't decide if it was better or worse than the coffee stain.

The door opened, and Angelina walked in—her silky dark hair pulled up into a ponytail, her lips painted the shade of red she seemed to love, dressed impeccably in a tailored black skirt suit and red-bottomed heels. A pair of pearl earrings somehow completed her look. I was envious of how put-together she looked, especially while I was desperately trying to clean my skirt in the sink.

Today was not my day. "Hi," I said to her after she came out of the stall, washing her hands at the sink next to me. "It is *so* not my day today."

"Hey, Zo." She dried her hands before readjusting her ponytail. Her eyes drifted down to the stain I was trying to get out—

and the fact that I was standing in the bathroom in just my spandex shorts. "Need some help?"

I sighed, holding up the wet skirt. "I spilled coffee on it this morning on my way in. I was already running late, so I didn't have time to go back and change. Sometimes I keep a spare outfit at the office, but…" But I'd worn it earlier this month, and with everything going on, hadn't replaced it yet. Groaning, I appraised the wet skirt. There was no way I'd be able to put it back on. It wasn't going dry fast enough, even if I could get the stain out of the fibers.

She winced. "Been there. I might have an extra spare in my office. Want me to check?"

"Oh, *yes*." I nodded immediately. "That would be great, actually. You're my hero. Nic and I have a meeting later." I didn't want to show up to a potential client meeting with a stain on my skirt.

"I got you. Wait here."

Ten minutes later, I was back at my desk, wearing a skirt that was only slightly too tight for my frame. Angelina had a few inches on me, and she was all legs, but I'd take that over a wet skirt with a stain. Or worse.

After sitting down, my personal cell phone started ringing, and I let out a strangled sound when I saw who was calling me. *Why was everything happening on the same day?*

"Amma?" I asked, my voice short as I answered my mother's call.

"Zofia. I'm glad I caught you."

"Hi. I'm at work," I said, massaging my forehead.

"I know, I know. I'll be quick."

Said every mom ever, I thought, holding back a snort. My patience was running thin this morning, probably why I snapped out, "What is it?"

"Remember the guy I was telling you about the other week? My friend's son—the lawyer? He's agreed to meet you!"

I winced. "Oh." I'd tuned most of her offer out, mostly because I'd been too busy staring at Nic and thinking about the way he'd used his tongue. *Definitely not safe for work thoughts.* I definitely needed to get laid. "I don't really think I'm interested—"

"Nonsense. You're thirty years old and single, Chellam. There's no reason for you not to meet him and see if you two have a spark." I had to remind myself that at my age, she'd already had three kids. She and my dad had moved to Oregon from India with no support from their families. "What is the worst that could happen?"

Samir, that was what. Another failed engagement, for the whole extended family to know about. Getting my hopes up that someone could support me and my dreams, only to find out they just wanted a perfect little housewife.

I could see through the glass doors into Nic's office. He was sitting at his desk, focused on the screen in front of him, chewing on the end of a pen. Damn, even that was sexy.

We should get married.

We should get *married.*

It was crazy.

Unless… Maybe it wasn't so crazy, after all? Maybe Nic had been on to something, and I'd been too quick to shut him down. It wouldn't be real. My mom would be happy, and I'd be free to live my life. Nothing would have to change.

Wait, was I actually considering it?

I tipped my head up, looking at the ceiling.

Maybe it wasn't the worst idea, if it was really fake.

The worst thing had already happened. My heart shattered into a million pieces.

I could survive a fake marriage with Nicolas, couldn't I? We'd spent a night together, and the sexual chemistry between us had been crazy.

Damn. I really was considering this.

Nic's eyes met mine through the glass, and I offered him a weak smile.

"I'm actually—I *am* seeing someone." I blurted it out before I could think better of it, eyes still trained on Nicolas. "It's still pretty new, so I didn't want to tell you until I was sure, but—"

"Is it serious?"

I looked at the photo of the girls and me from Napa that was sitting on my desk. It had been taken in the bar the last night, everyone dressed in short cocktail dresses with bachelorette themed sashes. A few minutes later, Nic asked me to dance. Even though I'd known it was a bad idea, I still hadn't been able to say no. "Mhm. Very serious."

"Oh! Good! Well, you'll have to bring him by sometime. What's his name? Where did you meet him? When will you bring him to dinner?"

"*Amma.*" My voice was sterner than I had meant it to be. "Sorry. I just—I really have to go. I'm at work and have a meeting I have to prepare for."

And I really needed to have a discussion about all of this with my boss before I said anything I'd regret. My heart wasn't the only one broken when I'd ended my engagement—my mom's had, too.

Her frown was practically audible over the phone. "*Zofia—*"

I sighed. "Okay, *okay.*" I looked over at my boss, raking his fingers through his blond hair in the way he always did when he was stressed. "Nicolas. His name is Nicolas, alright?"

Oh. God. *I'd done it.* I was doing it, apparently.

"Nicolas… like the man you work for, Nicolas Larsen?" She sounded shocked. Which made sense, considering she had no idea I was even interested in him. And I wasn't—not *really.*

I held back my wince. "Yes. I gotta go. Love you."

Then I promptly hung up the phone, horrified and mortified about what I'd just done.

What was Nicolas going to say?

He was going to think I'd lost my mind.

I knocked on the door to Nicolas's office, trying to figure out what I was going to tell him.

So, I know you joked about getting married last week, but I accidentally implied to my mother that we were together. In a serious relationship. I tugged down the front of Angelina's skirt that was already riding up my thighs. *No biggie though! I'm sure she'll forget about it in a few days… or two to five years.*

Nothing was going right today. I definitely hadn't thought this through. I wanted to go outside and scream—and then maybe cry. My ruined skirt was the least of all my worries, and yet it seemed to be the crack in the iceberg. I was so off-kilter today that I'd actually thought his idea sounded like a good one.

"Come in," he said, though I knew it was nothing more than a formality anymore between us.

"Hey," I said, walking in and sitting down on the chair in front of his desk. Fuck, this skirt was determined not to stay put. I tugged it down again.

He eyed my outfit, but said nothing.

"Angelina let me borrow a skirt," I offered, even though he hadn't asked. "You know, after my coffee spilled this morning."

"Looks nice," he said, voice tight. I scrunched up my nose, knowing it absolutely did *not*.

"So," I swallowed, not sure how I was going to get the words out.

"So…" Nicolas propped his elbows on his desk, resting his head in his hands. "What's up?"

"I might have done something less than optimal," I admitted. *Terrible. Please don't fire me, bad.*

He frowned. "What? Normally, you're the one who puts out fires for *me*. Whatever it is, I'm sure we can fix it."

I winced. "Maybe not *that* kind of problem, Nic." Unfortunately, this had nothing to do with work.

"Oh. Okay." Nicolas leaned against his desk, casually crossing his arms. "What is it? I've got your back."

I looked down at the skirt, picking a loose thread instead of keeping my eyes locked on his ocean-blue eyes. They were the perfect shade of turquoise that I wanted to drown in. "I might have… accidentally… sort of told my mom I was seeing someone."

"You what?" he raised an eyebrow. "Who?"

"You." I made a face. "I told her I was seeing *you*."

His face morphed into one of surprise. And then amusement. And then—confusion. "But we're not? The whole marriage thing, I—you said it was a terrible idea, us together."

"Yeah, I know." I wanted to bury my face in my hands. "I'm sorry. She was just trying to set me up with this lawyer, and I'm sure he's a perfectly nice man, but after everything, I just—"

I couldn't stop thinking about it, clearly.

Maybe that was why I'd told my mom what I did.

Now it was his turn to wince. "I thought we agreed it was a stupid idea, and that we'd forget about it."

Crossing my arms over my chest, I glared at him. "I don't know how you think I could forget you suggesting we *get married*, Nicolas." Seriously, the suggestion was practically ingrained in my brain. I was going to be knee-deep in boxes if I kept using retail therapy to deal with it. And potentially credit card debt, because I didn't have a billionaire giving me unfettered access to their card. "So, I panicked a little. It's fine. I'll figure it out. Really. I thought maybe if I told her I was seeing someone, she'd get off my back for a bit. Just like you said." I knew I was rambling, but I couldn't seem to stop.

"And it worked?" He raised an eyebrow.

"Sort of. I mean, now she wants to meet you. Asked when you'd be coming to dinner."

I was surprised how quickly he responded, "Okay."

"Really? Because I can put her off, tell her no, and then say we broke up." It would be *mortifying*, but worse would be if I told her I had lied from the beginning. After my ex, she might literally disown me. But she'd get over it, right? At least I had brothers to give her grandkids.

Somehow, that didn't stop her from harping on me about them.

He shrugged. "Sure, why not? Your family seems great. You're all close. And this would be great for both of us. The board needs to see me in a serious relationship. We can use this to our advantage."

I frowned. "But we're not… *actually* seeing each other."

"They don't have to know that."

"So we're actually going to lie to everyone?" I squinted my eyes. "Even our friends?"

"It doesn't have to all be a lie. We could…" Nicolas drummed his fingers against his desk. "We could actually get married. That part wouldn't be fake."

"So now we've gone from fake dating to seriously getting *married*?"

Nicolas nodded. "I know. I know it sounds crazy, but hear me out. We *can* actually make a contract. One with favorable terms for both of us. And when we've both gotten what we need out of the relationship…" He grimaced, as if realizing how it sounded. "If either of us decides we want out, or we meet someone else, we can get a divorce. No questions asked."

"You really want to be fake married to me? Your *assistant*?" Maybe I'd hit my head this morning, and it was all just a dream. That would feel more realistic than our current conversation.

"Make no mistake, Zofia. The relationship might be fake, but the marriage will be real. Legally, you'll be my wife."

A little shudder ran down my spine. *Why did I like the sound of that?* "And if I say yes?"

"Then, when I come to meet your parents… we'll tell them the good news. That we're engaged."

"This is all moving so fast." My head hurt. I needed a drink. Or maybe more caffeine, after I'd spilled the first one. Something to figure out why I was actually considering saying yes to this fake engagement, this fake *marriage,* with the man who signed my paychecks. The man I brought coffee to every morning, not because I had to or because he'd ever asked me to do it, but because I liked to.

He stood up, coming to kneel in front of my chair, taking my hand in his. "We don't have to do this if you don't want to. If you're not comfortable…" Nicolas trailed off.

I stared into his eyes—the deep turquoise-blue ones that had held me captive in Napa. The night I couldn't get out of my mind.

If I said yes to this crazy scheme, to marrying him, it felt inevitable that we would end up in bed together again. I knew it was a line we shouldn't cross. This was only going to be fake, and like it or not, one of us was going to get attached if we had more nights like those.

"No, I…" I massaged my forehead. It *was* a good idea, all things considered. My parents would be happy because I'd be married, and well, the rest of it was stuff we could figure out later. "I'll do it," I told him. "I'll marry you."

Humming, he pulled out a piece of paper. "We can write it all out." Nicolas reached for a pen. "Let's outline our contract, *wife.*"

And if the tingle in my stomach from that one word held any indication of my future with this man, I was already in trouble.

8
nicolas

On the outside, I was the perfect picture of calm and collected. The suave executive who had worked on a multitude of mergers and acquisitions.

On the inside? I was *ecstatic*. Turns out I liked the idea of calling her my *wife* far more than I thought I would. Was this inevitable from the first moment she'd joked about it?

I held out the pen to her, and she just stared at it. "What?"

"I figured you'd want to write it down."

"Because I'm your assistant?" Her eyebrows practically rose to her forehead, her arms still crossed over her chest.

Her blouse covered her cleavage, but the motion still pushed them out, giving me flashbacks to when I'd had my mouth all over them, running my tongue all over her perfect tits. *Fuck.* Thankfully, I was behind my desk, so I could rearrange myself in my pants without her knowing I was getting hard just from the thought of her nipples.

"No." I shook my head, letting out a small laugh. "Because my handwriting is shit, and you know that."

That got me a small smile. "Okay, fine. Hand it over." Zo took the pen, and I slid the piece of paper over to her.

She started writing out in script across the top: *Nicolas &*
Zofia's Marriage Contract. And then she furrowed her brows at
me. "Do we *really* need to write this down? I don't think either of
us is going to forget what we agreed to."

"Seemed fitting."

"Why?"

I interlaced my fingers and placed my hands on the desk.
"Isn't this what they do in all those smutty romance novels you
girls like to read?"

"I—" Zofia opened her mouth and then closed it again.
"Still." She looked away, out the large windows that looked onto
downtown Portland. "How do you even know about that?"

Frowning at her, I tapped my fingers on the desk. "I pay
attention."

I'd been friends with Angelina and Gabbi since college, and
they'd *always* loved to yap about books. They didn't bother
filtering themselves around me, either. While at first I'd found it
uncomfortable, eventually I'd realized it was great to learn what
women liked. It still didn't tell me what the woman sitting in
front of *me* liked, though, and maybe I craved that information
most of all.

What made her tick? What made her tell her mother that she
was seeing *me?* I'd thought I'd have to plot and scheme to get
her to agree to this marriage, but she'd come to me of her own
volition.

"Right. Forget I asked." She drummed the back of the pen
against the desk. "What kind of wedding were you thinking?"

"Never really thought much about what my wedding would
look like." I shrugged.

Mainly because I'd never really imagined getting married.
Sure, ideally my closest friends would be there, but the important thing was the woman sitting across from me. My *bride-to-*
be.

"My mom's going to hijack our plans to plan some big

event." She gnawed at her lip. "I'd prefer something more…low-key."

"We can do low-key," I reassured her, figuring she probably didn't want to waste a big wedding on a fake marriage. It would make more sense this way. "We could go to the courthouse."

"Yeah. The courthouse works." She nodded, starting to write, then paused, looking up at me. "When would we get married?"

That was a good question. I rubbed my chin, feeling the slight stubble growing in. "Maybe in a few weeks, after we're back from the conference? We can pitch it to the board as a whirlwind romance. After working so closely together for the last year, we fell in love and decided we couldn't wait to get married."

"Okay." She nodded. "That works for me, I guess."

Zofia's eyebrows drew together. "What do we tell everyone at work?" She gestured towards the rest of the office. "Our coworkers? Everyone."

I shrugged. "Whatever you want. We can play pretend in public, and in private, we can just be *us*. Professionally, nothing has to change." The board would know, and her parents, of course. But I could keep it quiet in the office if she wanted.

Though selfishly, I didn't want that. I wanted her to be mine. I wanted my ring on her finger. She had such elegant fingers, like the rest of her, and she deserved to have a diamond adorning them. If I had my way, she'd be dripping in them, but damn, I was getting ahead of myself.

"What about our friends?"

I furrowed my eyebrows. "What about them?"

"I mean, do we invite them? When do we tell them that we're…" She couldn't even say the word, could she?

"Together?" I gave her a pointed look.

"Everyone's going to find out." She leaned back in her chair, her fingers toying with the gold hoops that she wore in her ears. She was always wearing gold jewelry—something I'd noticed a long time ago. "If we tell the board, Angelina and Benjamin will know—and so will all our friends."

"Yeah." I combed my fingers through my hair on the back of my head. "You're right."

"I know," Zo groaned. "Maybe we *should* wait until after the wedding."

"Wouldn't you want them there?"

She shrugged, helplessly. "I don't know. We're going to have to figure out *how* to tell all of them. As far as they know, we're just boss and assistant."

"We're more than *that*, Zo."

Her eyes met mine again, and I wondered if she could see the heat simmering in mine. "We're going to tell the same story to everyone, right?" Her nose scrunched as she seemed to ponder the thought.

"Probably makes the most sense if we keep it consistent with everyone."

She bit her lip. "Yeah. Fewer chances for one of us to slip up." Zofia gave me a pointed look and then added two more points to the paper.

"We can't tell anyone this is fake," Zofia said, remarking as she tapped the pen against the desk. "It would ruin both of our reputations if that came out."

"Agreed." I'd definitely be in deep shit with the board if they suspected. "Which means we have to sell it in public."

"Right." She frowned, like she hadn't considered that we'd need to make people believe we loved each other enough to have a whirlwind elopement.

I looked over what she'd written so far.

1. The two agree to get married in a small, simple ceremony, with only their closest friends present (if possible).

2. The marriage will take place in late August or September.

3. Information about the fake relationship will be consistent based on the story chosen by both parties.

3a. No parties shall be privy to the contract or any of the information within, including the false nature of the marriage.

4. Public displays of affection shall be limited to hand holding and hugging.

"No kissing?" I interrupted as her pen paused over the paper. "Zo, we're going to have to kiss, or no one's going to believe that we're *married*. You know that, right?"

"Fine." She let out a small groan. "But no tongue."

Can't promise that, gorgeous, I thought, but kept it to myself.

She scribbled an addendum underneath the previous bullet.

4a. Kissing is acceptable only when required and agreed upon by both parties.

"And you'll move in with me after the wedding, of course." It slipped out, but it made more sense the longer I thought about it.

"I'll… what?" Zofia froze. "What about my apartment?"

"No one's going to take it seriously if we say we're living separately."

We had to keep up the rouse. But I kind of loved the idea. It meant I'd get to spend more time with her, and maybe we could explore our physical connection again.

She scowled. "I have a cat."

"I know." There was a framed photo of Duchess on her desk, and if she thought I didn't listen every time she brought up her cat, she was crazy.

"You have a dog."

"So?" Cooper was my golden retriever. He was only a few years old, but he truly was man's best friend. "They'll be fine." Coop got along with everyone; I was pretty sure he'd be trying to love on Zo's cat the first day they moved in. He'd always loved other animals.

"*Fine*. I'll move in once we're married. But I'm not sleeping in your bed."

I bit my tongue, knowing that if I pushed too far, she'd pull back entirely. "I've got plenty of guest rooms."

"We can't have sex again," Zofia said, shocking me. "I'm already your assistant, and if I'm going to be your fake wife, too, that'll get too complicated. We can't complicate this with sex."

I didn't know why I hated that so much. Especially when that was exactly what we were proposing—a *contract* marriage. No complications, no feelings. Definitely no love. Maybe I just felt possessive of her because the chemistry between us was insane.

I had to remind myself that we weren't doing this because of what had conspired between us in the bedroom.

"Fine," I barked out, knowing I'd come to regret my next words. "No sex. But while we're married, I expect you won't be sleeping with anyone else, either. If word got out that either of us were cheating on the other…"

Her face seemed to turn gray, like she'd lost color. "Of course not, Nic. I know it's not real, but I could never betray you like that." There was hurt in her eyes, and I wondered who had put it there.

5. Zofia agrees to move into Nicolas's apart-

ment after the two are legally married. She will sleep in her own room.

6. Sexual relations will not be a part of the relationship, nor will they be expected by either party.

"How long?" Zofia asked, looking down at the paper.

I knew what she was asking without her having to elaborate.

"For people to take the marriage seriously, I think two years would be sufficient."

"And then what?"

I thought about what I'd told her before.

When we've both gotten what we need out of the relationship...

If either of us decides we want out, or we meet someone else, we can get a divorce. No questions asked.

"And then... we can amicably divorce." The words tasted like ash on my tongue. As much as I wanted to give her an out—a way to maintain her autonomy and freedom—I also wanted her tied to me.

My ring on her finger.

My last name as hers.

Now that I'd gotten those ideas into my head, there would be no getting them out.

Zofia winced, though she didn't put her pen back down to add another clause. "I don't want to lose my job after this ends. I know we'd be divorced, but..." She toyed with the small gold hoop in her ear.

"Hey." I placed my hand over hers. "You know I'll take care of you, right? I'd never let that happen."

She let out a breath. "Right." Her eyes met mine. "We're really doing this, then."

"Guess we are."

7. The Marriage will last for two years unless either party wishes to terminate the contract sooner, no questions asked, or both parties agree to extend the length of the contract.

She signed her name at the bottom and then slid the paper over to me. "Time to sign on the dotted line, *fiancé.*"

I grinned. *Damn,* I liked the sound of that.

"Can I help you?" The man standing in front of the glass counter looked in my direction, and I tried not to get distracted by all the sparkly items surrounding me.

I shoved my hands into my pockets. "Yes. I'm looking for an engagement ring." Swallowing roughly, I stepped up to the counter.

I was really doing this. *Buying Zofia an engagement ring.*

A real ring for a fake relationship, for this crazy scheme that somehow didn't feel so crazy at all.

If it was going to be anyone, it was going to be Zo.

She could keep it after we ended things and sell it or whatever. I didn't really want to think about that, even if we'd put it in the contract.

Maybe the contract had been a stupid idea. After I'd signed it, Zo had slipped out of my office, and I'd locked it in my personal safe for safekeeping. I didn't need anyone getting their grubby paws on it to make a mockery of the woman who would be my wife.

"What's your budget?"

"No budget," I responded, thinking about the enormous sum in my bank account. "Just want to get the perfect ring."

Most guys I knew with that kind of money would blow it on things like sports cars, but I'd hardly spent any of it. Maybe because I didn't feel like I deserved it. I was lucky enough to come from money, and even though I'd made my own, I could never bring myself to spend it.

Until now.

The guy's eyes lit up with delight. "Alright. Are you looking for something custom?"

Custom meant it could be one of a kind. Just like Zofia was. "What's the timeline on something like that?" I tapped my fingers against the glass display case.

"Normally four to six weeks at baseline, but for more complex designs with intricate details or if we need to source a specific gemstone, it could be more."

I frowned. "That might be a little tight." Especially with the timeline we were working with.

"We have a selection that you could choose from in house."

"Oh, that would be great."

He nodded, turning to a display and unlocking it with his key. "Do you know if she prefers gold or silver?"

"Definitely gold." Zo was always wearing gold jewelry, from tiny hoops to bangles and different gold rings on her fingers.

"Perfect." He slid a tray of rings with gold bands onto the counter in front of me. "Take a look at these and tell me if there's anything you like, and we can go from there."

I took my time picking out the right ring, wanting something perfect for Zofia.

My assistant, and soon to be… *my wife.*

9
zofia

NICOLAS

You good?

ZOFIA
Yes.
Still processing, I guess.

NICOLAS

I know.

But it's going to be fine, I promise.

ZOFIA
You say that now, but…

NICOLAS

Trust me, gorgeous.

I'll make sure you never regret agreeing to
marry me.

ZOFIA
Fake marry.

NICOLAS

Sure.

See you soon.

I didn't know how to feel. We'd promised nothing would change between us, and then I'd gone and told my Amma we were dating. We'd said nothing would change, and then we'd somehow gotten fake engaged.

So, maybe I was freaking out… just a little.

The time on the clock blinked back at me like the countdown to my doom.

"It's just dinner," I reminded myself as I paced back and forth on the carpet. "Dinner with Nicolas. Your boss. Who you told your mom is your boyfriend. No big deal."

Tonight, Nic was coming to dinner to meet my family for the first time, and I was introducing him to them as my *fiancé*, not just my boss.

Duchess jumped on my bed, kneading the soft white comforter with her paws as she started to purr, a telltale sign that she wanted pets.

"Hi, sweet girl," I cooed, scratching between her ears.

I'd tried on practically every outfit in my wardrobe, and nothing felt *right*. It was beginning to actually feel like fall in Portland, and I wanted something casual but still cute.

"What the heck do you wear to tell your parents you're getting married to your boss?" I groaned, wishing she could answer me.

Instead, all I got was a small meow and white kitty fur on my abandoned outfits.

The worst thing was that ever since I'd told my mother we were in a relationship, she'd been so *giddy*. Like she was happy, just knowing I was seeing someone and wasn't alone. Like my relationship status alone helped reassure her that I was okay. A sinking feeling settled in my gut, knowing we would be lying to everyone we cared about. What was I going to do when they all found out exactly what *was* happening?

When we had to play pretend for real?

I was scared to find out. Especially since I was still trying to figure out our new normal ever since we'd signed the contract—ever since I'd spent the night in his bed, really.

That nagging voice in my mind kept reminding me what we'd agreed to. In less than a month, he was going to be my husband. What was I thinking, saying yes to marrying the man who signed my paychecks?

I rubbed my empty ring finger, wondering what it would feel like to wear his ring.

To be his wife in name only. No feelings—no love. I already felt guilty. What would I feel like when we actually tied the knot?

"Just a contract," I reminded myself, muttering to myself as I cleaned papers off my desk. *No feelings.*

Finally, I settled on a soft cotton light pink sundress with pockets and straps that tied into bows on my shoulders.

I did a little twirl and then turned to my cat, still curled on my bed. "Good?" I asked her, not expecting an answer. Still, when she gave me a little chirp in response, I took that to be cat for *yes.* Duchess was one of the most vocal cats I'd ever met, which was one of my favorite things about her. I loved how loving she was, and how if I meowed at her, she'd meow back, like we were having our own little conversation.

My favorite wedge sandals were sitting next to my purse, just waiting to be slipped on.

I checked the time again as my hand drifted to the small gold pendant that hung around my neck. I ran it back and forth across the chain.

There were only a few minutes left until Nicolas was picking me up, and I was trying to get a handle on my emotions before he arrived.

It shouldn't have been strange, considering we normally drove together to work events, but it felt different knowing we were going to my childhood home. Knowing that this wasn't a work event, and we were going to have to act like we were in love.

Me. In love with Nicolas Larsen. I snorted. Unlikely. "Isn't that a funny thought, Duch?"

She gave me a little *mrowf* before jumping off the bed, likely in search of a mouse toy to chase around the living room. Or a hair tie, because my girl was easy to please.

The doorbell rang, and I sucked in a deep breath.

He was here.

When I opened the door, I found my fake fiancé grinning, leaning against the wall with a bouquet of flowers in his arms.

"Hey." I ignored the little flutters in my stomach.

"Hi." His eyes trailed up and down my body. "You look gorgeous."

I looked down at my dress, hiding my smile. "Thank you. Not so bad yourself." He was wearing a red short sleeved button-up shirt and slacks. He was still dressy, but it was a far cry from his typical office attire of a three piece suit.

Nicolas handed me the flowers. "These are for you."

"You didn't have to do that," I insisted. "It's not like this is real."

He shrugged. "I wanted to."

I buried my face into the peonies, inhaling the sweet scent. "Let me just put these in water and then we can go." I carried the bouquet into the kitchen, rooting around for a vase under my sink. Nicolas followed me inside, and Duchess was immediately all over him, rubbing herself on her legs.

"Hey, pretty girl," he murmured, reaching down to run his hands over her fluffy coat. "It's nice to finally meet you."

Duchess meowed in response, tilting her head back as he kept petting her.

It was strange to think that in the past year, he'd never been inside my apartment. But why would he have needed to?

"She'll keep you there all night if you don't stop." Once the flowers were in water, I came back to stand beside him, watching how my cat was all over him.

I couldn't even blame her, because look at him.

His short-sleeved shirt showed off his arms, forearm porn that should really be illegal. Nic had muscles that I never in a million years would have suspected a tech guy would have. Arms I'd tried hard to forget ever since that night in Napa, because I couldn't be dwelling on it and keeping things professional.

And wishing for a repeat was not in the cards.

That was why I'd made it clear to him that we weren't having sex as a part of this arrangement. Because if we had sex, I knew I'd get attached. And this wasn't a forever marriage. We weren't getting married for love.

So I couldn't let that happen.

Nic chuckled. "Not the worst place I could be."

I hoped he meant that.

He stood up and gave me another once-over. "Got everything you need?"

I grabbed my purse, a light sweater, and slipped my feet into my shoes. "Yeah."

"Great." He offered me his arm. "Shall we?"

Slipping mine through his, I couldn't help but feel like a teenager about to go on her very first date. And sure, this wasn't a date, but the way he was acting, the flowers… it felt like one.

Nic opened the car door for me, and I slid inside, immediately surrounded by the scent of his cologne. I took a deep breath in as he rounded the car, letting myself luxuriate in it for a brief moment before he got in the driver's seat.

Normally, when we travelled for work, we took the company town car. Nic and I would sit in the backseat so we could get work done, which meant that I'd never had him drive me around before.

"This is nice," I mumbled, appraising the car's interior.

I didn't know why I expected him to drive something flashy —like a sports car—but I was surprised to see him driving something practical.

"Thank you," he answered, his free hand—the one not on the wheel—resting on the console between us.

I crossed my legs, trying to ignore how my knee was bouncing, fidgeting as I pictured all the ways tonight could go horridly wrong.

The closer we got to my family's house, the more nervous I felt.

"Relax," he murmured, like he could read my mind. "It'll be fine."

I looked out the window, because I couldn't look at his face right now. "Are you sure about this?" I wrung my hands. "You can still back out."

"Of course. I'd do anything for you, gorgeous." His words were like a balm, one I needed to hear. "Besides, we signed a contract, didn't we?"

His hand slid onto my knee, squeezing lightly, and I appreciated the warmth before he removed it.

I wanted to ask him to put it back.

But that was too forward for a fake fiancée, wasn't it?

I winced. "I should probably apologize in advance for my family."

"It'll be fine," he promised. "We're a team, right?"

A team.

"Yeah." I turned to look at him, seeing a warm smile on his face. *This* was my Nicolas, I realized. Warm, reassuring, and caring. The one who never asked me to get him coffee, but I did it anyway, because I liked taking care of him. The one who made sure I ate lunch every day, often bringing my favorite sandwich or salad to my desk if we were too swamped to leave the office. The one who kissed me in Napa like I was the air in his lungs. "Yeah, we are."

He nodded as he pulled into the driveway, behind my brother's car.

"We should have practiced," I blurted out.

"Practiced?"

"Being a couple." This time, I winced. "Forget it." It was a stupid thought, anyway. I turned to open my car door, but Nic's hand on my thigh stopped me. I froze, staring at the way it looked, his skin against mine.

"I'll get it," he murmured, expression serious. His eyes slid to my lips. "And if you want me to kiss you, Zofia, all you have to do is ask." He winked, and then he was out of the car, leaving me feeling breathless.

What just happened?

Nicolas opened my door, holding out his hand. I placed mine in his, stepping out of the car. My parents house was large—a three story, including the daylight basement—and I knew just how hard they'd worked to give us a good life. They'd put three kids through college, wanting us to take advantage of every opportunity.

He was still holding my hand as we stepped onto the sidewalk. "Before we go inside, I have something for you," he murmured, reaching into his pocket with his free hand.

The one not holding mine.

I cocked my head to the side. "You do?"

He nodded, pulling out a black velvet box and flicking it open.

"Oh. Nic… You didn't have to…" I trailed off as I took in the ring.

"We're engaged, right?" He picked up my left hand, kissing

my knuckles before slipping the ring onto my finger. "Perfect fit," he murmured.

Fake engaged, I wanted to remind him, but I was speechless. The ring was beautiful. It was a yellow gold band with a large, oval stone, framed on either side with smaller stones. "I don't know what to say."

Nicolas grinned. "You don't have to say anything, Gorgeous."

"When did you have time do this?" I couldn't stop staring at it. "It's beautiful."

"Just like my fiancée. Now, come on. Let's go meet the family."

Showtime, I thought to myself as I watched the light catch my brand new ring. I could do this.

What was one little lie, anyway? It wouldn't hurt them. They'd be so happy I was finally getting married. They'd never need to know all we'd agreed to was a contract marriage with an expiration date.

I was contractually obligated to him—nothing more.

At least, that was what I kept telling myself.

10
nicolas

e're a team. Words that kept echoing in my mind, because like it or not, we were in this together. I was still holding her hand as she rang the doorbell to her parent's house, enjoying that neither one of us had broken that connection.

The ring I'd spent so much time deliberating on looked perfect on her finger. I'd probably gone overboard with the three carats, but it complimented her perfectly.

My entire life, I'd always assumed I would propose with my mother's ring. It was classic and elegant, but I didn't know what Zo would think if I'd given her my family's heirloom ring. It felt too real for a relationship that was formed on a piece of paper in my office, so I'd stuck with one from the jeweler.

It was the right choice. She was meant to wear that ring.

"Still time to back out," Zofia whispered to me as we waited for the door to open.

I shook my head. "Never," I promised her, squeezing her hand—and not letting it go. It was getting harder to keep my hands off Zofia. Especially after I'd gone out and bought her a ring. "You're stuck with me now, my dear fiancée."

She shook her head, slipping the ring off and tucking in her pocket. "You're going to wear that word out if you use it so much."

"Can't wear it out when you won't be my fiancée for very long."

The door opened, and I recognized Zofia's parents from the photo on her desk. She was the spitting image of her mom, though she was a few inches taller than her. "Hi Amma," she said, a forced smile on her face as she let go of my hand to hug her mom, and then her dad. "Hi, Appa." She turned to me. "This is my—" Zofia paused, like she didn't know what word to use. "—Nicolas." I gave them a warm smile. "Nicolas, these are my parents, Sahana and Kadal Narayan."

Her father was shorter than me, but his eyes swept over me like he was trying to decide if I was good enough for his little girl. *Fair enough*, I supposed. I definitely wouldn't think anyone was good enough for my daughter, either.

"Hi, Kutti." Her mom beamed at her before looking at me. "It's very nice to finally meet you, Nicolas. We've heard so much about you."

"Only good things, I hope," I joked.

Zofia raised an eyebrow, and I crossed my arms over my chest.

She patted me on the stomach. "Of course… *babe*."

"We didn't even know you were dating until Zofia told me," her mom said.

Zo looked over at me. "Well, when you spend so much time together, these things just happen. We both realized we had feelings for each other, and the rest is history."

It was a condensed version, but it stuck to the truth as much as possible—which was good. Less chance of slipping up. "Your daughter is the best thing to ever happen to me, Mr. and Mrs. Narayan."

I didn't know what I'd do without her—that was the truth.

"No need for formality," her mom said. "Please, call me Sahana. Kadal and I are just happy our Zofia is happy and letting us meet her boyfriend."

Babe? I mouthed at her as we followed her parents to the living room. I liked it. More than I should.

"I don't know," she whispered. "It just slipped out."

I hummed, wrapping an arm around her waist and tugging her into me.

"Besides, what's with *you*? Laying it on a little thick, aren't you?"

"We're supposed to be in love," I reminded her.

"Akka!" One of Zofia's brothers wrapped her in a big hug, interrupting our conversation. "It's good to see you." All the worry seemed to melt off of her as she embraced her family, hugging her brothers and then her sisters-in-law before she introduced me to all of them.

Her oldest brother—Arjun—and his wife had two toddlers who were playing quietly on the carpet, while her younger brother, Kavin, who had gotten married recently, had his wife tucked into his side, who was sporting a small baby bump.

It was easy to see why her mom was eager for Zofia to settle down and get married, especially being surrounded by her family. I was an only child, and I had no idea how much pressure it must be to feel like you were competing with siblings on major life events.

Sometimes I wondered what it would be like if my mom hadn't passed away when I was young. I knew they'd struggled to conceive again, and then she'd been diagnosed with ovarian cancer. But sometimes I couldn't help but wonder what if?

Maybe if we hadn't lost her, my dad wouldn't have been such a workaholic.

Maybe he'd been a more attentive father.

Zofia's family dynamic was completely different than mine.

Her parents were warm—and it was clear how much they all loved each other. Even if her dad was a little quiet. Though she'd explained he was an engineer, and to expect that. He loved his technology, and I wondered if that was why Zo had ended up working for the company after college

Her brothers and sisters-in-law all were warm and welcoming towards me. If I'd worried about what they'd think—if they'd accept me—I shouldn't have.

After a few minutes of chitchatting, we all settled down at the dining room table. Zofia's mom had made a traditional Tamil dinner—sambar, her mom told me, which had a soup-like consistency and was made with lentils, vegetables, and spices, and served with rice. There were also several side dishes, including kovakkai poriyal, which was stir fried tindora—a type of gourd.

"Everything looks great, Sahana. Thank you." It smelled heavenly, and I was more than happy to dig in.

"So, Zofia, you said you had news?" Her mom asked after all our plates were filled.

"Oh." She looked over at me. "I thought we'd wait until after dinner—"

"Nonsense." Her mom waved her off. "You brought your new boyfriend, and we are all dying to know what you have to share."

I cleared my throat, taking her hand in mine. "About that."

Her dad was frowning at me, like he was worried I'd come to announce I'd knocked up their daughter. Thank fuck we'd used a condom in Napa. Kids were definitely not on the table.

Zo turned to me, eyes wide with panic. I took her hand in mine, kissing the back of it softly. "Zofia's actually not my girl-friend. I asked her to marry me, and she said yes."

She slipped her ring back on and held up her hand. "Surprise?"

It was deadly quiet as the whole family stared at us—until they seemed to realize that we were actually serious.

"My baby girl is getting married?" Her mother looked like she was going to cry as she stood up and came around the table to hug my fiancée.

"Yeah, Amma. I'm getting married." She patted her mom's back as she looked over at me, giving me a small smile.

"No wonder you didn't want me to set you up with someone," she said. "You could have told me you were in love. After Samir, I wasn't sure it would ever happen again."

I could practically feel Zofia's wince.

Samir? Was that an ex of hers? She'd never mentioned her past relationships, especially not a man who she'd obviously been serious enough with that he'd met her family.

After her mom pulled away—returning to her seat—I squeezed her hand, keeping it in my lap. A reminder that we were in this together. *A team.*

Her older brother's wife—Priya—lit up. "Well, you have to tell us the story, Nicolas! How did you propose?"

"Oh." I looked at Zofia, wondering why I hadn't expected this. "I was actually—"

"He was a perfect gentleman," Zofia interrupted, looking at her ring. "We went out to dinner at my favorite restaurant downtown, and then he got to one knee and asked the question over dessert. Super romantic."

It was a perfectly acceptable proposal story, and it was a damn shame it was a lie. But also, fake me could have done better.

She deserved better than some hastily written out contract.

"Yeah. They brought out a dessert that had '*Will you marry me?*' written out on the top." I leaned over and pressed my lips against her cheek. "I had it handled," I murmured against her ear.

"Sorry," she breathed. "I panicked."

I gathered as much. It was strange, seeing her in this state. Normally, she was so calm and collected, but here, she seemed frazzled. "It's okay."

We pulled apart, and realized everyone was looking at us.

"I will have to start calling venues," her mom said, changing the subject. "When do you want to get married? Do you have any thoughts on the time of year?"

"Um." Zo looked at me. "We were actually thinking something small. Maybe just going down to the courthouse?"

The room was so quiet, you could hear a pin drop.

"The *courthouse*?" Her mom repeated, aghast.

Zofia nodded. "Yes, we don't need an entire production—"

"Nonsense."

Everyone else around the table was silent as Zofia faced off against her mother. "*Amma.*"

"But you're my only daughter. And your father and I want to give you away. What about all the traditions?"

"Appa can still give me away," she insisted. "I know it's not traditional, but maybe we can plan a bigger ceremony for a year or two after we're legally married? That way, you have time to plan it, and we can both have what we want."

She looked at me, and I nodded, backing her up. "Whatever Zo wants." I understood her hesitation to have her mom plan a large, expensive wedding, especially with the contract we'd signed. Still, I couldn't help but feel like I'd taken something away from her, intentionally or not.

"When are you planning on getting married?" Zofia's father asked.

"Next month, sir," I said.

"Next month?" Her younger brother's eyes widened as Zofia took a drink from her glass. "What, Akka, are you pregnant?"

Zofia spat out her water. "No." Her eyes widened. "No, of course not."

"Then what's the rush?" Her father said. "You could take the time to have a long engagement and get to know each other first."

I put my hand over Zofia's. "With all respect, I know you're Zofia's family and you want what's best for her, but I do too. This isn't an impulsive decision, not for either of us. I admire and respect your daughter, and I just want to make her happy."

"Good answer." Her father nodded. He turned to Zo's mom. "I like him. Seems like a fine young man."

After that, the interrogation seemed to slow, though I could still sense some lingering disappointment from Zofia's mother and discomfort from Zofia.

It made sense, now, why she'd been so nervous in the car.

But the hardest part was over now, so hopefully that meant she could breathe a little easier.

"So… that wasn't so bad," I said after we were both buckled into the car.

Zofia fidgeted with the ring. "It could have gone better."

"Sure, *babe*." I flashed her a grin.

She groaned, burying her face in her hands. "Don't remind me. I don't know why I said that."

"It's cute, Gorgeous. You can call me babe if you want."

Zo spread her fingers, peeking over at me. "I would like to forget that ever happened instead."

I hummed. "Not happening."

"At least my parents seemed to accept that we didn't want the whole production for our wedding. At least, not right away. Hopefully I can put her off, and before anything happens we'll…" She trailed off, and I knew what she meant.

"That's really what you want?" I asked, turning to look at her. "I don't want to rob you of an opportunity."

"I love weddings," Zofia admitted. "Angelina and Benjamin's was beautiful, and I had such a great time. But I've never been the girl who sat around planning my *own*." A shudder ran through her. "I don't want all that attention on me. Especially not when we're, well… pretending."

"Understandable. But if you change your mind, you know I'm okay with it, right? I know your family—and culture—are important to you. I wouldn't want to get in the way of any of that."

"This is why you're such a great guy." She bit her lip. "Why are you single, anyway?"

I shrugged, because I didn't know how to answer that. Not without giving away too much of myself. "Guess I was just waiting for the right woman."

She scoffed. "Well, if you find her, let me know. I'll be happy to bow out."

Instead, I picked up her hand, kissing the ring on her finger. "No getting out now, Zo. You're my fiancée."

"*Fake* fiancée."

"The wedding will be real. None of that will be a lie."

"I know." Her voice was quiet. "I'm still wrapping my hand around all of this." She held up her hand with the ring on it. "This is crazy."

"A little," I agreed. "But it looks good on you."

She looked down at her lap. "I won't wear it around the office yet. Not until after we tell our friends."

I hated that, but I understood. "I know. We'll tell them soon, yeah?"

Driving into Zo's apartment complex, pulling into a visitor parking spot. She didn't make a move to get out of the car. She looked over at me, fidgeting with the skirt of her dress—the pretty pink making her skin practically glow. I wanted to untie the straps, to kiss her bare skin like I had that night we spent together. But she'd made it clear what she wanted out of this.

And I was respecting her boundaries.

Didn't mean I couldn't look, though. Her lips were stained a dark red color, and they looked perfectly kissable. Worse, because I knew just how soft they were.

Her eyes darted down to my lips, and her tongue darted out, moistening hers. "Nic—"

"Your mom mentioned something about a… Samir?" I asked, tilting my head at her.

She looked flushed. "Oh. You caught that, did you?"

"Yeah. Who was he to you?"

Zofia didn't meet my eyes. "My fiancée." Her voice was quiet. "I was going to tell you about him, really."

"I believe you. You don't still have feelings for him, right?"

Her laughter filled the car. "*God*, no. It's embarrassing, really." She fiddled with the hem of her skirt. "It was an arranged marriage—normal in our culture, you know? Our families were friends, and we fell in love quickly. At least… I thought we did. He moved in with me, and we were living together as we planned the wedding."

She looked out the window. "Until I caught him fucking another woman in our bed. *My* bed."

"That's why I didn't want to get married. Why I didn't want my mom to set me up again. I can't… I can't go through that again."

Oh, fuck. It was obvious I'd completely misread the situation. "That's why you reacted the way you did when I said we'd be faithful to each other. Because he wasn't faithful to you. I'm so sorry, gorgeous." Reaching over, I grabbed her hand, interlocking our fingers before kissing it. "I promise I would never do that to you." I couldn't imagine having such a beautiful woman at your side and not being satisfied. Not thinking she was *enough*, when she was… everything. She deserved to be someone's everything, and yet I was a selfish bastard for making her stuck with me.

She gave me a sad smile. "I know, Nicolas."

It was all I could offer her—and yet, somehow, I knew it wasn't enough.

11
zofia

After bringing Nicolas to meet my family, it felt like the dynamic between us had changed once again.

He'd been amazing, and I didn't know why I was surprised. I'd always known how charismatic he is, from that very first day. He was always a charmer—probably why he'd been able to talk me into being his assistant despite my reservations.

I didn't even want to think about how he could just flash that brilliant smile of his and have practically any woman falling at his feet.

Mostly because I didn't enjoy thinking about Nic with other women, especially not in his bed.

Which was strange, because I'd technically never been in *his* bed either. Not really. So why was I feeling so possessive over my fake fiancé—and my husband to be?

That's not what this was, I reminded myself. Fake nuptials or not, Nicolas and I weren't real. Ours was built on trust and mutual respect, but not on love. That was what we both wanted. It was just a contract—something I needed to remember on nights like tonight.

I lay on my bed, cuddled up with Duchess, petting her soft fur.

My phone vibrated with a text, and I pulled it out from underneath my cat. I shouldn't have been surprised that he was texting me, but it made my heart flutter. Just like it had when he'd given me the bouquet of pink peonies earlier this evening.

NICOLAS

Having cold feet yet?

Sitting up, I rested my back against the headboard as I typed a reply.

ZOFIA

No. Are you?

No.

Good.

Great.

I had fun tonight.

Me too. More than I thought I would. Even if I thought my parents were going to lose their minds when you told them we wanted to get married next month.

Your family is pretty great.

Even if your brother thought we were having a shotgun wedding.

Good thing we're not, right?

I bit my lip, wondering why the idea of having a child with him didn't sound so bad. *That* was the craziest thought I'd had all night, so I quickly shoved it away.

Yeah.

Anyway, I just wanted to check in before bed. I'll see you at the office tomorrow.

Good night, Nicolas.

Good night, Zofia.

Sweet dreams.

I fell asleep with a smile on my face, trying to ignore the fact that I was a little giddy over the man who was going to be my husband.

I tucked the ring Nicolas had given me into the velvet box, leaving it on my dresser. My hand already felt bare without it, but wearing it to work—when we hadn't told anyone else about our engagement, fake or not—didn't make much sense. Still, I rubbed my ring finger, wondering how when I'd worn it for less than twenty-four hours, it already felt like it belonged there.

Nic was in the middle of a call when I got to the office, and I settled at my desk, beginning to go through emails and making sure his calendar was set. We had a shareholder meeting later in the day that we'd need to prep for later. We had a lot of events and travel coming up, not to mention trying to figure out where *our* wedding fit into all of that.

I was also already working out the details of our annual charity gala, held every winter. It was one of my favorite parts of my job. Since Willamette Tech didn't really have an event planning department, I got to partner with Marketing whenever we had anything coming up. I *loved* it.

In another life, I like to think I would have become an event planner. One where I didn't have bills to pay or worry about where my next paycheck was coming from. Unfortunately, I didn't have the luxury of being born a billionaire—not like Nic— so I'd picked my job based on practicality, even though I'd wanted to get an event planning certificate and follow my passion.

Maybe someday.

After all, I wouldn't be Nic's assistant forever.

It wasn't the first time I'd had that thought—of course, I wouldn't be an assistant for the rest of my life—but it *was* the first time I'd considered the fact that I was his assistant... and I'd agreed to be his wife.

"What's wrong?" Nic asked as he perched against the side of my desk. He was wearing a navy blue suit today, a fancy watch on his wrist, and he looked every bit the executive that he was. Well built, tall, and handsome as ever, even with the freckles that made him look rather boyish—all part of his charm.

This was the man who was going to be my husband.

My mouth was dry. I'd forgotten how to speak, apparently.

I knew Nic. After working for him for a year, I understood him almost as well as I did myself. In all that time, I'd never seen him with a girlfriend. Never in a serious relationship.

Last night, after he'd found out about Samir—a shortened version, at least—he reassured me he'd be loyal. Deep down, I'd never had to worry about that. Somehow, I knew he wouldn't be a bad husband. Maybe because he had the biggest heart of anyone I knew. I'd never heard him speak in a harsh tone with anyone, and he was always smiling, reassuring his employees.

"Zofia?" He looked down at my ring finger and frowned, and I knew what he was thinking, but what was I going to do? Scream to the entire office that we were engaged? That he was *mine*?

That I'd done what no other woman could before—making an honest man out of Nicolas Larsen, playboy extraordinaire? I quickly brushed away the thought. *No. Absolutely not.*

The possession was a startling, sobering thought. He wasn't really mine.

I cleared my throat. "Sorry. Nothing. Lost in thought, is all."

"Was it your mom again?" He frowned. "I can talk to her, if she's pressuring you—"

"No." I waved him off. "She's fine. Taking the whole thing better than I expected, honestly."

His teeth dug into his lower lip. Soft, pink plush lips that had been surprisingly welcome against mine. Lips I'd have to kiss again, considering he was going to be my husband. But that was all playing pretend, and it wouldn't mean anything.

Soon, everything would change. Part of me couldn't wait. I looked down at my empty ring finger, missing the weight of it.

What did that say about me, that I couldn't wait to play pretend? For a while, I could imagine that he really wanted me, and it wasn't just a marriage of convenience.

Like we hadn't signed a contract with an end date in mind.

God, I needed to think about something else. *Anything* else. He hadn't kissed me last night—not on the lips, anyway—but I couldn't get it out of my mind. Maybe it was because he'd been so sweet, holding my hand and telling me we were a team.

We'd always been a team, but recently things had shifted. I didn't feel like his assistant, even if he depended on me to keep everything together… This felt like *more*.

"I have an idea," Nicolas murmured, his voice a welcome rasp against my ear. His voice was deep, and it made my nipples pebble in my bra, which thankfully was padded enough that they wouldn't show in the air-conditioned office.

"What?" I asked, but he didn't explain further.

"You'll see. Come on." He extended a hand out towards me, and I took it, rising from my desk chair.

"Where are we going?" I asked Nic, following him towards the elevator.

"Lunch."

I gave him a look. "Well, obviously."

I'd never met someone as food motivated as Nicolas. He loved to eat. In every sense of the word.

He gave me his signature grin—one that made me feel things I shouldn't be feeling, like he knew *exactly* what dirty thoughts I was thinking.

"Live a little, Gorgeous," he said, interlocking our fingers as we walked out the front door and onto the sidewalk. It was a beautiful day in Portland, so I thankfully didn't need a coat, even though I'd brought one into the office with me.

"Okay." I resisted rolling my eyes, instead enjoying the fresh air and sunshine, and the feeling of Nic's hand in mine. It was warm, his grip firm, and I really didn't hate it. Especially not because it felt like his fingers fit mine perfectly.

Maybe I shouldn't look too deeply into that. Definitely not.

"I was thinking we could hit one of our favorite food truck spots," Nic told me.

"Sure. Sounds great." There was so much good food in Portland, and I loved being able to try new places often. So did Nic—though I wasn't sure I'd ever met a food the man wouldn't eat.

As we walked through downtown, he never let go of my hand, always keeping me on the inside of the sidewalk. Even better was how he slowed his pace, keeping in time with me. Even though I was tall for a woman, at five-foot nine, Nic had a good five inches on me, and his legs were a lot longer than mine.

He really was the perfect gentleman.

Nic's eyes caught mine, and his eyes lit up, his face breaking out into the most brilliant grin.

My heart fluttered, because *damn him*. He was always calling me gorgeous, but I couldn't deny just how handsome he was. He knew it, too.

Those panty-melting smiles probably worked on lots of girls over the years. My mood soured. I didn't want to think about everyone else. Not when I'd been with enough men in my life to count them all on one hand—including Nicolas. I *liked* sex, but I was a committed relationship kind of girl. I didn't have one-night stands.

Until Nicolas.

Though I was starting to feel like I didn't really know how him at all.

I knew his reputation with women. Had heard stories about his past exploits—when he'd had a different woman on his arm for every event. He was still a giant flirt, but I had such a hard time reconciling those stories with the man next to me today. Maybe because he seemed to have everything together now, and I hadn't seen him flirt with another woman in the last year.

He'd struggled in the beginning to adjust to the role of CEO. Partially because his dad had sprung it on him sooner than he'd ever expected, but we'd found our groove. Still, I couldn't imagine leaving him to fend against the wolves without me. Like it or not, he needed me.

Just like he needed this marriage.

I knew Nic planned to tell the board, but I wasn't sure what he was waiting for. I was fine with it, with no one knowing yet, because I wasn't ready for everything to change once again. We'd gotten used to our new normal after Napa—after spending that night wrapped up in his arms—but this would change *everything*.

After we ordered and got our food, he led us over to a picnic table, nestled against the backdrop of the city. No matter where you went in Portland, there were trees and greenery everywhere. It rained almost the entire year—it felt like a constant drizzle every month except summer—but that made the scenery unbeatable.

"This is just what I needed," I said, taking a deep breath before diving into my food.

Nic smiled at me as he took a bite of his own food. "Good. You looked distracted, maybe a little nervous, and I wanted to fix it. You're always doing so much for me, and I wanted to do something for you, too."

"Oh, Nic. You don't have to—"

"I know what you're giving up to marry me, and I don't want you to regret it." He shook his head. "So just let me, okay?"

I kissed the back of his hand, because what else did you say to that sort of thing? I wanted to tell him I wasn't giving up anything. That I'd long ago resigned myself that I'd never have that. Especially when I loved my life and didn't want someone else to change it. Instead, I just said, "Okay. Thank you."

He smiled at me, and for the moment, it felt like everything was going to be okay.

12
nicolas

We were really doing this.

"Hey." I leaned against my car, grinning at her. It was easy to act like this—to be the cocky, playboy guy everyone loved. It was far harder to be real, to divulge every truth about myself and lay myself bare in front of the woman I wanted, the woman who was *mine*, and yet I couldn't have.

"Hi." Zofia gave me a small smile, suitcases ready at her side for our trip to Vegas.

That was when I realized—*she was wearing it.* My heart practically skipped a few beats with the realization that Zofia was wearing my ring. Why did that satisfy some primal part of me?

Why did I like it so much that the ring I'd painstakingly chosen looked so perfect on her?

"You're wearing it."

She rubbed it absentmindedly, like she was still trying to get used to it. "Yeah. I just figured, well… We're doing this, aren't we? It's like a practice run before we tell the rest of the world."

"Yeah." My voice was rough. It felt like we were discussing a business contract, not our *marriage*. "Ready to go?"

Zofia turned, looking back at her apartment. "Yeah. My

brothers are going to come over this week to check on Duchess. So…" she hummed, rocking on her heels.

"We should probably practice," I blurted out.

"Practice?" Zofia froze, her eyes wide. "Practice *what?*"

I shot her a look. "You know what, Gorgeous." My hands wrapped around her waist as I pulled her between my legs, trying to ignore how fast my heart was pounding.

"Why do we need to practice?" Her voice was calm and collected, totally the opposite of how I was feeling inside.

"Because we want people to think we're in *love*, Zo. This will never work if we can't touch each other openly." I brushed a piece of hair behind her ear, and she bit her lip. "It's not like we haven't before," I reminded her.

She shook her head, her hands curling over the edges of my desk. "We agreed—"

Letting my hands rest on her thighs, I rubbed them absent-mindedly, watching her eyes dip down to my lips. "I know," I said, voice soft. "Do I… make you uncomfortable?"

"Oh, Nic. No." Zofia shook her head. "Of course not. You never have. That's not the problem."

"So what is?" I was well aware of how husky my voice sounded, how close together we both were.

"You know what," she said, echoing my sentiment.

Yeah, I was pretty sure I did. "Kiss me," I begged. "All I can think about is having your lips back on mine."

"Nicolas—" She gave a weak whimper of protest, but didn't stop me when I slid my hand around the back of her neck, pulling her closer to me until our lips were almost touching.

"Tell me to stop," I murmured. "If you don't want this, push me away. We can tear up that contract right now and pretend like none of it ever happened. But if you want this—want me—then kiss me, Zofia."

Her lips were on mine before I could blink, soft and warm and inviting, everything I'd dreamed about over the last few months. Zofia wrapped her arms around my neck, kissing me harder, our mouths devouring each other in what promised to be a repeat of before. I groaned into her mouth as she opened for me, her tongue sliding against mine, the kiss turning deeper, more urgent.

She tightened her hold on the back of my head, fingers gripping my hair as I pulled on her bottom lip with my teeth before kissing her again, lips moving against hers like I couldn't get enough.

Because I couldn't. When we pulled apart, panting, I rested my forehead against hers.

"Think that's good enough to convince them?" she asked, nipping at my bottom lip one last time.

It was a reminder of what this was. *Practice.*

Fuck. I smoothed a hand over my face, trying to calm my body's reaction to her mouth on mine. My cock was already half-hard in my pants, pressing against the zipper angrily.

"Yeah, gorgeous. Kiss me like that, and I don't think we'll have any problems with people believing we're in love."

I willed my erection to go away, trying to think of the least sexy things possible. Anything but my fake fiancée, standing next to my car, lips swollen from kisses. Our *no sex* rule was definitely going to be the death of me.

And we had a flight to catch.

"Showtime," I told her, opening the door for her. I pressed a kiss to her forehead before rounding the car, buckling myself in.

It had been hard enough to keep my hands off of her in the office these past weeks. Now that we were fake engaged, and she was wearing my ring? It was a temptation almost too hard to pass up.

But I needed to.

After this week, we'd get married and she'd move into my place. She'd be so deeply entrenched in my life, I couldn't possibly get her out.

I needed her like I needed air.

But we had an agreement, and I knew it wasn't like that for Zo.

So I wouldn't push her. I was letting her have the reins because I knew what I wanted—*her*.

For better or for worse, for richer or poorer, in sickness and in health.

And yet, even knowing what we agreed, she still wasn't mine.

Which is why I wasn't allowed to touch her. Wasn't allowed to feel her skin against mine.

Because it was irresponsible to give in to this heat between us again.

13
zofia

While it wasn't the first work conference Nic and I had attended together, it *was* the first one where I'd had his ring on my finger. At first, I'd considered taking it off, but after Nic's reaction when he'd found me wearing it this morning, I didn't have the heart to.

The plane ride to Vegas was two hours, and since we'd taken the company jet, we had the benefit of being alone on the flight, with minimal crew there to assist us if we needed anything. Mostly, we spent the flight on separate sides of the aisle, both engrossed in our own little worlds. I was reading a book that the girls had recommended to me. I'd been working my way through the series slowly, and was finally on the last book. The main character took no shit, and I loved that about her.

Nicolas had his laptop out and a pair of headphones in, busy working on some sort of report, giving me the chance to study him unabashedly.

He was gorgeous; it was undeniable. Between those deep turquoise blue eyes and his soft blond waves and that brilliant smile. I adored his little smattering of freckles along his nose and cheeks, faint in the winter but darker every summer when he spent more time in the sun.

We were so different that sometimes it felt easier to point out those differences than to find similarities.

But I couldn't deny how part of me called to him. We were dancing around each other, and I wasn't sure how much longer either of us could resist the temptation. It was getting harder to deny that I wanted him, and I wasn't sure I *wanted* to, either.

Especially after that practice kiss that left me panting, an ache between my legs I knew I'd never be able to fulfill on my own.

Nic went to check us into our room, leaving me in the lobby with our bags.

When he came back, it was with a grimace on his face.

"What's wrong?"

"There was a mix-up with the reservations." He ran his fingers through the long blond strands, holding up a singular envelope of room keys. "We were supposed to have two rooms, but they only have one."

I frowned. "I definitely booked two—"

"I know. They overbooked, I guess? He upgraded it to a suite for the trouble, but we're going to have to share."

My eyes darted down to my ring. "Oh. Well, I guess then let's go get comfortable, *roomie*." I supposed it was practice for when I moved in with him, after all.

"Zo—" he protested as I grabbed the keycards out of his hand.

Nic grabbed the bags as I headed towards the elevator that would take us up to our room, ignoring the butterflies I had thinking about sharing a room with him. The last time we'd shared a bed, I'd discovered just how good he was with his tongue. And his fingers. And—

Fuck, I was not supposed to be thinking about how much I wanted him inside me again. Especially not when I could feel the heat of him against my back.

I opened the door, the full reality of our next few days staring back at me. It was a fantastic suite—with a separate living area with a couch, plus a kitchenette—but it was very obvious from my quick perusal that our bed choices were very limited.

Whirling around, I stared at him. "There's only one bed."

"I was trying to tell you that. They only had a king suite available."

I almost laughed. The girls would get a kick out of this.

"What?" He furrowed his eyebrows.

"Nothing." I waved him off. "It's a popular romance trope. The girls would find it hilarious." Though at least three of them were probably more than happy to share a bed with their significant others, since Gabbi and Hunter were now dating, too.

I wouldn't be surprised if Charlotte and Daniel weren't far behind.

Technically, we wouldn't be either, considering we were getting married. *Fake married,* I tried to remind myself. Just a contractual marriage, not a real one.

And yet, nothing about *this* felt fake.

The room felt smaller, somehow, with Nic's presence next to me, the smell of his cologne invading all of my senses. He smelled like driftwood and clean laundry, and I couldn't get enough of it.

"So, I guess we're sharing a bed," I said, unable to tear my eyes off it to look at Nicolas. I was afraid that if I did, he'd see too many things I wasn't ready to share yet.

He brushed a lock of hair behind my ear, his mouth dipping dangerously close to my ear. "We've shared a bed before, Zo."

"That was different," I protested, my words almost a whisper.

"How?"

"We weren't… *engaged* before." I looked down at the ring on my finger. It was a constant reminder that none of this was really real. That there was a contract we'd signed, saying we'd both play along.

"Shouldn't that make it better, gorgeous?"

I shrugged. "It's all fake, anyway."

"Zofia." His voice was stern.

I shook my head, still not looking at him. "It's fine. I'm going to live with you soon anyway, right? Let's just unpack and then head down to the mixer."

Nic let out a huff, but didn't argue with me.

Trying to ignore how his presence lit up my body, I unzipped my suitcase, hanging up my dresses before opening a drawer and sliding my folded bras, underwear, and pajamas inside. We didn't speak as we organized our things, and I had to admit there was something almost comfortable about the silence.

"I'm gonna go freshen up," I murmured to him, a change of clothes in my arms before heading into the bathroom. It was huge, complete with a large tub and a waterfall shower, and I was already looking forward to enjoying the bathtub later.

Nicolas was being a perfect gentleman. So much so that I wanted to scream. Would it really be so bad if we ended up in bed together again? We were getting married after all.

Why had I been the one to say *no sex*? Especially after that kiss. And *oh*, I'd be replaying that kiss every night once I slipped under the covers of my bed. Like that spark had somehow grown into a raging inferno, and I couldn't ignore it anymore.

Every time his hand brushed mine. Every time I caught him staring at me from across the room. Every time my heart sped up when he leaned over my desk, and I could smell his cologne.

Heat pooled in my veins, remembering what it was like to

have him wrapped around me, to have him inside of me. It was all too much. And yet, I wanted more. Needed more.

Alone, in the dark, I could admit what I wanted. What my body craved.

All I knew is I needed to keep my distance, because if today was any indication, it was already feeling harder and harder to stay away.

Now that we were sharing a room, it was going to be even harder.

After checking into the conference and getting our name badges, we were swept into the welcome mixer. The room was crowded with other CEOs and business executives alike who worked in the technology industry, all dressed impeccably in suits. They were eager to network and make connections, and I knew just how important things like this could be for securing future contracts.

All the men in suits together made me wonder if I had a thing for guys in suits suddenly. Maybe it was competence porn, because I knew they were just as smart as they were handsome.

But it was hard to deny that there was only one man I wanted to take me home at the end of the night.

Only one man whose ring I was wearing.

"Nicolas," I murmured, tugging on his hand before we could get pulled into conversation with anyone.

"You okay?" He asked, brushing a strand of hair back behind my ear.

I nodded. "Of course. I just wanted to check how *you* were doing with all this."

His mouth opened and then closed, like he didn't know what to do with that information.

Then he smiled. "Good. Even better, because you're here and I don't have to do this alone." He dropped a kiss to the crown of my head. "Just don't abandon me."

"Never," I promised.

Nic nodded. "Let's go get a drink." He interlaced his fingers through mine, tugging me towards the bar.

"Larsen." A dark haired older man approached us as we sipped on our drinks a few minutes later. He had a younger woman on his arm, who was sporting a small baby bump.

"Sinclair," my fake fiancé grinned at the man. "Good to see you."

He nodded, rubbing his dark beard. "You remember my wife, Tanya?" She was beautiful—blonde and slender with a giant diamond ring on her finger.

Nic turned to her, murmuring, "Of course. So nice to see you again," before turning back to me. I gave him a small smile. "Zofia, this is Robert Sinclair, founder of Sinclair Industries—and his wife, Tanya."

"Oh, it's nice to meet you," I said, holding out my right hand for him to shake it. I knew the company well—they were based out of NYC, and one of our biggest competitors in the industry.

"And who might this be, Larsen?" He asked, a hint of amusement.

Had Nicolas come to these kind of events before with women on his arm? I hated the thought immediately, even though I'd only been his assistant for the past year. I was attributing my jealousy to the fact that I had his ring on my finger, not because I was worried he'd slept with his previous assistants.

Nic's arm wrapped around my waist. "This is my executive assistant, Zofia Narayan." His hand splayed possessively over my hip, and I found I didn't hate it. "And my *fiancée*." The tone of his voice left nothing to the imagination.

I curled my hand over his bicep, giving them both a tight smile.

"Fiancée?" Robert Sinclair's face lit up with delight. "Oh, we absolutely have to catch up. I need to hear all about this."

Nic nodded towards the edge of the restaurant, where an empty booth waited. He pressed his palm onto my lower back, guiding me towards the table.

"He's friends with my father." His voice was low, barely audible over the chatter in the room. "We have to—"

I nodded. "I know," I reassured him.

We settled onto the bench, and Nic slid his arm around my waist, tugging me closer to his side.

"Comfortable?" He murmured in my ear, like he was making sure I was okay.

I nodded, trying to relax into him, though my body was like a live wire, and all it would take was one spark.... "Yes," I murmured. My drink was empty, and I sat it on the table, crossing my hands in my lap.

Nic's hand still rested on my hip, that arm curled around me, and he made no move to remove it.

"Want another drink?" His breath warmed my neck, goosebumps erupting down my arms.

Nodding, I looked at him, wondering if he looked *extra* handsome tonight, or if it was just my hormones crying at the sheer proximity to him. Nicolas might have been two years younger than me, but he was all man. And I liked it more than I should.

The waiter came by, and he ordered me another glass of the wine I'd been drinking without even having to ask. I appreciated that—how attentive he was, always checking on me to make sure I was okay. It reminded me of how my father had always doted on my mother, and I softened even more at the thought.

I was aware we were playing pretend, but I couldn't deny the thrill it gave me to have him touching me so openly. To have his hands on me.

Sliding my hand onto his jaw, I pressed a kiss to his cheek. "Thanks, honey."

He chuckled. "You're welcome, gorgeous."

"I'm dying to hear how you two met," Tanya said, the first words I'd heard from her all night besides our short introductions.

Nic was the one to start. "I walked in to her office and begged her to be mine."

"His *assistant*," I clarified.

My fake fiancé smirked. "Yeah. When my dad told me his plan to retire, I knew I needed to step up my game. I'd had some trouble with my previous string of assistants, and I'd always noticed her and her excellent work ethic." He grinned at me, and I felt my cheeks flush. I knew it was all a lie, but maybe I liked the idea that he'd always noticed me, even throughout all the years where we'd hardly known each other.

Our new glasses of wine were placed on the table, as well as some appetizers that the guys had ordered.

Tanya sipped on a glass of ginger ale, since she was pregnant. Watching the two of them and how tenderly he treated her made me wonder about my future. I couldn't help but wonder how Nicolas felt about having children. We'd never actually talked about it. Did he even want children?

I knew why he'd chosen to go through with a fake marriage, but I had no idea why he didn't just try to have an *actual* relationship.

His hand squeezed my hip, and I refocused myself on our current task, both of us going back and forth as we gave our fictional story of how we fell in love over lunches and working long hours together in the office. How we didn't want to hide our relationship anymore, and we couldn't wait to get married.

The thing was, it didn't feel entirely fictional anymore.

After about an hour of visiting with them, I rested my head on his shoulder, enjoying being able to act so freely with him.

"Do you want to get out of here?" Nic asked, his lips brushing over the crown of my head.

I nodded, heat pooling in my lower abdomen as Nic's hand rested in the small of my back. It warmed me through to my core, and I was desperate for more.

After tonight, I wasn't sure if I could keep insisting on my no sex rule. Especially when all I wanted was his hands on me and his mouth on mine.

We made it back to the suite before he pounced, pressing me up against the door. Nicolas kissed my neck, and I had to hold in my moan.

I'd been dreaming of his touch ever since we'd left Napa. Couldn't believe how much I craved it, but it was like the second he touched me, I was on fire.

"Liked when you called me honey," he rasped, his hands on my hips. "Wanted to kiss you all night."

I wrapped my arms around his neck, my eyes intent on his. "Then what are you waiting for, *honey?*"

"Fuck, gorgeous." He pressed his forehead against mine. "Share the bed with me tonight," he pleaded.

"This isn't real," I reminded him, but there was no real heat to my words. Yet, even with my protest, I didn't make a move to step away from him when his mouth trailed over my skin.

"What happens out there might not be real, but this certainly is."

I looked down at the ring on my finger. *Was it?*

14
nicolas

on't think about any of that," I told her, pressing a kiss to the side of her lips. "Just think about me. How good I can make you feel."

Her eyes shut, her head leaning back against the door, and I tugged on a tight curl.

She was so beautiful, I couldn't believe it. I couldn't believe she was wearing my ring on her finger, that all night I'd had my hand on her. It was impossible not to when she looked like that, knowing that for better or for worse she was going to be mine.

"God, you in this fucking dress," I murmured, tracing a finger down her neck and over her collarbone. The champagne satin clung to her every curve, showing off her incredible body. "I can't fucking stand how beautiful you are, baby." She tilted her head to the side, giving me access, and I pressed a kiss to the soft skin of her neck.

"Nicolas," she gasped. "I want to make an amendment to the contract."

"Oh yeah?" I trailed my lips down her soft skin. "Which part?"

"The *no sex* part," she said, letting out a whimper as I brushed her straps off her shoulder.

I hummed. "And what do you propose, my darling fiancée?"

Her eyes were dark when they met mine, her pupils practically overtaking her dark brown irises. "That you fuck me."

"*Fuck*, gorgeous. Is that what you need?" I unzipped the back of her dress, letting it slide down her body in a ripple of fabric, baring her beautiful body to me. She wasn't wearing a bra, and I let out a groan at the sight in front of me. "You need to be fucked?"

"*Yes*," she moaned. "Please." Her pretty brown nipples were perky and hard, begging for attention from my mouth.

There was no way I could deny her. I grasped her chin with one hand as I tugged her body into mine with the other. Wrapping my arm around her body, I let my palm settle on her lower back, groaning at the feeling of her skin as I brought my lips to hers, kissing her deeply.

Her hands explored my chest, tracing up my abs until she reached the top. Zofia's hands tightened on my shirt collar. "Need this off." She fumbled with the buttons, finally reaching the bottom one before pushing it off my shoulders and letting it fall to the floor.

She brought her lips to my chest, kissing down lower as she dropped to her knees, unzipping my pants.

"Zofia—" I protested.

Her eyes met mine as she looked up at me, looking sexy as sin in only her panties, kneeling in front of me. "Let me," she murmured. "I didn't get to taste you before."

I smoothed her hair away from her face, bringing a fistful of her hair up into a ponytail as she pulled my hard cock out, her tongue darting out to run over the tip. She wrapped a hand around my shaft, slowly pumping up and down as she took the crown into her mouth, closing her lips around it.

Groaning, I tightened my grip on her hair. "If you don't stop, this is going to be over way too fast."

Her eyes sparked with amusement, and she took me in deeper, her hand dipping between her legs, pushing her panties aside to dip her fingers inside her pussy. Fuck, but knowing she was turned on from sucking my cock only spurred me on more. Gripping her hair, I helped her work herself up and down my length, coating it in her saliva.

Finally, when I could feel my balls tightening, so close to release, I pulled myself out of her lips, desperate to be inside her instead.

Pulling her up, I crashed my lips on hers, not caring if I tasted my pre-cum on her lips, and then lifted her into my arms, carrying her to the hotel bed. "I need to be inside you," I grunted, setting her down on the comforter. Making quick work of my pants and underwear, I climbed up onto the bed next to her, hooking my thumbs into her panties.

Her eyes met mine as I dragged them down her gorgeous long legs, baring her sweet cunt to me. Groaning, I buried my face between her legs, inhaling her scent and lapping up her arousal, swirling my tongue over her clit until she was moaning for more.

My cock was hard as steel, and I rocked against the mattress as I ate her out, desperate for relief.

Relief that would only come when I was buried inside my wife-to-be's pussy.

I'd been desperate for her all night, and this was better than I remembered.

"Oh, fuck, Nic," she shuddered, and I could feel how close she was when I slid two fingers into her entrance, working them inside her as I sucked on her clit. Her walls clamped down around me as her orgasm hit her, and I kept massaging her with my fingers through it until she was dripping and pliant and absolutely *needy*, bucking her hips against my face.

"That's it," I cooed. "Soak my face. So sweet, I want your taste on my tongue every day."

Zofia let out a whine when I pulled my fingers out, resting back on my knees as I appraised her, watching as her chest rose and fell quickly before her breathing evened out.

Her dark, tight curls were spread out around her, a stark contrast to the white comforter. Zofia's warm brown skin *glowed*, even in the hotel room lighting. She looked like a goddess. I was pretty sure that if Aphrodite had a human form, she would look like Zofia Narayan.

"Beautiful," I praised, thinking that word paled compared to her. "The fact that I haven't had you in my *own* bed yet is a damn shame," I muttered, thinking about all the things I wanted to do to her once I had her in my house.

"*Yet*," she said, like it were the key word.

She gave me a sly smile as I reached down, fisting my cock, tugging at the length a few times. "Damn right. Because if the no sex rule is gone, I'm going to fuck *my wife* every chance I get. No more holding back, Zofia." There was no way I could after having her again.

These last few months had been torture, and I was just glad we were finally putting each other out of our misery.

My girl nodded in agreement. "No more holding back."

I pulled out a condom from my bag, glad I had the foresight to pack some. Rolling it down my shaft, I positioned myself between her hips, notching my tip at her entrance. "Yes?"

She nodded eagerly. "*Yes*. Please, I want to feel you."

The head slipped inside, and I couldn't ignore the feeling of rightness as her body enveloped me.

"Ah, fuck, baby." I groaned, resting my head against her shoulder as I pushed inside of her. "You're so damn tight." I had to close my eyes as I got used to being inside her once again, not wanting to come yet.

She let out a moan as I slid inside to the hilt, my hands

resting on her waist, holding her tight. "Maybe you're just too *big*."

I chuckled. "No need to inflate my ego, gorgeous."

Zo reached up, sliding her hands into my hair and tugging my mouth down to hers. "Less talking," she rasped. "More fucking."

This time, we both groaned as I drew out before slamming in again.

"Been wanting a repeat of this ever since that first night," I admitted, a rasp against her skin as I thrust into her, over and over. "Wanted to wake up next to you and bury myself in your perfect pussy again. Even though I knew it was wrong."

She cried out as I slammed to the hilt, unable to hold my hips back from rolling against hers. The room was filled with the filthy sounds of us fucking, skin against skin, and the bed frame creaked with each roll of my hips as I pumped inside her.

"I wanted you too," she admitted, her fingernails digging into my shoulders. "Even when I knew I shouldn't want my *boss*."

Her inner muscles squeezed around me, and I cursed. "Need you to come again before I do," I told her, dropping my head to her gorgeous tits. "Touch your clit. Let me feel you clench around my cock."

I sucked her nipple into my mouth as she reached down, her fingers rubbing against that little bundle of nerves as I rolled my tongue over her hardened peak, lavishing it with attention. With a wet pop, I switched to the other side, until both her breasts were shiny from my saliva.

"So fucking pretty," I murmured, my thumb rubbing her brown nipples. "These deserve to be worshipped every day." I pressed a kiss to each swell, resolving myself to do just that.

That was a husband's job, right? To satisfy his wife.

And fuck if I wouldn't satisfy my woman.

I focused on shallow thrusts inside of her, rocking against

that soft spot that made her moan louder as she circled her clit. My hands were so tight on her hips, keeping her in place, that I thought she might have bruises from my fingers, but I *liked* that.

Liked the idea of marking her with my fingerprints, with bruises I put there, as much as I liked her wearing my ring and telling people she was *mine.*

"Mine," I grunted, dropping my open mouth to her neck as I buried myself inside her, holding her tight to my body.

Zofia wrapped her legs around mine, giving a small whimper of pleasure. "I'm so close, Nic," she said, her eyes fluttering shut.

My lips were a breath from hers. "I want to watch your face as you come," I told her. "As you give me your pleasure."

"*Ohmyg—*" she cried, her cunt clenching me tighter, spasming around me as her orgasm took hold. Her back arched off the bed, ankles tightening around my waist like she wanted me deeper. It didn't take much more for me to follow behind, not when the fluttering sensations around my cock felt better than anything else I'd ever imagined.

It was all her—all Zofia.

"That's it," I soothed, pushing hair back from her forehead as we both collapsed back onto the bed, sweaty and spent. "Such a good girl."

She mumbled something incoherent, and I knew I needed to get up—to take care of the condom, to make sure Zofia was taken care of—but for the moment, all I wanted to do was hold her. To keep her in my arms, feeling her there, knowing that she wouldn't disappear the next morning.

Knowing that I might not have her forever, at least I had tomorrow.

Even though no part of me wanted to give her up.

Zofia was cradled in my arms when I woke, the way I wished we could have woken up months ago. Sunlight streamed in through the large windows, illuminating the bedroom, allowing me to appreciate her soft features in sleep.

I wouldn't complain now. Not when last night had been everything I'd wanted for so long.

I didn't move, not wanting to wake her, and just admired my view. Neither of us had bothered with clothes after we'd gotten cleaned up last night, so her shoulders were bare, her curls spilling down her back.

She stirred in my arms, and I pressed a kiss to her shoulder, trying to ignore the way I was already hard from her body's proximity to mine.

"Good morning."

"Mmm." She turned, nuzzling her face into my neck. "It is."

Her ass was pressed against my cock, erect and desperate to be back inside her, as if I hadn't spent most of the night inside her. She stretched out like a cat, pushing further into my erection, and I groaned. "*Fuck*, baby."

Zofia smirked at me as I gripped her hips, stilling them. "Let's get married."

She blinked as she sat up, the sheet falling off her as she turned to look at me. She held up her left hand—the one with my ring—like that meant something.

"I already said yes, Nicolas. Remember, we signed a contract?"

Of course I did. That was why I felt so crazy possessive over her, after all.

"I mean, right now. *Today*. We're in Vegas. Let's just go do it. I don't want to wait anymore to call you my wife." I gave her my best grin, doing my best not to stare at her tits, which was difficult because they were *incredible*. Sucking on them last night as I thrust inside her was better than I'd ever imagined it could be, and I wanted to see if I could make her come just from that next time.

I pulled her onto my lap, the sheet in between us as she straddled me.

Zofia wrapped her arms around my neck, her fingers combing through the back of my hair. "I don't even have a dress here."

I shrugged, letting my hands rest on her waist. "You remember what I said about shopping? I'm sure we can find something." In fact, I'd already researched bridal boutiques before we'd ever left Portland, wanting to take her somewhere to let her look at dresses anyway.

This would just be the icing on the cake.

She frowned, pausing her fingers in my hair. "You're… really serious, aren't you?"

I squeezed her hips. "Yeah, Zofia. I am. Be my wife. Marry me. *Today.*"

Zofia looked over at the clock, her dark brows suddenly furrowed. "Don't we have conference sessions and meetings today?"

I shrugged. "Fuck those. We'll play hooky."

She laughed. "Who are you, and what have you done with Nicolas Larsen?"

"What can I say? Being an engaged man has changed me. And I really want to spend tonight eating my wife's sweet pussy."

Zofia smacked my chest, but I could see the amusement in her expression. *She was enjoying this as much as I was.* "Okay. Okay. *Fine.* But are we really going to do this without our friends?"

I kissed her lips once, twice. "We can have a party when we get back. I don't need the whole big wedding." *I just need you.* "All I care about is that you're the one on the other end of the aisle."

"I have to admit, it sounds easier than having to figure out all the logistics…" Zo's hand draped over my chest. I wondered if she could feel how rapidly my heart beat for her. How hard I was for her. How much I *needed* her. "Alright. Let's get married, then." She shook her head in exasperation. "This is *crazy*."

Zofia tried to get off me, but I kept her on my lap and pressed a kiss to her cheek. "Maybe. Or maybe it's exactly how we're meant to do this." I grinned, nipping her lower lip before kissing her softly. "Before we do anything, shower with me."

She gave me a look. "We won't get out of here for a while if we shower together, Nic, and you know it."

"Worth it," I grinned, trailing my lips down her neck. "Besides. I didn't get enough of you last night." I sucked one of her nipples into my mouth before standing up, keeping her in my arms as I walked towards the large shower.

Getting upgraded to a suite had its benefits. This was one of them. I set Zo down on her feet as I reached in, turning on the waterfall shower that I definitely wanted to take advantage of while we were here.

When it was warm, I pulled her inside with me, letting the water run over us as I wrapped my arms around her body, tugging her against me.

"I don't even want to leave the room today," I said against her skin.

"Down, boy," she said, her fingers scrubbing into my hair. "You can worship me again later."

"Bet." I grinned. That was a promise I would definitely keep.

15
zofia

Despite Nic's efforts, we didn't skip the entire conference that day, even though I knew how antsy he was to say *I do*. I didn't know what had changed between us, with him, but I liked it.

Especially if it meant that we could have a repeat like last night more often.

After the sessions ended for the afternoon, I headed out to shop—in the private town car that he'd hired for me. I still wasn't used to the way he wanted to pamper and spoil me, giving me his black American Express credit card to buy anything I wanted. This was all new, and I didn't know how to react. I'd never been with someone like Nic before. He didn't throw his money around, and even though I knew his bank account had a lot of zeros after it, sometimes I forgot how wealthy he truly was.

I closed my eyes as I pulled on the white satin dress, loving the way the soft fabric felt against my skin. True to his word, Nicolas had found a few different bridal boutiques and made appointments for me as a surprise—*before* he'd come up with the crazy idea of getting married before we left to go home.

"What do you think?" The sales associate asked me as I stared into the full-length mirror. The dress was calf-length and had an off-the-shoulder design with a structured bodice.

I looked like a *bride*. Before I'd left the room this morning, I'd pinned my curls up on my head, and when the sales girl helping me slid a tulle veil on a comb into the back of my hair, I knew *this* was the dress.

Fiddling with the gold pendant around my neck, I nodded. "It's perfect."

"You look beautiful," she told me, resting her hand on my arm. "Your groom is one lucky man."

"Thank you," I said, unable to take my eyes off the mirror. "But I think I'm the lucky one."

After a few extra stops, I arrived back to the suite, dress bag draped over one arm, and my shopping bags in the other. There was a beautiful bouquet sitting on the table, and I reached out, brushing my fingers over the petal. When I turned, I found my husband to be watching me, leaning against the doorframe.

"What are these?" I asked him as I took in the flowers, setting my bags down on the bed.

He looked nervous, and it was adorable. Most of the time, I could forget that he was two years younger than me, but times like this, it was obvious. "I thought you'd want a bouquet, so I called and…" Nicolas shoved his hands in his pockets. "It's too much, right?" He cursed.

"You didn't have to do this," I whispered. The bouquet was made of peonies, lilies, baby's breath, and the gesture made my eyes water. "They're beautiful."

Nic grinned. "Beautiful flowers for a beautiful woman."

"Thank you," I croaked, feeling overwhelmed with emotions.

He pulled me into his arms, holding me tight. "Anything for my wife."

"Not your wife *yet*," I reminded him.

He just grinned at me, his hand rubbing soothing circles on my back. "Tonight, Zo."

I nodded and took a deep breath, inhaling his ocean-scented cologne. "Tonight."

The little white chapel loomed in front of us, and I smoothed down the front of my dress, feeling nervous all the sudden.

"Having second thoughts?" he murmured at my side. I turned to look at him, appreciating how handsome he looked in his three-piece black suit with his blond hair combed back. He'd let it grow out a little, and I loved it was long enough for me to run my fingers through.

I frowned at him. "About what?"

Nicolas's lips dipped close to my ear. "Our wedding."

"No." I shook my head. "I'm still game as long as you are."

He chuckled. "That's good to hear, but not what I meant." His finger caressed under my chin before urging it up, forcing me to look at the decor. "I mean about *this*. *Eloping*. Not having a big wedding. The ceremony, the flowers, the dress."

Sure, part of me *wanted* all of that. Especially after going to Angelina's wedding this summer in France. But then I thought about the wedding I'd been planning with my ex, and how awful it had been, calling all the vendors to cancel.

"I don't need that," I answered, knowing I couldn't go through the heartbreak of that again. "It's beautiful, don't get me wrong, but…" That was a *real* wedding, and ours was *fake*. I squeezed his hand. "This is fine," I promised.

Fine was good enough for a contract, wasn't it?

"Okay." He looked like he was resisting reaching out to touch me. "If that's what you want."

My chin dipped in a nod. "It is."

Nicolas looked away. "Right."

"No Elvis," I specified, narrowing my eyes.

He laughed, his hand wrapping around my neck, bringing us together before he dropped a kiss to my lips. "Agreed, Gorgeous. No Elvis. Just us."

"Just Zofia and Nicolas," I whispered.

"Ready to marry me?"

"Yes."

And surprisingly, I was. Maybe it was the dress, the veil, and the bouquet he'd so thoughtfully gotten me, but I felt like a bride.

It was crazy that I was about to be someone's *wife*. Contract or not, Nicolas was going to be my husband.

He laced his fingers through mine, and we walked in the chapel, finishing the rest of the process, though Nic had called earlier to set most of it up. We'd chosen to do the photo package as well, so we had something to prove our wedding had actually *happened* and was legit. With our wedding certificate in hand, we waited to be called up.

When it was our turn, we walked hand in hand into the chapel. I felt like I was clinging to him like he was my lifeline. In some ways, maybe he was.

The officiant looked at us, and after we nodded, started the ceremony. "Zofia and Nicolas, we are gathered here today in the heart of Las Vegas to celebrate your love and commitment to one another."

We'd opted for something simple, which I preferred. I didn't need all the bells and whistles for a marriage that wouldn't last over two years. I clutched the bouquet in my other hand tighter, my heart racing a million miles per hour as they went through the words.

"Repeat after me," the officiant said to me, and I nodded, swallowing roughly.

Holding Nicolas's hands, I couldn't look away from his eyes, wondering what this might feel like if it were real. "I, Zofia, take you, Nicolas, to be my husband, to have and to hold from this day forward, for better or worse, for richer or poorer, in sickness and in health, to love and to cherish, until death do us part."

My husband-to-be did the same, squeezing my hand before he started. "I, Nicolas, take you, Zofia, to be my wife, to have and to hold from this day forward, for better or worse, for richer or poorer, in sickness and in health, to love and to cherish, until death do us part."

Our officiant looked between us, her eyes warm. "Do you have rings?"

Nicolas shook his head. Biting my lip, I pulled the gold band I'd bought him today out of my dress pocket—along with my engagement ring. "Here," I whispered. I could see the question in his eyes, the surprise that I'd gotten him a ring, too.

But it was only fair, fake or not, that I returned the favor.

"These rings are a symbol of your love and commitment, an unbroken circle symbolizing an unending, committed love," she said as we slid them on to each other's ring fingers.

I'd gotten used to how the engagement ring looked on me, but it felt different now. More *real*, somehow.

"By the power vested in me by the State of Nevada, I now pronounce you husband and wife," she announced. "You may now kiss the bride!"

Nicolas stepped closer, one hand cupping the back of my neck and the other resting against the small of my back, as he pressed his lips against mine, soft and firm. It was tender and precious, like he knew exactly what I needed in that moment. He pulled back, resting his forehead against mine. "How do you feel, *Mrs. Larsen*?"

I couldn't help but let out a giggle. "Like you should take me back to the room, *Mr. Larsen*."

He grinned. "Anything for my *wife*."

He picked me up into his arms and carried me bridal style out of the chapel.

The door slammed shut behind us when we finally made it back to our hotel room later, after an entire session of photos and consuming the best fast food and milkshake of my *life*. Maybe it was just because I'd been starving, or how greasy it was, but it was delicious.

Also delicious? My husband in his wedding suit. My husband wearing the ring I'd bought him. My *husband*, period.

It had been hard to focus as the photographer had reposi-tioned us, as we were tangled up in each other, when all I wanted was for him to shed his golden retriever persona and be the man who fucked me like no one ever had in bed.

I was impossibly turned on, incredibly horny, and desperate for more.

His lips found mine in a desperate kiss, one that was hot and heavy and all tongue. He sucked my lower lip into his mouth, teeth dragging over skin, and I let out a soft moan.

"Fuck, the things you do to me," he muttered, hands grip-ping my hips. "Need to fuck my wife."

"Yes," I agreed. "Please." I let my head fall back as he kissed down my neck, wondering why we hadn't been doing this all along.

"Turn around." His voice was a rasp, so low that my nipples hardened. "I want to see you."

I put my hand on his chest before he could unzip me, feeling shy all the sudden. "Wait. I, uh... I have a surprise for you."

He raised an eyebrow. "You do?"

I nodded, thinking about the pretty lingerie set I'd seen in a window earlier today and had bought on a whim. What if he hated it? Maybe it was too forward buying lingerie for our wedding night, but I wanted to feel beautiful. And it had looked so good on, making me feel confident in my skin in a way I hadn't in a long time.

Nicolas adjusted his erection in his pants before taking a step back. "Okay, gorgeous. You've got five minutes before I come get you." He winked, heading into the bedroom to sit on the bed.

I slipped into the bathroom, unzipping the dress myself and hanging it up in the closet. Pulling my hair out of the updo, I gently fixed my curls before opening the bag I'd purchased earlier. The white lace and sheer mesh babydoll slid free from the tissue paper, and I put it on before I could second guess myself again, and then changed into the panties. It was gorgeous, with little pearl detailing on the top, and I ran my fingers down the fabric, appreciating how it looked on me.

The stark white popped against my skin, and I loved the way it hugged my curves.

When I slipped out of the bathroom, I found Nic lounging on the bed, suit coat and vest discarded over the back of a chair. He'd loosened the top buttons of his shirt, giving just a peek of his chiseled abdomen.

"Wow," he rasped, sitting up. "You're…" Nicolas trailed off. "*Radiant. Stunning.* The most beautiful woman I've ever seen." I was pretty sure I'd never forget the look in his eyes as he caught sight of me, like he couldn't look away.

"You like it?" I did a little twirl for him.

"Like it?" He shook his head. "*Like* isn't a big enough word, Gorgeous."

I smoothed my hands down it, feeling nervous. "I wasn't sure if it was too much. Maybe it's crazy, but I wanted to have something special for our wedding night."

He let out a strangled groan. "Come here, baby." My heart fluttered at the pet name. He'd used it last night, too, and it made my insides melt.

Walking over to the bed, I stood between his legs. He ran his hands up and down my body, from my hips to my breasts, his face in rapt attention.

I let my hands rest on his shoulders, shutting my eyes and breathing him in.

He kissed my neck, his thumbs hooking through the waistband of my pretty lace panties, and I moved to straddle his lap. Nic picked me up, shimmying us backwards until his back hit the headboard.

"We're *married*," I whispered, slowly unbuttoning the rest of the buttons on his shirt.

He grinned, helping me take his shirt off before his hands slid up to cup my ass. "I don't know what I did to deserve you," he murmured, his fingers rubbing back and forth underneath my underwear.

My core pressed over his erection, and I let out a moan, only a few layers of fabric separating us. How was it possible that I'd taken him last night, and I was already desperate to have him inside of me again tonight? Except it felt different this time. Maybe because of the vows we'd given each other. We didn't love each other—not like that, anyway—but this felt special.

If it was my one and only wedding night, I wanted to remember it.

I tilted my head down to kiss him softly, my tongue running across his lips before his joined mine, sweeping through my mouth. He brushed his tongue over mine so sweetly and gently, his hands tightening on my ass, my hips, rubbing me against his hard length as we kissed.

I'd never understood dry humping before—it never really seemed that exciting—but there was something different about it now. Maybe because I was closer to coming than I ever had been without extra stimulation, and I was out of my mind. No man had ever made me as wet as Nic did, something I was trying not to look too deeply into.

Because my fake husband was my ideal man. He was just my type, physically and intellectually. Nicolas could challenge me at every turn, keep me on my toes, and he respected my decisions. He depended on me, and maybe that was the hottest thing.

His hips thrust up, and I let out a gasp against his lips as the fabric scraped over my clit. "Yes," I cried. "Again." Nic repeated the motion, and I moaned. "So good."

"Do you think you can come like this?" he asked, rolling his hips, pushing his cock against me as his fingers tightened on my skin.

"I—Yes." I was so close. Holding onto his shoulders, I bucked my hips faster, grinding down on his hardened length, chasing my release. My whole body was on the edge and begging for it. It was like a bolt of lightning when my orgasm hit me, the friction and pressure too good to hold back, and I slumped against him, needing a moment to catch my breath.

"Fuck," he murmured, his hands resting on my lower back and rubbing softly as he stilled. "You're incredible."

I reached behind me, going to unhook the babydoll, but Nicolas's hand stopped me. "Leave it on," he said, his voice hoarse. "It's beautiful—*you're* beautiful, and I want you on top of me. Want to stare at my beautiful wife in her wedding lingerie as she rides me." He brushed a few strands of hair away from my face.

"Are you sure?"

"I've never been more certain about anything," Nicolas responded, his eyes full of heat.

I shimmied backwards, just enough that I could pull the zipper down on his pants, pushing his boxers back to free his erection. Wrapping my fist around his length, I pumped it a few times before running my tongue over his tip, lapping up the bead of pre-cum there.

He groaned, hands holding me in place, and then I was straddling him once more. I could feel how wet I was from my climax, and I knew I wouldn't require any extra lubrication to fit him inside of me. Pushing my lacy thong to the side, I positioned his tip at my entrance, sinking down onto it, already feeling so fucking full.

I groaned. "You feel so good." I wiggled myself down deeper, taking a few more inches.

Nic thrust upwards, burying himself, and then he cursed, gripping my hips. "Fuck, Zo. Condom."

Shit. In my lust-filled haze, I hadn't even thought about protection. "I'm all good," I told him. "It's been a while since I've been with anyone, and my last test was all clear."

"Me too." He cupped my cheek. "I've never had sex without condoms before, and I—" He swallowed roughly. "I haven't been with anyone in over a year. Haven't even looked at another woman since you became my assistant."

I gasped, and then let out a moan as the motion brought him in direct contact with my g-spot. "Right there," I moaned. It felt so good like this, even better than I'd ever thought possible. I rocked my hips, placing my hands on his abdomen.

He groaned, wrapping me up in his arms as he sat us up, pulling me off his cock. "Are you on anything?"

"No," I whispered. Birth control made me anxious, even when I'd tried a ton of different types, and I hated how it affected by body. "I don't like the way it makes me feel."

"Zofia," he croaked, lips finding my neck. "You can't tell me that."

"Tell you what?" I gave him a soft smile, pressing my lips to his shoulder.

He shook his head. "We should be safe."

"I know," I groaned. What he was saying *was* the smart thing. But damn, if it hadn't felt insanely good to have him inside me bare.

But me getting pregnant during our fake marriage was a terrible idea—kids weren't part of the plan. Not when we'd be getting divorced in two years—or sooner if he found someone he wanted to marry instead.

He pressed a kiss to my forehead. "Let me put a condom on, and then we can continue." I nodded, watching as he reached over to the nightstand, pulling one out of the drawer. I took it from his hands, tearing the wrapper and rolling it on before he laid back down on the bed, pulling me back on top of him.

Once again, I guided him to my entrance, sinking down and taking the entire length of him in one movement. Letting out a loud moan, I dug my fingernails into his abs, my knees resting on either side of him as I rocked back and forth, each movement making my breasts bounce in the lacy top.

"That's my pretty bride," he praised, his hips raising to meet mine with every rock against him. Each thrust was incredible, even if I missed feeling his warmth inside me. "So gorgeous as you ride my cock, wife."

He continued praising me as I rode him, sliding up and down on his length and not caring about the whines that continuously slipped from my lips.

"Gonna come again," I gasped, and then his thumb was on my clit, pressing down hard enough to give me the pressure I desperately needed until I gushed, coming all over him.

Nicolas let out a grunt as my pussy contracted and fluttered around him, still pulsing from the orgasm, and he wrapped me up in his arms, bringing me down onto his body as he followed close behind with a roar.

We stayed like that, with him murmuring praises into my ear and me pressed against his bare chest, until we fell asleep, Nic still buried deep inside me.

16
nicolas

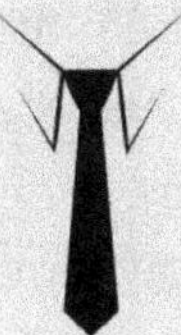

There was no better feeling in the world than being inside my wife bare. Those few moments I'd been inside her without a condom had been *life changing.*

When she'd told me she wasn't on birth control, and I'd know she was unprotected, I almost came inside her right then and there. The idea of seeing her full of my seed, growing our child inside her—it was almost too much to resist.

I didn't know where the thought came from. Maybe after seeing Robert with his pregnant wife, some part of my brain had short-circuited.

Or maybe deep down, it was because I knew that it would fulfill the requirements of my trust fund and allow me to have access to the rest of my inheritance. Still, I couldn't put that on her.

I wouldn't force her to make a decision like that—especially in a fake relationship.

So I pulled out, putting a condom on before sinking back inside my wife.

She was truly mesmerizing in that white sheer lace lingerie, and I couldn't get enough. Part of me still couldn't believe that she'd said yes to marrying me today, let alone going shopping for something for tonight.

"How are you feeling?" I asked my wife, whose only response was to hum, stretching out in our bed.

Picking her up, I carried her into the bathroom, running us a bath in the large tub. I'd seen her make eyes at it ever since we'd arrived, and I wanted to help her relax—especially since I planned to put my mouth on her later.

Helping her out of the lingerie, I pressed my lips to the parts where the fabric rubbed on her skin, praising her and worshipping her with my mouth. I wanted to feel her come on my tongue, but that would come later. I held her hand as I guided her into the warm water, sliding in behind her. My body curled around hers, and I wasn't sure I'd ever felt so close to another person before.

"This feels surreal," I said against her ear.

She let out a contented sigh. "What does?" The words were a murmur, barely audible.

"Knowing we're married and can do that whenever we want." I pressed a kiss to her shoulder, so fucking glad we'd gotten rid of the no sex rule.

Zofia let out a small laugh. "You're incorrigible, Nicolas Larsen."

"You like it, Zofia Larsen."

Her eyes fluttered as they met mine. "Say it again," she whispered.

I pressed my lips to her neck. "*Zofia Larsen.*" I loved the sound of it, maybe a little too much. "Remind me why we haven't been doing this every moment we could since June?"

She let her head fall back, resting on my shoulder, as I traced circles on her thighs. "Because you're my boss, and I'm your assistant, and sleeping together would have made things *way* too complicated."

"But marrying me didn't?"

"You know what I mean."

I hummed. All I knew was I'd wanted her ever since I'd known her, and now she was finally *mine.* Her ass was pressed firmly against my cock, already perking up again at her proximity, but I tried to ignore that, letting myself treasure the moment.

"Why did you want to elope?" Zofia whispered.

How much could I tell her without revealing the full spectrum of my feelings? "I thought maybe this would be better. Less pressure on us." I intertwined our fingers, bringing her hand up to my mouth, kissing over the ring I'd given her. "Was it okay?"

"It was perfect," she admitted. "And you're right. This was easier."

"And now you're all mine," I answered, thanking the contract for giving me this. She let her eyes fall shut, not saying anything else, and I pressed a kiss to her shoulder.

Even if it was only for two years, I was going to savor every moment with her.

"Morning," she murmured, her big brown eyes blinking up at me with an expression I couldn't quite place.

"Morning, wife." I kissed her forehead, soaking up every moment.

She yawned. "We have to go home today."

Home. I liked the sound of that. Running my fingers through her hair, I enjoyed our last moment waking up together like this.

We'd spent the last two days of the conference wrapped up in each other, barely leaving the hotel room besides for the mandatory sessions and dinners we had to attend. It was the best work trip I'd ever been on.

"I don't want to leave," I admitted. "I enjoy being here, just the two of us."

She smiled up at me. "Me too, Nic."

Here, the rest of the world didn't matter. Here, there was no one we we'd be faking for. No one to convince that this was *real*. And yet, somehow, it felt more real than anything else in my entire life.

Like all along, I'd been waiting for this.

This moment. This woman.

Kissing her softly, I pulled back. "Will you move in once we're back?" I wasn't sure why I felt so nervous, but I realized wanted her to *want* to live with me.

She gave a hesitant nod. "You really think Cooper will be okay with Duchess? Because my cat hates everyone but me."

I laughed, thinking about my independent girl and how her cat was just like her. "Yeah, baby. Cooper loves cats. And we can build her a little kitty paradise, too. It won't just be my home, Zo. It'll be yours, too." I pulled her into my arms, enjoying the feeling of her bare skin against mine, her nipples rubbing against my chest. "I don't want you doubting that, or thinking I don't want you there."

Zo rolled over, wrapping her arms around her pillow and baring her creamy, warm brown skin to me. The sheets rested just above her ass, where I wanted to sink my teeth into her flesh. Unaware of my filthy thoughts of taking her one more time before we left the bed, she nodded. "Okay. I'll move in this week." Zo wrapped her arms around my shoulder. "It's in the contract, anyway."

I winced internally at the reminder, but she wasn't wrong. "Alright. Time for breakfast, and then packing before we hit the airport." I dropped a soft kiss on her lips before getting out of bed and heading towards the shower.

"Without me?" She called.

I laughed. "You know we'll never leave the room if we shower together."

She mumbled something under her breath, but she knew I

wasn't wrong. We were insatiable, and I was pretty sure it would only get worse once she was living under the same roof as me.

Would she share my bed after she moved in? Before this trip, I'd figured this marriage would be so in name only, but it was clear the attraction between us wasn't going anywhere. I couldn't deny the chemistry anymore, even if I wanted to.

I'd have to be insane to not want my wife.

It was a zero to one hundred shift in energy on the plane versus our flight to Vegas earlier in the week, and I was glad there was only a small crew on the plane; that way we wouldn't be interrupted during the flight.

Zofia sat in the chair next to mine, my hand resting on her thigh, and when I looked over, I caught her biting her lip.

The romance book she was reading—one she'd probably planned to make a lot more progress on by the pool in Vegas, if only I'd been able to keep my hands off of her—was resting in her lap, completely ignored. She'd dressed in her usual attire this morning—pencil skirt, white button up blouse, heels, with all her hair secured in a clip to the back of her head.

No matter what she wore, I was more attracted to her every single day.

By the time the plane was in the air and the captain turned off the fasten seatbelt light, Zofia stood from her seat, her book falling on the floor—forgotten.

"Zo." My breath was rough as she kneeled in front of me. "What are you doing?"

Her eyelashes fluttered. "We didn't get to *play* this morning, husband."

"Here?" I sucked in a breath as she unzipped my pants in response.

Her hand slipped into my boxers and wrapped around my cock, and I wasn't sure I'd ever seen a hotter sight. She closed her lips around the tip, sucking on it as she slid her hand up and down, moaning around my length as she felt me harden in her hand.

Her other hand dipped between her legs, and I knew they were playing with her pretty little pussy, her arousal dripping on her fingers.

"Oh, *fuuuck*," I groaned, my hand cupping the back of her head. I undid her clip, letting her curls spill down her shoulder as I slid my fingers into them, holding her in place as she licked down my shaft, coating it in her saliva. "Such a good assistant, sucking your boss's cock," I said, the words spilling out of me before I could think better of it.

Her eyes were full of heat when she stopped and stood up in front of me, her fingers smoothing her curls. "You like that?" she asked, looking amused.

Wordlessly, I nodded, trying to wrap my hands around her waist to pull her back onto my lap, but she stopped me.

Zofia unbuttoned her top slowly, like she was giving me the best strip tease of my *life*, letting it fall to the ground before pushing off her skirt, too. Then she was standing in front of me in only her pair of fuck me heels and lingerie. The red bra and underwear were both lace, and my mouth was watering.

"*Gorgeous*. You're going to be the death of me, baby." I let out a groan as she stepped forward, hands making quick work of my tie and shirt. I loved how much she appreciated my abs —it made the time I spent staying in shape completely worth it.

She gave me a sly smile, taking a step forward, bringing her knee onto my lap as her hands slid up my bare chest and onto my shoulders.

"Naughty girl," I said, reaching out to hold her waist as she slid onto my lap. My cock was pressed against her stomach as she ran her fingers through my hair, kissing her way down my chest.

"It's my job to take care of you," she started, her tongue flicking over my nipple, "as your assistant."

This role-play was way too hot, and I imagined being back at the office, pushing her down over my desk and taking her right there. Letting my cum run down her thigh as she flittered about, so there was no doubt who she belonged to.

My cock was weeping at the thought, desperate to be inside of Zofia.

I gathered her hair into my fist, forcing her eyes to meet mine. "And as my *wife*."

She moaned. "Yes."

"Fuck, gorgeous. I need to be inside you." Pushing her panties aside, I thrust two fingers into her, not surprised that she was soaking. Her insides sucked me in as I scissored them, then pumped into her until she was whining, begging for more. "Shhh," I reminded her. "Be quiet, or the pilot will hear the boss fucking his assistant."

Her body shuddered as I kept fucking her with my fingers until I felt them squeezing around me, wishing it was my length instead. Zo dropped her mouth to my shoulder, her sounds lessened as she sucked on my skin, sure to leave a mark.

I wanted her to, just like I had her ring on my finger. Fuck, I loved seeing it there. A surge of possession went through me, and I pulled a condom out of my wallet, pumping my cock twice before rolling it on and positioning myself at her entrance.

We'd run out of the ones I'd bought, and I'd had to buy a box from the hotel gift shop, because there was no way I was going to stop now that we'd given in to the heat once again.

My eyes caught hers, and she nodded. "Please, I need to feel you."

There was no denying us this. Not when we were both this needy for each other. I pushed inside her, her insides easily accommodating the stretch of my size, especially thanks to the added lubrication of her climax.

"You feel so perfect," I said, my eyes closing shut as she grasped my shoulders, both of us stilling as we luxuriated in the feeling.

Then we were both moving, rocking her back and forth on my length, punctuated by a roll of my hips up into her or her moan as I pressed against her cervix, wishing I could fill her with my cum.

If this marriage were real, I'd want nothing more than to put my baby inside her. The feeling was only growing more and more desperate, and I knew I needed to be careful. I couldn't force something like that on her. It was her body—her choice. Not mine. No matter how hot the idea of her knocked up with our baby was.

And fuck, what was wrong with me? I wasn't sure I'd be a good father, let alone know if I really wanted kids.

Leaning forward, I sucked her breast into my mouth through the lace fabric, lavishing her nipples with attention as I alternated between the two before finally unhooking the bra, letting it fall on the floor. I lost track of time with her in my lap, her nipples in my mouth, her cries spurring me on like music to my ears. I'd made her come a second time from her breasts, and I could feel her growing close again.

Her climax hit the same time the captain came over the speaker. "We're beginning our initial descent into Portland..."

Zo's eyes met mine, and we both groaned as I followed right behind her, unable to hold back with the exquisite squeeze of her cunt around my cock. "Yes, baby," I praised. "So fucking good for me."

"I can't believe we just did that," she murmured as we pulled apart. She raised herself off of me, collecting all her clothes and pulling them back on. Still, her hair was mussed, and she looked like she'd just been fucked.

"So fucking hot," I told her.

I got rid of the condom before tucking myself back into my pants, still half-hard and wanting to go again, and re-buttoned my shirt. We both buckled ourselves back into our seats, and when she looked over at me, we both burst out laughing.

"Best flight ever," I responded before leaning over and pressing a kiss to her lips. "Definitely not one I'll ever forget."

17
zofia

october

As soon as we stepped off the plane, my phone pinged—it was a message from the group chat I was in with Angelina, Gabbi, Charlotte and Noelle.

ANGELINA

ZOFIA AVANTHIKA NARAYAN.

We need to have words, babe.

What's this I see about you and Nic GETTING MARRIED?

SPILL. I WANT ALL THE DETAILS. Leave nothing out!

GABBI

Wait wait wait. Hold on. Zofia and Nic got married??? WHEN?

ANGELINA

This weekend, apparently.

CHARLOTTE

Did we know they were together? I didn't think
we knew they were together.

GABBI

No, Char. We did not.

ANGELINA

I suspected, though.

Nicolas has always had puppy eyes for her.

NOELLE

Definitely not what I thought I'd be opening up
this group chat to find.

But congrats, Zofia!

ZOFIA

Sorry, I'm just getting off the plane.

I was going to tell you all, I promise.

It was a spur-of-the-moment thing. We didn't
exactly plan it.

ANGELINA

Still, without us??? I'm hurt.

ZOFIA

I know. But it's not like I was going to call you
and demand you fly to come to our wedding in
Vegas.

ANGELINA

I would have.

ZOFIA

How did you even find out?

ANGELINA

Your lovely husband posted about it. On
Instagram.

I looked over at Nic who was grabbing our luggage before we headed towards the waiting towncar. "You posted that we got *married*?"

He shrugged, shoving his hands in his pockets. "Yeah. Was I… not supposed to?"

"We didn't even tell everyone yet." I showed him the texts from the girls, which were still continuing. I ignored them for now, not wanting to give more of an explanation yet. "They're freaking out."

Nic's phone buzzed next. "It's the guys," he chuckled. "Guess I'm about to get the same thing."

My phone started ringing. "Oh, fuck me." I pressed the answer button. "Hi, Amma." I looked at my new husband, and he winced.

"You got married this weekend?" She asked, her tone full of hurt.

"I'm sorry. I was going to tell you once I got home and had a chance to come over. We decided to elope instead of worrying about the whole civil ceremony at the courthouse." Nic locked eyes with me as I said, "We'll still plan a big ceremony and you and Appa can give me away, I promise."

She sighed. "Okay. As long as you're happy, Kutti."

"I am." Nic squeezed my hand next to me, and I shared a few more placating words with my mother, promising we'd come by for dinner one night this week, before we slipped into the car.

"I guess the cat's really out of the bag now," I said, blowing out a breath.

"No going back," Nic said. "We're in this together, remember?"

Leaning over, I pressed a kiss to his cheek before he put the car in reverse. "We are. I'm on your team—always."

He gave me a warm smile. "And I'm sorry for not telling you about the post. I just wanted everyone to know." He picked up my hand, kissing it, before resting his on my thigh.

I looked at the photo he'd posted—one of the two of us from the chapel, and the caption was a simple *my wife* with a red heart emoji and the date we'd tied the knot.

"You're forgiven," I said, knowing I wasn't really mad. "I was a little blindsided, but it's like ripping a bandaid off. Now it's over, and we don't have to hide anymore."

Part of me liked his possessive streak, how he wanted everyone to know I was his. I knew it had to do with selling our fake relationship as *real,* but I liked to imagine he did it because he actually felt something for me. My heart fluttered as I looked over at my husband, one hand on the steering wheel.

He laughed. "No more hiding our fake relationship, huh?"

I wished it didn't hurt. That calling it fake didn't make me want to cave in on myself. Especially with how insatiable we were. We'd fucked on every surface of the suite over the long weekend, including in the bathtub, and used an entire box of condoms, and even though I was sore and my body ached *every-where,* I still wanted more of him.

It was a sobering thought, because how was I supposed to be married to him and want him this bad when it was all a lie?

He pulled up to my apartment complex, pulling into a spot, and before I could open the door, there he was, offering me a hand.

"Go get some rest," he said to me at my door, pressing a kiss to my forehead. "Tomorrow, after work, I'll come over and we can start packing you up to move in."

"Alright," I said, swallowing roughly. I didn't know why I was so nervous about living with him, but I was. Maybe because it would be a lot harder to hide my feelings there. That was why I'd had the no sex rule in the first place, dammit. Neither of us was supposed to be catching feelings, and it definitely wasn't supposed to be *me.*

Even putting up barriers to protect myself, I still worried about my heart if I let myself fall into the fantasy. That was why I had rules. Because getting attached, letting myself believe in a future that wasn't promised… I couldn't do it again.

Ever since the wedding, everything felt different. Heightened, somehow.

"Yes." He grinned, looking like an excited golden retriever wagging his tail. "I'm looking forward to living with my wife, Gorgeous." He winked. "See you in the morning."

"Okay," I whispered, and he pressed a soft kiss to my lips, not letting it go any farther, before walking back to his car, leaving me to wonder if I'd just made the biggest mistake of my life…

Or the best.

"I *knew* it," Gabbi said when she walked into my office the next morning, wrapping her arms around me in a hug. "Let me see that ring!"

"I still can't believe you got married without us," Angelina mused as she swung her legs from where she was perched on the edge of my desk. After her meeting with Nic this morning, she'd hopped up to that spot and hadn't left since.

Not that I was complaining. I loved having friends close enough that they gossiped at my desk with me.

I felt sheepish as I held out my hand, her eyes alight as she inspected my engagement ring. "We were trying to keep it secret," I said, going with Nic and I'd agreed upon story. "You know how it is. It's not exactly against company policies, but it is frowned upon to date your superior. And he's about as superior as it gets."

She looked over at her best friend. "I know what you mean. Benjamin told Hunter he wasn't allowed to touch me." She rolled her eyes. "Like that was going to keep us apart."

Angelina shrugged, like she didn't have any control over her husband's actions. Man was obsessed with her, so honestly, I understood that.

"You're perfect for each other," I said.

"You and Nic are too," Gabbi said, squeezing my hand. "We've known Nic for years, and honestly, I've never seen him smile as much as he does around you."

I scrunched up my nose. "He's *always* smiling."

Gabbi grinned. "Exactly. Still, I just can't believe you didn't even tell us you were engaged."

"It was definitely hard to keep it from everyone. I would have loved if everyone was at the wedding, but… is it bad that I kind of loved that it was just us?"

"I'm so happy for you two. Besides, after planning a wedding, I definitely understand why you'd want to elope." Angelina snorted. "It was magical—besides me getting a little too tipsy since everyone kept handing me alcohol—and I'm so glad to be married to him." She flicked her eyes over to Benjamin, who was still talking with Nic. "Even if he drives me crazy most of the time."

"Yeah," I responded, twisting the ring on my finger. I was still getting used to wearing it, and sometimes I'd catch myself staring at it while I was at work. Luckily, no one had caught me yet. "It just felt… right. Besides, I insisted to my parents that we'd still plan a traditional wedding ceremony. They've already done it twice, but those were for my brothers, and I know how important it is to them."

"Hey, people thought we were crazy planning ours in less than six months, and it all worked out."

I laughed. "You *were* crazy. Speaking of events, I've already started planning the charity gala. You in to help me this year?"

"Of course. It's my favorite event of the year. Tell me what needs to get done on my end, and I'll have it all to you."

"You're the best," I told her, marking that off my to-do list.

Delegation was everything in my job, but I didn't want to give up the gala.

She brushed her ponytail off her shoulder. "I know." Angelina winked, standing up and looking at Benjamin. "Alright, let me go rescue the boss from my husband. Otherwise, those two will probably be in there all day." Her face curled into a mischievous smile as she looked at me. "Our husbands. Wow. That's crazy to say." She shook her head, letting out a small laugh. "Anyway, I'll see you later, babe. We'll have to get everyone together for dinner some time this week."

"After I'm all moved in with Nic, I'd definitely be down for that."

"If you need any help, let us know," Gabbi said. "I'm sure the guys would all help."

I hadn't even considered asking, and I felt so touched. "Thank you. I… I'll probably take you up on that, actually."

She hugged me and then squeezed my hands. "We've got you, Zo. Always."

"That's what friends are for," Angelina told me.

I'd never felt so lucky to have them in my life.

It took until Friday until my apartment was completely packed up. Nic had called the guys, asking for help with some of the heavy lifting.

Since we'd agreed to be married for two years, I'd broken my lease instead of subleasing it, not wanting to deal with the additional headache. It was up soon, anyway, and it made more sense financially. I'd rather put the rent money into savings for a future business or a future college fund than waste it on rent when Nic had a perfectly good house.

It was strange seeing my entire life packed up into boxes, all the pictures and decorations gone off my walls. It looked like I'd never even lived here, even though I'd spent the last few years in this one-bedroom apartment.

The last loads were already packed up in Nic's car, Matthew's truck, and Hunter's jeep. My extra furniture was already at Nic's place, and we'd dropped it off the rest at a used furniture store to be sold. I kept the heirloom antiques I'd gotten from my family, and sentimental things I didn't want to part with.

The only thing that remained was Duchess's cage, and after I walked out the door, I'd officially be living with my boss. And my fake husband. I looked down at my ring finger, at the ring he'd given me. I was giving up *everything*. My independence, my privacy. The place I'd called my own.

This was the place where I'd picked myself up after my life had fallen apart—after Samir had cheated on me, and I hadn't been able to keep living in the place where he'd slept with someone else in my bed.

Picking up Duchess, I stroked between her ears as I surveyed the place one last time. I was surprised that I didn't feel upset, knowing I was about to say goodbye. But I wasn't the same girl I'd been when I first moved in. That girl was gone, and now I was someone else entirely.

Unexpectedly… A wife.

A title I never thought I'd have after I broke off my engagement. It still gave me goosebumps to think about, even if Nicolas loved to call me *my wife* like it was going out of style. Secretly, I loved it.

What was even more surprising was the way I was crushing on my fake husband, even when I knew I shouldn't.

Was this a terrible idea? After the last week together, I realized maybe it wasn't so bad to have someone else by my side. Especially when that someone else seemed like he existed solely for my pleasure.

I was changing little by little, every day. He was changing *me*.

"You look deep in thought," Nic said, curling an arm around my middle. When I looked down, I saw his wedding band resting against his skin, and it made my heart flutter.

"Just thinking about Duchess adjusting to a new home," I said, not wanting to relay the rest of my internal thoughts.

He nodded. "My dad's going to be glad when I grab Cooper. He loves him, but I know he's a lot." Since he'd been at my apartment every night this week, he'd asked his dad to watch his dog, and I knew he was also looking forward to having him back.

Nic had brought his golden retriever into the office a few times, and he was a big, lovable goofball. The dog had extremely high energy levels and *loved* all the attention he got every time— practically the opposite of my sweet, docile cat.

"I don't know how you think they'll co-exist," I muttered under my breath.

Especially when I looked at my now-empty apartment, my cat clutched in my arms. Petting her fur, I tried to give her soft words to help her relax, but I was pretty sure that I was trying to comfort myself more than her.

"It'll be great, Zo," he told me. "Just like us." He grinned. "You'll see."

I bit my lip. "I guess."

He pressed a kiss to the exposed skin of my shoulder.

"Are you ready?" Nic's breath warmed my neck, and I turned, finding him with a question on his face. "Because if you're not, we don't have to do this. I know we're married, and we have the contract, but—"

"Yeah. It's time to move on." I looked around one last time. I was leaving my past behind—and that felt freeing in a whole new way. Squeezing his arm that was wrapped around me, I nodded. "I'm okay, really. *Better* than okay." How could I not be, with someone as caring and thoughtful as him as my husband?

We hadn't talked about our Vegas sex-fest, but I'd noticed that Nic had carried all of my clothes and personal items directly into his room when he'd been unloading, leaving no question of where I'd be sleeping every night. After a week of sleeping alone, I was looking forward to sharing a bed with him again. He was like an extra cozy blanket, and I loved falling asleep with him spooning me, or waking up draped across him.

"Let's go home, Nic," I told him, a slight rush coming at the words.

Ever since things had ended with Samir, I'd had no long-term relationships where we'd lived together or shared a bed. It had just felt too intimate, too *real*.

And now I was doing all of that with a *husband*. It was crazy how fast life could change.

Nicolas nodded, interlacing his fingers through mine. I left the empty apartment behind, heading towards the next chapter of my life.

18
nicolas

*L*eaning on the doorway to the living room, I caught sight of Zofia, sitting on the couch, laptop in her lap and her cat curled up next to her. "Hey. I was thinking about making dinner. You hungry?"

It had been a few hours since our friends had helped us finish moving Zo's stuff in, and after unpacking for a few hours, she'd stopped to take a break. Knowing her, though, the break also involved work stuff—and I wanted her to *actually* take a break.

She looked up, giving me a shy smile as she shut the computer lid. "Oh. Hi. Yeah, I could eat."

"Great. I was thinking breakfast for dinner. Any objections?"

Zofia shook her head, stroking Duchess's back before standing off the couch. "Works for me." Her blanket fell onto the floor, baring her long, slender legs to me. She was wearing a pair of shorts and an oversized t-shirt, so opposite from her usual work attire, and I was a little obsessed.

I wanted to pull her shorts down and bend her over the couch, burying my face in her sweet pussy and eating her out until she cried my name.

My dick perked up at the thought. *Down boy,* I urged myself.

I needed to feed her first. Take care of her and make her feel at home.

Cooper nudged at my leg, whining at me. I scratched his head. "I'll feed you in a second, Coop." He barked in response, and I chuckled.

Zofia followed me into the kitchen, settling onto a barstool as I filled a bowl with food for him before pulling out the pots and pans I needed to make food.

"This is weird," she said, scrunching up her nose.

"Living together?" I asked, frowning.

"Yeah. Besides my ex, I've never really lived with anyone before. You know how that turned out. And now you're being all... *domestic*."

I looked down at myself, wearing my favorite soft blue t-shirt and a pair of jeans as I pulled ingredients out of the fridge. Maybe I wasn't the only one who was used to our usual business attire. "I'm just trying to be a good fake husband," I told her. "Can't let my wife go hungry."

"Do you want help?" she asked, rounding the corner. "I know my way around the kitchen. My mother instilled a love of cooking in me since I was a young girl. I loved making Tamil dishes with her."

I blinked. "Are you sure? You don't have to."

She nudged me aside with her hip. "Yes. Just tell me what to do, *husband*." She winked.

"You want to cut up these? I was going to make omelettes." I gestured to the spread of toppings. "You can have whatever you want inside."

"Sure." She picked up a knife. "I got this."

I laughed. "Great. And, for the record, I've never lived with anyone besides my parents and roommates in college as well. And it's been a while since the latter."

"No... long-term girlfriends?" Zofia asked, and I could see the curiosity sparked in her eyes as I cracked eggs against the bowl.

Shaking my head, I chuckled to myself. "No. I had a girl-friend in high school, but things ended pretty quickly when we both went to different colleges. After that, I only saw people casually. I knew couldn't devote enough time to a relationship." Grabbing the whisk, I whipped the eggs till they were well-mixed.

She hummed, slicing through the bell peppers as I added salt and pepper to my bowl. "So there's no one who got away?"

"No." *There's only you, Zofia Larsen,* I wanted to tell her.

But that was too much, too soon. Too much for our fake marriage, that felt less fake by the day. Especially with her under my roof. With her shoes next to mine in the entryway. Her clothes in my walk-in closet.

"What about you? I know you didn't want another arranged marriage after your asshole ex, but I don't understand how someone like you didn't find someone already." I added some butter to the pan, letting it melt before I added the egg mixture.

"Someone like me?" Zo furrowed her brows, turning to look at me. "What does that mean?"

"Smart. Successful." I wanted to touch her, but I kept my hands to myself. "Beautiful."

"Oh." She looked away, her bottom teeth digging into her lower lip. "I don't know." She went back to chopping the bell peppers into smaller pieces. "I guess you could say I didn't prioritize dating for a long time. And then suddenly I was thirty and still single. But I don't regret it."

"You don't?"

She shook her head.

"Why not?"

"Nicolas." Her voice was soft, but full of need.

I stepped towards her, curling a finger under her chin. "Tell me, Gorgeous." My voice was rough.

Her lips opened, but no sound came out, and then my hands

were on hers, bringing her mouth to mine. She let out a moan as I swiped my tongue through her mouth, savoring her taste, like caramel and coffee.

I pulled back, noting her heavy-lidded eyes, and pressed another soft kiss to her lips. "Food first," I said, readjusting myself before turning back to the pan. "What do you want?" I asked.

She fiddled with the hem of her shirt. "You."

I chuckled. "Me too, but I meant in your omelette." After making sure the eggs were set, I added in some ham, cheese, bell peppers, and bacon to the middle of the pan, continuing to cook it evenly.

"Oh." Zofia looked flustered. "I, uh—that looks good."

"Okay." I nodded, smirking at her, plating the first omelette after it finished cooking. "Eat." I drew my eyes down her body, leaning in to whisper in her ear. "You'll want the energy for later." I winked, scooping up a bite onto the fork and extending it to her.

Zo sucked in a breath, taking the bite. Her eyes never left mine as she chewed, finally letting out a moan. "This is *so* good."

Grinning, I held up another bite, thinking about how I wanted to have her make that sound again later in bed.

I repeated my process to start another omelette, only to find Zo holding a forkful up to my lips. "Here. We can share," she murmured. I closed my mouth around the tines, maintaining eye contact with her as I chewed and swallowed, just like she had with me.

"Mmm," I said, enjoying how domestic the action was.

When her plate was empty, I filled it back up with the second omelette, both of us taking turns feeding each other. I was so turned on, and the action was hotter than I'd ever expected. I pinned her against the counter, lifting her up to sit on it, and stood between her legs. "One more bite," I told her, holding the fork to her mouth.

"I'm so full," she pouted.

"Not how I usually like hearing those words, but I'll take it," I said, feeling satisfied.

She pushed at my shoulder. "Perv."

"You like it." I nipped at her lower lip.

Zofia hummed, wrapping her arms around my neck. "Maybe."

"You love the way your husband fucks you," I said against her mouth. "Admit it."

She closed her eyes as I kissed down her neck. "Yes," she said, winding her legs around my torso.

I carried her up to our bedroom, setting her down onto my bed—*our* bed, now.

She frowned when I stepped back, opening the drawer of my nightstand.

"Nic?"

"I have something for you," I confessed, pulling out the box I'd picked up earlier.

"What? Nic, really, I don't need anything—"

Opening it, I pulled out the band before snapping the box shut. I stepped closer to her, grabbing her left hand and slowly slid the wedding band down onto it.

"*Oh.*" She stared at it, as if mesmerized by the gold and diamond band. It was in the shape of a crown, made to stack perfectly with her ring.

"I'd ordered it at the same time as your ring," I admitted. "But it was back ordered, and it only just came in. I went to pick it up during lunch. I was going to give it to you earlier this week, at the office, but..." I wanted it to be more private.

"It's beautiful. But you didn't have to..."

I brushed her hair back behind her ear. "Of course I did. My wife deserves the best, doesn't she?"

"Nic—"

Stepping between her legs, I tugged her into me, pressing my lips softly against her forehead. "I'm sorry it took so long. I wish I'd had it in Vegas."

She let her forehead rest against my chest. "Every time I think I'm used to *us*, you surprise me like this."

"Happy one week anniversary, Gorgeous."

Zofia laughed, pushing my shoulder. "You're ridiculous."

Yeah, I was. Because I was obsessed with my wife, contract or not, and I never wanted her to give that ring back. If this was what it took, it was so worth it.

"Do you like it?"

"Yes." The word was quiet, but there was no missing it.

"Then it was worth it." I kissed her cheek. "Now that you're all moved in, I was thinking we could celebrate with everyone soon? Maybe dinner with our friends?"

"I'd like that. Ang, Gabbi and I were talking about it at the beginning of the week." She smiled, inspecting the ring again. "My parents are already asking me when we're coming over for dinner."

I winced. "My dad is too." I ran a hand through my hair. "Looks like we have a *lot* of people we have to apologize to, huh?"

"No apologies," Zo said, standing on her tiptoes and kissing my jaw. "No regrets, either."

"Good." I pressed my lips to her forehead. "Now, I want to get you out of these." I tugged on her shirt, guiding her to sit back down on the bed.

"I—" She bit her lip, drawing in a breath. "Do you think us having sex is a good idea?"

I paused, taking the time to look into her eyes. "Do you not want to?"

"It's not that. I just worry that we're complicating things. We signed a contract for a reason, right? We're helping each other."

"I think giving each other orgasms definitely counts in the *helping* each other category." Smoothing a hand down her hip, I moved to kneel in front of her. With my head resting on her knees, I looked up at her. "I never want you to do something that you don't want to do. If it doesn't feel good, or you're not into it, we'll stop."

"That's not it at all," she insisted, her fingers running through my hair, nails scratching softly against my scalp. It felt incredible. "I just feel like so much is changing so fast, and I don't know where we stand anymore."

"You're my wife," I responded, placing a kiss on the inside of her thigh. "I'm your husband."

"And my boss," she whispered.

"You've always been so much more to me than *just* my assistant, Zofia. Even if sometimes I want to fuck you like you're not."

"Oh?" Her eyes heated, hands tugging on my shirt and pulling it over my chest. "Tell me more."

I pulled her thighs apart, humming. "When you come into the office wearing those tight pencil skirts, I want nothing more than to bend you over my desk and slide inside of you. My sexy, *tempting* little assistant." Pressing my knuckle to her clit through her clothes, I rubbed slightly. "And then I want to send you back to your desk, my cum dripping out of you for the rest of the day, reminding you who exactly you belong to."

Zofia let out a moan. "You'd like that, wouldn't you? My dirty girl."

"Yes, *sir*," she said, and my cock twitched in my jeans. "Please."

"Fuck, Zofia." I rubbed my face against the inside of her knee. "You don't know how much you affect me. This last week I was hard almost all day, knowing you were sitting outside, wearing my ring."

"You could have told me," she whispered, hands trailing down to my face.

I shook my head. "I wanted to give you time to rest after Vegas. Your poor pussy took quite the pounding."

She laughed. "Yeah, but I liked it." Zofia tugged me up, bringing my lips to her mouth. "Now remind your *wife* exactly whose she is, husband."

"My pleasure."

And then I stripped her out of her clothes, all too eager to be inside my wife.

19
zofia

*H*ow is everything?" Angelina asked, brushing her long, dark hair off her shoulder. She normally wore it up in a ponytail or a bun, but I liked this more relaxed version of her. It seemed like her honeymoon had done some good, at least.

"Good. I mean, obviously we're adjusting." We'd been living together for a few days, and the news that we were married had spread like wildfire throughout the company. "There's been some gossip about why I married Nic, and it's just been a lot." The two of us were at lunch, and I was glad to escape the office. It felt stifling right now, especially when it seemed like everyone was looking at me or whispering about me.

"People need to mind their own damn business." Angelina scowled. "What have they been saying? If it makes you feel better, I haven't heard it."

"That I married Nic just for his money, or to get ahead in the company." I hated people thinking I was *less* because I'd married him. Of course, they didn't know it was all fake, but it should have been seen as more.

On the bright side, the board was happy he had settled down

—even if they were upset we hadn't disclosed our relationship beforehand.

She winced. "That doesn't even make sense. Have they not seen how he is around you? I've never seen him act like this with anyone else. He's *obsessed* with you. Do you know how many times I caught him staring at you this morning?"

I bit my lip, trying not to think about that too deeply. "He told me he'd never really had a long-term girlfriend—not since high school—so I can understand how this is all new for people. No one expected us to get married so soon."

She nodded. "I think losing his mom when he was young affected him more than he likes to admit. I wasn't sure he'd ever commit to someone, honestly." She frowned, and then added, "Not that I don't think he can commit, or he can't be loyal. He's just always been the biggest flirt. I always thought he hid his actual feelings behind that smile, though."

"I know what you mean." Not that there were feelings—because he definitely didn't love me. "I've been trying to keep it from him because I know just how upset he'd be if he found out what people were saying."

It wasn't just my reputation—it was his, too.

He wasn't the guy people loved to make him out to be. The man I'd once thought he was. Maybe because I'd witnessed his behavior, over and over, and it showed just how loyal and committed he was to me? For a contract relationship, he'd given it one hundred and ten percent.

It was fake, but it felt so real. Our relationship in the bedroom just kept getting better and better. I couldn't believe how explosive sex between us was.

I'd never been with a partner so dedicated to my pleasure, so insistent on my orgasms that he'd put off his own.

"Other than that, though?" Angelina asked, quirking an eyebrow.

"It's been… great," I admitted, feeling a warmth in my

cheeks. "We cook dinner together almost every night. Did you know he can cook? Because I had no idea. With how often we went out for lunch, I never would have guessed that." I'd realized really quickly how many things I didn't know about my husband, despite working for him for a year. I sucked in a breath. "Honestly, I was a little nervous about moving in together. But it's better than I imagined."

"It's definitely an adjustment, living with someone new. But when you love someone, it's worth it." She grinned. "Plus, the sex is *great*."

"Angelina!" My eyes widened.

She shrugged. "What? It's true. You can't tell me that the sex isn't way better after getting married. And living together means you can do it whenever you want." She smirked. "I mean, hello, you've seen my husband. Nic's not my type, but even I can appreciate a fine male specimen."

I looked away. "Yeah," I mumbled. It *was* great. And that was the problem.

Because it wasn't real. And no matter how many orgasms we traded, it still didn't change the fact that my feelings for him were rapidly developing.

She chuckled. "Guess all those billionaire romances weren't wrong. Did he give you his card?"

"Maybe," I mumbled.

"Oh my god. He totally did. You're living the dream, babe."

I rolled my eyes. "You're ridiculous." Those books couldn't even compare to Nicolas, anyway. "And we should get back to work."

Angelina hopped off my desk. "Probably." She squeezed my hand. "Congrats again, Zo. I'm thrilled you two are together. Selfishly, because now I'm not the only one who's married, but also because you belong together."

"Thank you," I said, though I couldn't ignore the unsettling feeling in my gut, the one that reminded me we were lying to everyone.

For the first time since we'd made our agreement, I hated that we had. Because I didn't want it to be fake. I desperately wanted this to be real. Wanted the things I felt for him to be reciprocated; wanted to not be living a lie. But that wasn't how things were.

I might have been his wife, but he didn't love me, no matter how caring and affectionate he was. That had to be enough. Asking for anything else was too much.

NICOLAS

Hey, do you have a minute?

ZOFIA

Yeah, what's up?

Come to my office.

I stared at the ping on my computer, my mind instantly wandering to Nic's confession from the other day. It made me hot just thinking about his secret fantasy, just thinking about him bending me over his desk and having his wicked way with me. I'd never been this wanton before him, but it felt like I'd unlocked an unknown part of myself, and I couldn't get enough of him.

Why?

I need your help with something.

Standing up, I headed towards his office, swaying my hips as my heels clicked on the tile floor. He watched as I walked in, locking the door behind me and making sure all the blinds were closed.

"Zofia." His voice was low—gravely.

A shudder of excitement ran through my body at playing out his fantasy. Ever since he'd confessed it to me, I'd been unable to get it out of my mind.

"Yes, *sir*?" I asked, batting my eyelashes as I pulled my hair out of the clip, letting it fall down around my shoulders as I brushed my hands over his shoulders. He looked stressed out, and I wanted to take his mind off of it.

"What are you—"

I sat on the desk in front of him, leaning against the wood. "I heard you needed my help."

His eyes were deep, swirling with desire. "You did, did you?" Nic smirked, towering over me, planting a hand on either side of me.

I nodded, tugging my tight gray skirt higher up my thighs. "Maybe I can be of some… assistance? That's my job, right?" I wrapped a hand around his tie, tugging his face towards me.

Close enough to kiss.

"I always need you," he admitted.

I fluttered my eyelashes as he wrapped a hand around my thigh, slowly inching towards the place where I wanted him most.

He groaned as his fingers brushed over my core, already ready for him. "You're not wearing any panties."

Shaking my head, I grabbed the bottom of my black turtle-neck, pulling it off and dropping it on the floor. My bra followed, and then I leaned back on his desk, pushing my hardened nipples towards him.

"*Fuck*," he cursed, standing up, pushing my skirt up to my hips. "My dirty little assistant, did you come in here to get fucked by your boss?"

"Uh-huh," I nodded.

He lowered his mouth to my nipple, dragging his tongue over the peak. "So pretty."

I dropped my head back as he thrust his fingers inside me, finding me already soaked for him. "I need *you*," I told him, feeling like I was admitting something of my own. A truth that I couldn't take back.

I *did* need him. I needed him more than I could explain. Like air.

"Who do you need?" His free hand closed around my neck, holding me in place.

I let my eyes lazily drag down his body. "My husband."

He groaned, dragging our mouths together before kissing me roughly as his fingers continued to pump into me. "Such a good girl," he praised when we pulled apart.

I let out a strangled cry as he suctioned his mouth back on my breasts, alternating between them as he worked me higher and higher.

When I was right there on the edge of my orgasm, he stopped, pulling out before spinning me around. My hands landed on the wood, my back arching as he pushed my legs apart. I could hear the clink of his belt, followed by the zipper on his pants, and I whimpered, wanting him to fill me up.

I pushed my ass backwards as he brushed the tip through my entrance, gathering up my arousal and coating himself in it. "Yes, yes," I said, dropping my forehead onto the desk. "Give it to me."

"Just the tip," he said, pushing inside me slightly. "And then I'm going to put on a condom."

I whimpered, feeling him stretch me. "More," I begged.

"Zofia," he groaned, hands gripping my hips as he gave me a few more inches. "You feel so good."

Nic gave a few more pumps, his hips snapping against mine, before he pulled out. I heard the condom wrapper, and then he was inside me again, sliding to the hilt. We both groaned as he filled me. He fucked me hard and fast, the brutal pace of his punishing thrusts bringing me back to the edge of my orgasm within minutes.

My climax rippled through me, a moan tearing from my throat, and Nic grunted, letting out a garbled curse.

"Come inside," I told him, playing into his fantasy. "Fill me up."

I could feel him throbbing inside me, still rocking his hips as he fucked me through his orgasm.

He bent down, pressing a kiss to my spine, before pulling out. "So goddamn perfect," he praised me.

After taking care of the condom and disposing it in the trash can, he handed me my bra, helping me back into it. He tucked himself back into his pants, leaving them open.

"I like you like this," he murmured, tracing a finger down my cheek.

"Like what?" I asked, pulling my skirt down and holding my top over my breasts.

He grinned. "Freshly fucked."

I shook my head. "Now we just have to hope your office was soundproof enough that no one heard us."

Nicolas shrugged, zipping his pants and redoing his belt. "Maybe I wanted them all to hear. That way, they know you're mine." His gaze was heated as he stared at me. "Don't want anyone getting any ideas about my wife."

"Fake wife," I reminded him, thinking about the contract sitting in his office.

He looked away, face stern. "Right. Of course. It's all about keeping up appearances, right?"

"Nicolas…" My voice was soft.

He shook his head. "For better or for worse, right, Zofia?"

Right.

It was the reminder that I needed—remembering just what we were to each other.

Or… what we'd never be.

"Are you sure about this?" I asked, standing in front of the door to my parents' house the next day. It had been two weeks since I'd come over for dinner with everything we'd had going on, and I felt terrible about that.

Especially considering we'd gotten married.

"Breathe, baby. They love you," Nic said. I looked up at my husband as he rubbed his thumb between my eyebrows, like he was smoothing away the worry.

My heart was fluttering in my chest, and I sucked in a breath, letting my eyes dip down to his perfectly kissable pink lips. Lips that I'd memorized over the last week. Lips that had been all over my body. A rush of heat flooded my system, and I tried to tamper it down.

"Zofia…"

"Nicolas," I murmured, hyperaware of where we were. Married or not, we were on my parent's doorstep. "We shouldn't —" I closed my eyes. After yesterday, I wasn't sure I could keep pretending. Not when everything felt too real, and I didn't know how to handle it anymore.

I was trying to remind myself that we had an end date. I couldn't get attached to him.

He shook his head, like he was remembering where we were. "Right. Sorry."

Which was good—because I needed a moment to steel myself before having to put on a cheerful front for my parents.

The door opened, and there was my mom. "Chellam," my mom said, arms open wide as she engulfed me in a hug. She smelled like *home*, like incense and jasmine and the laundry detergent she'd used my entire life. I pressed my nose against her shoulder, inhaling her scent.

"Hey, Amma." I tightened my grip around her, grateful for my mother's support. "I missed you."

She pulled apart, smiling at me before brushing her thumbs across my cheeks. "And my new son-in-law."

"Hi... Athai," he said, addressing her as the Tamil name for mother-in-law. I was touched. He hadn't asked me, which meant even more to me. My mom wrapped him up in a hug as well.

"Oh, I like him a lot," she said to me. She patted his back, opening the door for both of us. "Come on in."

Nic took a deep inhale. "That smells amazing."

She smiled at him. "I made Zofia's favorite."

"Amma." My cheeks were warm. "You didn't have to."

"Nonsense. It's not every day your daughter gets married without telling you."

"It's my fault," Nic said, wrapping an arm around my waist. "I didn't want to wait any longer to call her my wife."

She chuckled. "I remember when my husband was like that, too."

"He was?" I asked, surprised. My father was fairly subdued. He fit the engineer stereotype to a T, though he'd always been loving towards his children, I still couldn't imagine him that passionate.

My mother gave me a secretive smile. "Oh, yes."

We followed her through the house, and I rubbed at my back, letting out a small wince. It had been hurting all day, and as much as I was happy to spend time with my parents, I was looking forward to getting home and taking a hot bath.

It was strange how quickly I already thought of Nic's house as my home.

He frowned, watching me. "You feeling okay?"

I rubbed at it, letting out a small wince. "Yeah, just a back-ache." I waved him off. "It'll go away after I take something, I'm sure." My back normally started hurting before I got my period, which was due any day now, so I was used to it.

"If you're sure…"

I nodded, standing on my tiptoes to press a kiss to his cheek. "I'll take a warm soak when we get back. I'll be fine, I promise."

"Okay." His hand rubbed over the spot on my lower back, and I almost moaned in enjoyment.

Unluckily for me, because my husband's hands could have performed miracles, my mom interrupted us, talking about some of our family traditions. Many of our extended family were Hindu, and Diwali was only a few weeks away. Even though my family wasn't super religious, I still had a lot of friends who were practicing, and it was a common topic in our household.

The holidays were just around the corner, and I wondered what Christmas would look like with Nic. I didn't even know how he celebrated, which felt like something I needed to remedy.

"You know," Nic said at one point while my mom got up to check on the food. "Halloween is almost here."

I nodded. "Yeah. The girls mentioned something about a party? They also told me that costumes were mandatory."

He laughed. "Oh, they *definitely* are. They always go all out. It's fun."

I bit my lip. "So, should we…"

Nicolas's face broke out into a grin. "My gorgeous wife, are you asking me if I want to do a matching couples costume with you?"

Trying to look nonchalant, I shrugged. "Maybe. You know, if you want."

His lips brushed under my ear, his breath hot on my neck as he murmured, "*Yes.*" His smile was so warm it made me feel gooey inside.

What I wouldn't give for this to be real. I felt empty inside, knowing our marriage was in name only, because lately it felt like everything did only made these feelings grow?

Feelings I wasn't supposed to have.

And I realized I wanted this—for *real*. I wanted to know that I'd walked down the aisle to the man of my dreams.

A man I was in love with, who looked at me as if I was the reason the sun rose in the sky every morning. A man who thought I was as integral to his life as *breathing*. A man who loved *me*.

Which was why I needed to protect my heart.

Because, Nicolas Larsen might not break my heart…

Unless I fell in love with him and he didn't feel the same way.

The way my heart was fluttering, I knew it was in danger.

20
nicolas

My wife stepped out of our room, a green dress wrapped around her curves, her dark brown hair in an elegant and yet sexy updo. *Stunning.* It would be hard to keep my eyes—and my hands—off her all night.

I couldn't help myself, letting my eyes trail down her body appreciatively. "Gorgeous, you... you look beautiful." I swallowed roughly.

"You think it's okay?" She asked, frowning, turning to look at herself in the mirror.

I wrapped my arms around her waist, kissing her neck. "I think you're perfect. You're a goddess, and I don't even deserve to breathe the same air as you." Zofia was the most beautiful woman I'd ever seen, and I was damn lucky she even allowed me to be in her presence.

She rolled her eyes. "Laying it on a little thick there, huh, Nicolas?" Zofia lowered her voice to barely a whisper. "I already married you."

I wrapped my arm around her waist, tugging her to my side so my lips could brush over her ear. "Not a line, Zofia. It's the truth."

I had a strange caveman-like urge to mark her as mine, to make sure everyone knew exactly whose she was. Never mind that it was just a contract that bound us together.

We were more than friends, but was it too much to hope that we could have an actual relationship? To be a *real* couple? Maybe. What if I'd done things differently?

But I knew she never would have given me a chance any other way.

Either way, my ring was on her finger.

"I just want your dad to like me."

"He already likes you," I reminded her. *Just like I do.*

Fuck. I couldn't develop feelings for her.

For starters, because I knew exactly what this arrangement was. A contract marriage, only until we had what we wanted. But when I told her about my inheritance—about what I had to do to get it—would she still want to be my wife?

I wouldn't blame her if she didn't.

It was more than I expected from her, especially with the contract we'd made. There were no stipulations for what happened if we *stayed* married, though I didn't foresee that happening. Not when I knew why Zofia wanted this marriage— and why she thought I did, too.

Zo let out a little huff. "You know what I mean. As your *wife.*"

"How could he not?" I spun her around in my arms, letting my hands settle on her hips. "You're incredible."

She let her eyes flutter shut, and I pressed a soft kiss to the crown of her head.

I'd been letting her take the lead on physical intimacy ever since that moment in my office, and it was killing me—but so had being reminded that we were fake after being buried inside of her.

It was safe to say I was a little on edge.

"You were so great with my parents," she said, her voice a whisper. "I just want to be that for you, too."

I pressed my forehead against hers. "You already are, baby."

Her eyes held mine, and it was fucking magical.

"Okay." Her voice was soft, but she gave me a firm nod, her eyes bright. "Let's do this," she told me. *Strong.* I appreciated that strength—God knows how much it got me through every day.

We stood in the large, spotless kitchen of my dad's house—white, pristine, stainless steel everywhere. It felt like such a stark contrast to Zofia's family home. The Narayan house was warm, welcoming, and full of love. My father's place looked every bit the home of a billionaire—one who had never once cooked in his own kitchen.

I knew it for a fact, because growing up, we'd always had a private chef.

It had been humbling, starting college without knowing how to do anything for myself, but I'd quickly realized I needed to adapt if I was going to survive.

Is that what I was doing now? Trying to *adapt*?

I looked over at my wife, standing across me. She was making small talk with my dad's wife, who was heavily pregnant with their first child. She was only a few years older than me, and though I'd found it crazy when they'd first started dating, I could tell my dad did genuinely love her.

He let his hand rest on her belly, and not for the first time, I mourned the loss of my childhood—of the life I could have had, if we hadn't lost my mom when I was so young.

What would she say, if she was here? Would she be as enchanted with my wife as I was? I liked to think so.

Stepping in beside her, I slid my hand onto Zofia's lower back.

"Thank you again for having us, Kendra," she said, smiling at my step-mother. I had nothing against Kendra—she made my father happy, and she was a lovely person. But seeing her around made me miss the mother I'd never known, bringing up all the unresolved feelings that came with that.

"I'm so happy you two could finally make it." She rubbed her belly. "Especially since this little one is due soon."

My father chuckled. "Never thought I'd be becoming a father again at this age, but we're very excited."

"Do you know what you're having?" Zofia asked, leaning on me.

Kendra's face transformed into a blissful smile. "A girl." She looked between the two of us. "What about you two? Are you thinking about having kids anytime soon?"

Zo froze underneath me.

"I—uh—not yet," I said, rubbing her back in a soothing circle. "We're happy with it just being us for a while."

"Yep," Zofia agreed. "Not to mention work is about to get crazy busy." She gave an awkward laugh, gulping down water from her glass.

"There's no time like the present," my father said. "If you're always waiting for the right time, one day you'll blink and realize your entire life passed you by."

"We're still young, Dad," I reminded him. "We've got plenty of time before life… passes us by."

"I'm just saying. Some grandkids would be nice."

"You're about to have a baby," I reminded him. "Wouldn't it be weird if their niece or nephew was that close in age?"

It was surreal to think I was about to be an older brother. To a *sister.* I'd lived twenty-eight years as an only child, but that would change soon.

"I need a drink," I muttered in my wife's ear.

She looked up at me, chuckling. "We should have made a bet how long you'd last."

I scowled at her. "Not fair. You know me too well."

Zofia just smirked. "One could say spending a year in such close proximity would do that."

Squeezing her hip, I turned back to my father and Kendra.

Luckily, no one brought up us having a baby again the rest of the night.

Though I couldn't get the idea of Zofia, round with our child and glowing, out of my mind.

I waited for my dad to bring up my trust fund, the inheritance I'd needed to jump through hoops to get. Part of me wondered if he suspected that the relationship wasn't real— especially since it had been less than two months since he'd sat in my office, telling me I needed to settle down.

Of course, back then, I hadn't even been able to consider what it would like to be married.

Now, I couldn't imagine my life without Zofia.

Without her cuddled against my body at night, and her copious amounts of blankets strewn across my house. Even her adorable white cat, who always seemed to be asleep on one of my shirts. She was in so deep, and I couldn't imagine getting her out.

It hadn't even been a month since we were married, and I already hated the thought of parting ways after two years.

But how did I convince her to stay?

How did I convince her that we were worth it?

Especially when I didn't even know if *I* was worth staying for.

A few days later, back in the office, I watched as Zofia tidied up a stack of files while mumbling to herself. Things had been different between us ever since my dad's house.

Before that, I could almost believe that we were real newlyweds. I loved waking up next to her, spending our mornings together while sharing coffee and breakfast. Even better was having her home each night. Ever since we'd shared the omelettes together in the kitchen, it felt like things were real.

I couldn't get enough.

Maybe I had developed a slight obsession with my wife, but who could blame me? I spent all day with her in the office, and I still wanted more of her. *Craved* it, really. How was it possible to spend almost every hour of the day together, and want her by my side every night? I could blame it on our sexual chemistry, but I'd felt like this for a long time.

Even Cooper and Duchess seemed content with their new living situation. At first, my dog loved to sniff her cat, only to get swatted on the nose when he got too close. They were warming up to each other, though, because more than once I'd found the two of them both cuddled up in the same room, mere inches apart from each other. Progress.

If only I could say the same for us. It felt like we had two steps forward and one step back, like she was pulling away from me. *How did I fix this?* Fix... *us.* It felt like I was standing on unsteady ground. Any sudden movement, and I'd be swallowed into a sinkhole.

Deciding I'd stared at my wife long enough, I cleared my throat. "Hey."

She looked up, her face smoothing into a smile when she realized it was me. "Hi." She was wearing a pretty blue blouse with a tight black skirt today, and I tried not to think about how badly I wanted to drag her into my office for a repeat.

"You still up for going out with everyone this week?" I knew she'd been extra tired and hadn't been feeling great. "If you don't feel well, we can always cancel." Zofia had blamed it on stress, and I wondered how I could lighten her load. She was overworking herself, and it was my fault. If I could take things off her plate, would that help?

"No." She shook her head. "I want to go see our friends. Besides, this is the first time everyone's getting together since we got married. It'll be good to celebrate."

We were all getting together at Angelina and Benjamin's house on Friday, and I was looking forward to it. Especially after dinner with *both* of our parents this past week.

"If you're sure."

"Of course." She pressed a kiss to my cheek. "Now I need to get down to marketing and work on this with them, unless you need anything else from me?"

I shook my head, knowing she was hard at work finishing all the details for the annual charity gala. It was Zo's favorite event of the year, and I was pretty sure planning it was her favorite part of her job.

"You're good. Go." I tucked a curl behind her ear. "See you later at home."

What would I do without you? I wanted to ask her, but I didn't say it.

Because it felt too real, and we were just playing pretend. Part of me knew I couldn't keep her as my assistant forever—not when she was so talented and shined so bright. I was holding her back, and I knew it. I just needed to find her a new role, something that would bring her as much joy and excitement as planning this gala did.

And I knew just who to ask for help.

21
zofia

There was something comforting about being piled around the table in Angelina's house, surrounded by all our friends. After how busy the last few months had been, it felt like everything was finally getting back to normal, and I was grateful for that.

All ten of us were here—the usual suspects. Us girls, and our guys.

The only difference between now and the last time we all hung out is that I was now *married*. Matthew and Noelle had also just gotten engaged, plus Hunter and Gabbi were moving in with each other. She and Hunter had been sharing looks with each other all night, him stopping to whisper in her ear and her blushing. It was cute, and I was deeply envious of how comfortable they were with each other.

It felt like life was moving so fast, and I was just trying to be along for the ride.

I was happy to be with them—even if I had a stomach bug that I couldn't quite seem to kick. I'd been feeling awful all week. Between the exhaustion and then the nausea that had started, all I wanted to do was stay in bed. Which was probably why, while everyone else had an adorable cocktail in hand, I was sipping on a glass of ginger ale and popping Tums like candy.

"So, I think it's time for a new buddy read," Angelina said, eyes twinkling with delight as she looked at me.

"Oh, no," I said, figuring I knew where she was going with this.

She pulled out her phone, pulling up a book on her e-reader app. "I found the perfect billionaire romance. We *have* to read this one."

"You're determined to torture me, aren't you?" The guy on the cover even reminded me of Nicolas.

Noelle gave me a look of sympathy. "We could also do something Halloween themed, since that's next week."

"I'm always down for a fated mates book," Gabbi agreed.

Charlotte looked at Angelina's screen. "I think we should hear Ang out. It's her turn to pick, after all."

They rotated who picked their book to read that month. I'd determined that it was partially so they could force each other to read their favorite books as much as it was to keep things interesting.

Hearing Charlotte talk about the blue alien series she'd recommended had been enough for my eyes to open. Eight books later, I'd fallen down a rabbit hole.

"Now that I've finished the fae series, I think something set in the real world might be good," I admitted. "I just don't know if a billionaire romance would hit *too* close to home." I felt flushed, my cheeks warmer than normal, as I looked at my husband, surrounded by the other guys on the patio. There was no way I could tell them it was too similar because I was *crushing* on the man who I'd signed a contract marriage agreement with, and my emotions were all over the place.

Angelina frowned. "Everything's good, though, right?"

"Of course." Did my voice sound too high? "Everything's great."

Except for my marriage being fake.
And I'm pretty sure I'm falling for my husband.

After dinner, everyone was curled up on the couch, and I slipped outside, standing on the back patio, staring out at the stars.

Inside, everyone was smiling and laughing, while I felt like I was fighting an internal war.

I so badly wanted to confess everything to them. They were my friends, and I felt closer to them than I did to anyone—except for Nicolas, maybe. Though that was different.

But how could I?

How could I betray Nic's trust like that?

I couldn't.

Two years. That was how long we'd agreed to. I'd make it through, keep my head held high, and after it was over I'd figure out a way to move on. I tightened my sweater around myself, wondering if I even believed that to be true.

Would I be able to move on?

Would I be able to get over this feeling that I couldn't even name?

"Zofia." My name murmured against my ear in that deep voice made goosebumps break out across my arms.

I turned, looking up at him, into those gorgeous turquoise eyes that I knew so well, and my heart fluttered. Actually fluttered.

Damn him. He wasn't supposed to be this perfect.

"Nicolas." Was my voice more breathy than normal?

"Hey." He shoved his hands in his pockets. "I just wanted to check on you."

"Oh." I let my hand rest over my heart, glad no one else could hear the way it beat in my chest. "I'm okay."

Nic tucked a finger under my chin. "You keep saying that, but I'm not sure that's actually true." My eyes met his, and I *melted*. He looked down at my lips, and I ran my tongue over them, dampening them.

"You're confusing me," I admitted, letting the truth slip out. "I feel like I don't know what's up from down anymore, and I don't know what's real and what's fake."

"You and me, Zo," he promised, his thumb stroking over my cheek. "Just Zofia. Just Nicolas. None of the other bullshit matters."

I shook my head. "That's easy to say, but it *does* matter, Nic. No matter what our contract says—you're still my boss. And I'm still just your assistant."

His eyes darkened, interrupting me. "You've never been *just* anything, Zo. When will you get that through this beautiful head of yours?" He cupped both of my cheeks, holding me in place.

"This is what I mean," I mumbled around his hands. "Again, with the confusing me."

"Look, I know this is still new for both of us. But it's going to be okay."

"Even though we're lying to everyone and you're charming me by being the best fake husband ever?"

Nicolas laughed. "Yeah, baby. I've got you, I promise."

I looked up into his eyes, seeing the sincerity in them. That was my sign, wasn't it? Somehow, even without knowing exactly what I was freaking out over, Nic was here. Just as he'd always been here.

It came with the startling realization that I wanted him.

Not just as my fake husband.

But for real.

When had these feelings grown? When had we gone from friends to this?

Because dammit, I wanted everything. Not just casual sex and a contract marriage—for *good*. I wanted what Angelina and

Benjamin had. Watching them interact, how they bantered back and forth like it was their own personal form of foreplay, and seeing the deep love they had for each other felt like more than I could ever hope for.

If they could go from hating each other to being in love, it felt plausible for Nic and I too, right?

He doesn't want you like that, I reminded myself.

"Promise me this won't get complicated," I whispered. "Promise this won't ruin us."

He pressed his lips to my forehead. "I promise, my gorgeous girl."

Somehow, all I could focus on was the way he'd called me his.

At least for a little while, I could pretend he was really mine.

22
nicolas

*P*ortland was back to dreary fall weather already, making me wish Zo and I had taken a honeymoon instead of coming straight back from Vegas. Somewhere tropical sounded amazing—and not just because it meant I could see my wife in a bikini. Maybe I could plan one for her as a surprise. I pondered the thought, tucking it away for later.

Our celebration dinner turned into multiple celebrations—because Matthew and Noelle had gotten engaged over the weekend.

"I can't wait to marry you," Noelle murmured, turning to her fiancé, Matthew. He was a professor at the same university we'd graduated from. The two had met while she was finishing her grad degree there and working as a hall director, and they'd fallen in love. While they'd initially had to keep their relationship a secret, two years later, they were stronger than ever.

"Me too, sunshine," Matthew said, pressing a kiss to the top of her red hair. She beamed in response.

It was hard not to miss the way it felt like everyone was coupling up—I even wondered about Charlotte and Daniel, who seemed like they'd been dancing around each other for weeks. If he didn't make a move soon, she was going to end up with someone else. And I'd never seen either Angelina or Gabbi as happy as they seemed around the Sullivan brothers.

I saw how Daniel was glancing at Charlotte, and I wondered if something was going on there that we'd missed. They'd been best friends since her freshman year, and I'd seen them together in the dining hall more times than I could count before Daniel and I both graduated.

Maybe now he was actually going to make a move. It was obvious he was in love with her, even if he was lying to himself about it.

Was I doing the same, lying to myself about my feelings for Zofia, which had grown so big I didn't know what to do with them anymore?

Promise me this won't get complicated. Promise this won't ruin us.

Didn't she know how much it ate me alive to hear those words?

It *was* complicated. And that was the problem.

"Still can't believe you guys got married," Benjamin said, looking at my ring.

I sipped my beer, watching Zo laugh with the other girls, wishing *I* was the one she was laughing for. "You know what they say. When you know, you know." Or when you make a contract. *Semantics.*

"Amen to that," Benjamin said. The other guys murmured their agreement.

"I knew the second I saw her across the room that first day," Matthew admitted. "Stole my heart right then and there."

Hunter gave a noise of agreement. "I never thought I'd find my person, but she's my other half." He rubbed at the new tattoo on his forearm—a dragon, one that I knew matched Gabbi's.

The girls were currently gossiping, piled onto a couch in the living room, snuggling Angelina and Benjamin's new kittens. They'd adopted the two black kittens this last week, naming them after Batman and Catwoman—Bruce and Selina, respectively. It was a callback to their Halloween costumes last year.

"Not sure how we're going to top those," Benjamin admitted.

"Those were sick costumes," Daniel agreed.

I looked at my wife. Zofia was wedged between Angelina and Gabbi, who both looked like they were trying to soak up as much time with her as possible. I knew they'd spent a lot more time together when she worked in HR, back before I'd practically kidnapped her and convinced her to be my assistant.

I didn't regret the decision, though. Never had.

Was this it? Was this what life was all about?

Surrounded by the people who made me feel more at home than I'd ever been, I thought maybe it was.

Catching her eye, I raised an eyebrow as she bit her lip. I knew she still wasn't feeling one hundred percent, which was why I'd gone outside to check on her.

I'd told her we didn't have to come, but she insisted. She didn't want to miss out on time with the girls, and I loved how much they'd brought her into the fold. How well she fit in here.

These people were more than just friends—they were family.

One day, we'd all be gathered around the same table, our kids running around the house, playing with each other, growing up surrounded by love.

It was the startling realization that I could *see* it. Our future, so vividly. And I... wanted it.

It didn't scare me anymore, the idea of having a family. Maybe because it was *her*.

Maybe because she'd changed everything for me.

My girl. My gorgeous girl.

"Zo and I were talking about being Herc and Meg," I said, drinking from my beer.

"Last year, Noelle somehow talked me into Anna and Kristoff from Frozen," Matthew said.

I laughed. "Admit it—that's the perfect costume for you both.

It fits so damn well, dude." Especially when you added Noelle's love of chocolate and Matthew's grumpy contenance.

Maybe Zofia and I were a little more like Hercules and Megara than I wanted to admit, too. She was a strong, independent, beautiful woman, and I was hopelessly obsessed with her. Even when I knew she'd never feel the same way.

It was getting harder to deny the truth to myself. That I cared about Zofia as more than just a friend or my assistant. That I had feelings for her beyond being my fake wife.

Did I *love* her?

Was I in love with my wife?

The idea made me sweat. I knew what we'd agreed to. She'd married me to help me with the board, and I'd married her to help get her parents off her back. They'd forgiven me for eloping with their daughter, which was great, because I really enjoyed spending time with her family.

It was clear her mom could be a little overbearing—as many parents were—but she still had a deep, meaningful relationship with her daughter. Sahana Narayan wanted what was best for her daughter, and I wanted them to know that was me. There was no way I'd watch anyone else take my place at her side, not now—not *ever*.

Two weeks had passed since Zofia had moved in with me, and we'd quickly adjusted to the new routine. I loved driving into work with my wife. We stopped to get coffee together, and our relationship felt like it was moving forward. Could I even call it that, though?

There was always that nagging feeling in the back of my mind that she was pulling away from me. Sometimes I caught her staring at me throughout the day, and it made me wonder what she was thinking. Part of me wished I could read her mind, to know how she was feeling about all of this. I wanted her to confide in me, to share all of her worries and problems with me.

Still, work was better than ever. Our projects were coming

along great, and the board seemed happier knowing I was doting on my wife. It was easy to, because Zofia appreciated the little things more than any woman I'd ever met. She liked pretty lingerie and flowers, yes, but she also lit up when I brought her lunch or made her dinner after a long day. And who wouldn't want to spoil someone like her?

For better or for worse, Zofia was mine.

I just needed to prove that to her. If my plan worked out, I was hoping to surprise her with it soon. Being CEO meant I had some pull over how the company was run, and I knew it would be a smart move.

"I need your help with something," I told Benjamin, briefly explaining my idea. "Do you think Angelina would be willing to help?"

"Absolutely."

"I'm sure Gabbi would too," Hunter piped in. "The girls all love her, you know."

I'd never imagined that befriending Angelina in college—the stubborn yet focused girl she'd been—would have given me an entire friend group that felt more like family.

"Thanks, guys. I appreciate you."

"As an honorary member of the Best Friends Book Club Boyfriends and Husbands squad, we're happy to help in any way we can. Especially for Zo," Benjamin said.

"I thought we agreed that was a stupid name," Matthew grumbled, taking a long pull from his beer.

Ben raised an eyebrow. "You have a better idea?"

"Zo deserves the world," I told them. "And I know she agreed to be my assistant because I needed help last year, but I see how happy she is planning events and running around the office. When she gets bogged down in paperwork and sched-uling, I feel bad. She's great at organization, but it's not where she *thrives*." She'd been great at her job in HR, but even that wasn't the spark for her. I could see it.

And I'd be damned if I didn't do everything I could to make my wife feel fulfilled—personally and professionally.

Our conversation with the guys turned into conversations about the new academic year for Matthew, a new project Daniel was working on at his job as an engineer, and Hunter's job as a pediatric doctor up on hospital hill. I finished my beer when the girls came back over, sliding in between us.

Filling the empty spaces perfectly, like they all knew exactly where they were meant to be.

Zofia at my side. In my heart.

I kissed the top of her forehead, pulling her into me.

"We need a hockey team here," Noelle pouted.

Matthew laughed. "We can always drive up to Seattle."

"I agree," Gabbi said. "Growing up in Boston, I loved watching hockey. And now, reading all these hockey romance novels…" She let out a dreamy sigh as Hunter let his hands settle on her hips. "I'd love to go to a game again."

"Maybe when we visit your parents for Christmas, sweetheart."

"My cousin in Minnesota has a son who plays hockey. He's only six, but he's pretty good, from what she's told me."

"I didn't know you had a cousin in Minnesota," Zofia said, looking up at me.

I shrugged. "She's my dad's sister's daughter. We're not super close, so I don't even know the last time I saw her."

"That's sad." She ran her fingers through my hair. "I love visiting my cousins and family in India."

"One day, maybe I can go with you."

Her eyes lit up. "You'd really want to?"

I nodded. "I'd do anything for you, Zofia."

She shut her eyes, and I pressed a kiss to my forehead.

"Maybe we can go visit your cousin and see her son play, too. Who knows, maybe one day he'll be a pro hockey player, and we can go see his games."

I laughed. "You might be onto something. I'm sure if you said that to Rhodes, he'd probably be ecstatic."

"It's a plan, then," she said, pressing a soft kiss to my lips.

I just had to hope that we'd be together long enough for both of those things tho happen.

It was getting late when Zofia leaned her head on my shoulder, her eyes sliding shut for a moment.

"Hey, baby." I wrapped an arm around her waist, noticing the ashy tone to her skin. "You don't look so good." I pressed my hand to her forehead, but she wasn't hot to the touch. "You feel okay?"

"I'm fine," she insisted, taking another small sip of the ginger ale she'd been nursing all night.

I crossed my arms over my chest. She'd barely had anything to eat at dinner—I'd watched her pick at her food. "You're not fine." I frowned as she let out another yawn. "I think you should go home and get some rest."

She gave me a small pout. "I just need something in my stomach, and then the nausea normally passes after that."

"Will you just let me take care of you, gorgeous?" I begged. "Please." I hated that she felt sick. Hated that I couldn't make her feel better.

She buried her face in my shoulder, nodding into my shirt.

"I'm gonna take Zo home," I announced to the room as I stood up. "She's not feeling great."

"Oh, no." Angelina frowned. "Let me know if you need anything, babe?"

Zo gave her a forced smile. "I'll be okay once I get over this bug."

I picked her up, cradling her in my arms. "Nicolas," she

started, giving a weak protest, "you don't need to carry me. I can walk."

"Let me," was all I said.

"Okay," she murmured against my neck.

Heading outside to the car, I opened the passenger door, sliding her onto the seat before buckling her in.

She closed her eyes, leaning back against the seat as I drove towards our house, pulling over when I noticed a Walgreens.

"Why are you stopping?" Zo frowned as I pressed a kiss to her forehead, unbuckling my seatbelt.

"Just going to run in and grab a few things. You okay here?" Her head dipped in agreement before her eyes fluttered shut again. "Text me if you need anything," I told her.

Wandering through the aisles, I found some anti-nausea medication, an electrolyte drink, and some crackers, hoping I could get some food in her.

She'd barely had anything tonight except the ginger ale. Which… I grabbed a case of that, too.

After I paid, I dropped the bags in the backseat, offering her the bottle of Tums and a bottle of Pepto-Bismol. "Here," I said, keeping my voice soft.

"Nic." Her eyes filled with tears.

I reached over, rubbing my thumb over her cheek. "No crying, baby. I told you I want to take care of you. I know you don't feel good. You're not alone."

Zo's hand closed around the bottle of Tums. "I don't know what's wrong with me this week. I've been so tired, and now the nausea on top of it? Ugh. I don't even know why I'm crying."

"I'll run you a bath when we get home," I told her. "You can relax and read your new book." She always had a new one to read after hanging out with the girls. "And this weekend, we'll take it easy. I'll call your parents and tell them we won't make it to family dinner."

"Are you sure?" She still looked like she might cry. "I don't know what I did to deserve you."

"You exist," I said. "And that's enough." I kissed her forehead softly. "Let's go home."

It occurred to me I'd gotten so caught up in the fantasy that I'd failed to remember that this was all an act. That we were just pretending to be together—to be in *love*.

Too bad I'd actually fallen in love with her.

23
zofia

For the last week, ever since dinner with our friends, I'd been feeling extra tired, and I didn't know what was wrong with me. Nicolas had been so damn attentive, doting on me whenever he could, like the perfect husband. It was too much. The reminder that he wasn't really mine, that all of this was fake, was breaking my heart. Especially when I saw how good this could be.

Still, he hadn't said anything about changing the terms of our agreement.

A wave of nausea passed over me, and I pushed my club sandwich away. Gabbi, Angelina and I were sitting at a small bistro for lunch, back to our usual routine.

"You okay?" Angelina asked.

"Fine. Just haven't been sleeping great," I admitted. "And I think I caught some sort of virus."

"Weren't you sick at dinner last week, too?" Angelina frowned.

I nodded, toying with the gold hoop in my ear. "I thought it was just a bug, but it hasn't gone away. Maybe some weird flu strain is going around."

"Maybe you should go home early?" Gabbi offered. "I'm sure Nic wouldn't mind."

Angelina nodded in agreement. "Plus, it's not like you aren't already ahead in your work for the week."

I bit my lip. "I guess I could. I'm just so achy and exhausted, and then the nausea on top of that has just been the worst."

"Zo…" Angelina raised one perfect eyebrow. "Is there any chance you're, you know…"

"What?" I frowned as I popped two Tums into my mouth, chewing on them. "Sick? I don't have a fever, so I really don't know. Maybe I need to go to the doctor."

"I was going to say pregnant."

I felt all the blood rush out of my face. *Pregnant*?

There was no way I was pregnant, right?

Nic and I used condoms every time. Except, well… my cheeks warmed. Except when he'd slid inside me bare before putting on a condom.

"Pregnant?" I murmured, looking down at my lap. When was my last period? I didn't normally keep track of it, mostly because I hadn't been sexually active in *years*, and I definitely hadn't expected staying in Nic's bed. I did the mental math, realizing quickly that my period was late.

I sucked in a breath. "Oh, fuck."

Gabbi's hand came to rest over mine, and I appreciated the reminder that they were here. "Is this… not something you would want?"

I shook my head.

"Do you and Nic want kids?" Angelina's voice was soft. "I know you just got married, so I'm sure this is a surprise.

"That's the understatement of the century," I muttered.

"We're here for you, no matter what you need or how we can support you, babe."

My eyes watered. I'd been extra emotional lately—maybe

this was why. In fact, all of my symptoms added up. The cramping, the exhaustion, the nausea and vomiting…

"I can't be *pregnant*, you guys." I rubbed my forehead, letting out a groan. "What am I supposed to do?" I dropped my head onto the table. "Nic and I are… We… It's not even *real*."

Angelina and Gabbi both gaped at me. "What?"

"It's all fake," I blurted out.

"What's fake?"

I swallowed roughly before taking a long drink of water. "Nic and I's entire relationship. We made a contract. One that I'm *technically* violating by telling you guys, but what am I going to do?"

"Start from the beginning, babe," Angelina said, giving me a reassuring look. "And breathe."

So I did. I told them about the board not taking Nic seriously as a bachelor. How when my mom had called me to ask if I was interested in being set up, I'd blabbed and said I was in a relationship with my boss. That he'd proposed the whole thing, that we'd be married two years before divorcing amicably.

We hadn't mentioned kids in the contract. Hadn't discussed what would happen if this exact situation were to unfold.

"I can't be pregnant when he doesn't even want to really be married," I told them. "Let alone having kids with me."

"But…" Ang's voice was soft. "You *are* sleeping together, right?"

I nodded. "Yeah. It started at your Bach party, actually. Nic and I sort of… hooked up. We agreed it was only one night, but then in Vegas, one thing led to another, and…"

"I knew it!" Gabbi almost shouted the words, and I winced. "Sorry. But I saw you, you know… sneaking out of Nic's room that morning."

"You did?" I asked, surprised that I was only just now finding out. "Why didn't you say anything?"

Angelina poked her best friend. "Yeah, Gabs. Why didn't you say anything?"

"You lost your right to first access to all gossip when you moved out, Ang," Gabbi said, leaving Angelina pouting. "Anyway, it wasn't my secret to tell. And I didn't know exactly what was going on between the two of you this summer—not until Nic posted that you'd gotten married. I know you know I can't condone workplace relationships, especially those with a power imbalance like yours, even if it's not *technically* against the rules."

She was right—I knew better.

"We weren't at work on the trip," I said, defending myself. "Besides, we're friends."

"Mmm, I've heard that one before," Angelina said,. "Do you know how long I told myself that Benjamin and I were just friends? Friends with some really amazing, wonderful benefits, sure, because Benjamin loves to—"

Gabbi quirked an eyebrow. "You know I love hearing about your sex life, Ang, but maybe not in front of Zo?"

There was never a moment with these two where I wasn't amused—if not, slightly terrified. "It's fine." I shook my head. "So yeah, we were sleeping together, but in like a *friends who give each other mutual orgasms* kind of way." It was sex, plain and simple. "No feelings."

We weren't making love.

Sure, he always made sure my pleasure came first, and I'd never met anyone else who could bring me to orgasm so quickly with just his tongue alone, but still.

Angelina nodded. "Denial is a river, and it's *long*."

"You mean the Nile?"

"It's a metaphor, Gabs."

She frowned. "I'm pretty sure you stole that from the *Jungle Cruise*."

It was my turn to interrupt. "I'm not in denial. Nic and I *are* just friends. That's always been the foundation of this, even after we got fake married."

Angelina gave me an unconvinced look. "Are you sure about that fake part? Seeing the two of you together, I guess I just never would have guessed it wasn't real. The way he looks at you…"

Shrugging, I avoided eye contact with either of my friends. "That doesn't mean anything. It's all just for show—that was the deal. Nic's a good actor, I guess."

"And you?" Gabbi asked. "Were you just pretending, too?"

"I—" I looked away, unwilling to disclose the truth of my feelings. Because it wasn't real, and that was the most sobering part of it all.

"Why don't you tell him how you feel?" She suggested. "Maybe once he hears, everything will change."

Or I'd tell him, and he'd turn down my feelings, and everything would end. And then I'd have to move back in with my parents until I could find a new apartment, admit that I was now *divorced,* and have another failed relationship under my belt.

I stood up from the table, the nausea only growing worse. "Excuse me," I mumbled, running towards the bathroom in the back.

Where I promptly threw up.

There was no denying the fact that I was pregnant. The two pink lines looked back at me, practically mocking me.

After I'd left lunch, I'd texted Nic, telling him I was still feeling under the weather but that I was going home to rest. I'd stopped at a store and grabbed a few tests, wanting to be sure before I figured out what I was going to do.

I felt so stupid. I'd gotten pregnant with my *fake* husband's baby, and the worst part was I was also pretty sure I was in love with him. Had this ever really been fake? Ever since we'd signed the contract, we'd toed the line between us. Ever since I'd fallen back into his bed, I hadn't wanted to admit the truth of what we were doing.

Why had I agreed to this in the first place? I knew it was all supposed to be fake. That nothing between us was real. And yet I couldn't help but feel like I'd gone from being the person with all the answers to the one with all the questions.

Looking back, it was hard to deny the truth, especially considering how many nights I'd shared with him.

And now there was a tiny life growing inside me.

A child that I realized I desperately wanted, but one I never expected.

What was I going to do?

"Zofia?" Nic's voice called out, and my eyes widened at the stick in my hand.

I wasn't ready to tell him yet. I didn't even know how I truly felt about it, not to mention I had no idea what his reaction would be. Shoving it into the bottom of my makeup bag, I pulled the zipper shut before walking into the bedroom, finding Nicolas frowning, hands on his hips.

"Are you okay? I saw your text. When Angelina and Gabbi came back, and you weren't with them, I was worried about you."

No. No, I wasn't okay. We'd been careful, so careful, and now everything would change. "I-I think I ate something bad," I croaked out. "I figured I'd come home and lay down."

The second I'd gotten home, I'd kicked off my heels and peeled off my blouse and pencil skirt, feeling overstimulated and trapped in the tight clothes, changing into a loose linen pajama set.

Now that I realized I was pregnant, it explained a lot. Like why my breasts had been so tender and sensitive this last week.

"What's wrong?" He asked, that frown deepening. "Talk to me, baby."

But I couldn't. I was frozen. How would he react?

Neither one of us had planned for this. I didn't even know if he wanted to be a *dad*. We'd been married and living together for almost a month, and I hadn't even asked him if he wanted kids. What had he told his dad?

We're happy with it just being us for a while.

Which was not the thing someone who wanted them said, right? Pretending or not.

He'd insisted on using condoms, and it made me think maybe he didn't want them—or that he didn't want them with *me*. His fake wife.

The thought hurt that one day he might meet someone for real. A woman who he fell in love with who would wear his ring and have his kids, and I'd be forgotten.

I hated that.

Because he was *mine*.

I'd only known for a few minutes, but I already loved our little bean. Tears pricked my eyes, and I cursed myself internally.

Damn hormones. I wanted him or her, no matter what. I wanted to be a mom.

I just didn't expect it to happen like this.

"Do you want me to take you to the doctor? You've been sick for too long." He took a few steps toward me, his hand reaching out to brush the hair back off my forehead. "I hate seeing you like this."

I opened my mouth to tell him, but nothing came out. Instead, I shook my head, trying not to preen at the contact, at how much I loved every touch. "No. I just need to sleep it off, I think."

I hated I couldn't bring myself to tell him the truth.

"Okay. If you're sure." He pressed his lips to my forehead. "Want me to grab you anything for dinner?"

"Maybe. I'm not sure what I can keep down, though."

He offered me a smile that made my insides melt. "I'll bring you some toast and ginger ale. How's that sound?"

"Perfect," I admitted.

Nicolas helped me into bed, handing me my paperback off the nightstand, before heading back downstairs. "I'll be back. Text me if you need anything."

"Okay," I whispered, snuggling into the sheets as I watched his backside disappear out the door, appreciating the sight of his ass in those pants. And why shouldn't I? He was my husband, and he had a very nice one.

Struggling to keep my eyes open even as I read my book, I finally succumbed to sleep, waking up hours later to Nicolas wrapped around me and the light no longer coming in through the blinds.

"Nic?" I whispered, cuddling back into his hold. It was warm and comfortable, and I felt safe. I shouldn't have felt like this, but I couldn't help it. He was too damn perfect not to fall in love with.

"Yeah, baby?" He was stroking my hair.

I tasted bile in my mouth. I couldn't bring myself to tell him. Wasn't sure I could force the words from my lips.

Tomorrow. I'd figure out how to tell him tomorrow.

"Nothing," I murmured. "Now, will you hold me again?" I wrapped my arms around his middle, lowering my face to his chest and inhaling his ocean scent. It somehow made even the nausea fade, if only a bit.

"You sure you don't want anything to eat?" His words were a whisper as his fingers delicately traced down the bare skin of my back.

I shook my head. "Right now, I just need you."

Every few minutes, I'd stared at Nic's door, trying to will myself to go in there and tell him my life-changing news.

I'm pregnant.

And yet, I was frozen. Unable to move from the chair.

I'd gotten up early this morning—before Nic had even woken up—and slipped outside, watching as the sun rose over Portland from the front porch.

I knew how stupid I was.

How ridiculous it was to hope things would change. And yet, here I was.

I wiped a tear off my cheek.

Everything I'd thought would be a negative about being with someone had turned into positives with Nicolas. He'd never asked me to give up my career, to change myself. He supported me, cared for me—and I even liked the way he took care of me. It was a strange realization that I could be independent and yet still rely on someone else. I'd worried that people would think less of me, being in a relationship with the man I worked under, and yet, a month later, the reaction from everyone at the office had been overwhelmingly positive. Sure, there might always be whispers I was just sleeping with him to get a better position with the company—but both of us knew better. And in the end, that was the only thing that mattered to me.

He was nothing like my ex. I knew that down to my bones.

So why did I have this feeling in my gut that said everything was about to implode in my face?

I wasn't sure what I expected, but Alexander Larsen standing in front of my desk wasn't it. I hadn't seen him since the day we'd had dinner at his house.

"Mr. Larsen," I said, giving him a firm smile. "Nic's in a meeting right now, but how can I help?"

"I'm actually not here to see him, Zofia." He adjusted the cuffs of his shirt. "I'm here to see you."

I frowned. "You… are?"

He nodded. "I'm glad you two seem to be happy. I know Nic mentioned that you two had decided to wait to have kids until later, but I was hoping to change your mind."

Oh. I resisted curling my hand over my still-flat stomach. If only he knew. "I'm sorry, I just don't know why that's any of your business?" My brows furrowed. "Shouldn't you be focusing on your own child—you know, the one who's about to be born?" I'd never had a problem with Nic's dad before, but I was so confused as to why he was really here.

"Of course, it's my business," his father said, running his finger along the edge of my desk.

I wasn't sure I loved his tone. "What's that supposed to mean?"

He raised an eyebrow at me. "A few months ago, when I'd brought up the idea of Nic getting married, he told me he didn't even want a wife. And then, a month later, you had his ring on your finger. Don't you think that's odd?"

I crossed my arms over my chest. "I don't like what you're implying, Mr. Larsen."

Alexander shrugged. "Maybe he married you to get his inheritance after all."

"His *inheritance*?" I froze. "What?"

His eyes drifted to mine. "You didn't know?"

I shook my head. "No. I thought—the board said he needed to be more settled. Committed. And you—we—"

"It's one of the conditions for him to get his inheritance from his grandfather. A marriage—and a child."

My eyes widened. "What?" *What was happening right now?* Did Nicolas really marry me for *money*?

He didn't even know I was pregnant yet, but somehow, that was the other condition?

"I think I'm going to be sick," I murmured, sliding my desk chair over to grab the trash can from under my desk.

Alexander gave me a look. "Huh. I guess maybe I didn't have to come convince you after all."

"I can't—"

Footsteps interrupted my thoughts.

"Dad?" That was Nicolas's voice. "What are you doing here?"

I looked up into the eyes of my husband—my fake husband —wondering if the entire foundation for our relationship had been a lie.

24
nicolas

I looked between my father and my wife, who looked like she'd gone pale. "Dad? What are you doing here?"

He cleared his throat. "Just wanted to check in on you, Nic."

"What did you say to her?" I narrowed my eyes. "What did you say to *my wife*?"

"Nothing," Zofia said, voice quiet. Subdued. She was lacking her usual spark.

I frowned. "It doesn't seem like nothing to me. He upset you." I turned to my dad. "Leave."

He crossed his arms over his chest. "You can't tell me to leave when this is my company, Nicolas."

"It's mine now," I reminded him. "You retired to travel with your wife. So maybe go live your life and be the parent you should have been for me all those years." I poked his chest. "That baby deserves better."

He opened his mouth and then closed it. "I had no idea that was how you felt. I'm sorry I tried to give you a better life."

"A better life?" I laughed bitterly, the resentment I'd carried all these years bubbling up inside of me. For so long, I'd shut it down. It was only now, after being with Zofia, that I'd realize how truly fucked up it all was. "You were never home. I was raised by nannies and housekeepers. We lost Mom when I was three, but I might as well have lost my dad, too. This company was your baby, and I always came in second place." I threw my hands up in the air. "This is why I don't want to have kids. I don't want to fuck them up like you did."

My father looked dismayed, like he couldn't believe I'd said the words out loud. I knew they were ones I couldn't take back, but I was surprised how much better I felt after saying them.

"We'll discuss this later," he muttered, before turning around and leaving the office. Retreating back down the elevator with his tail between his legs.

Zofia's hand was over her mouth when she faced me again. "You don't want kids?"

"I thought we were on the same page with all of this," I said, frowning.

"Humor me."

I sighed, my hands running through my hair. "I don't know. I didn't exactly grow up with the best example of a dad. He spent more time at work than with me, and it didn't get better after my mom died."

"Your dad being a shitty parent doesn't mean you'll be a bad one," Zofia murmured.

"I know. I just… I'm just worried that I'm too married to my job and I wouldn't be able to give a child the attention they deserve."

"You give *me* plenty of attention. What makes you think a kid would be any different?"

I—I furrowed my brows. I hadn't considered that, had I?

"Nicolas, in the last two months, how many times have you stayed late at work? How many times have you forced your employees to work overtime to get projects done?"

I thought about it for a moment. "I… I haven't."

"Exactly. Because you're a good boss. A good *man*. And despite my initial reservations, a good husband. I have no doubt that you'd make an excellent dad."

"I'm confused, Zo." I reached for her, but she stepped back. "What did he tell you? Why are you asking me this? Kids were never a part of the contract. We both knew that."

"But what if things changed? What if I decided I wanted to have kids?" She shook her head. "I can't do this, Nicolas."

"Can't do what? Talk to me, please." Everything felt like it was cracking, falling apart. And I couldn't fix what I didn't know. "*Please*. Please, tell me how to make it better."

"You can't," she whispered. "He—he told me about your inheritance, Nicolas. The trust fund you're so desperate to have access to."

Oh. "Fuck." I ran my fingers through my hair, tugging at the strands. "It's not what you think, I promise."

Her eyes filled with tears. "I need *you* to tell me. Not him."

I shook my head. "I don't—didn't want to lose you."

"I'm such an idiot," she said, tilting her face towards the ceiling. "Any of it. Was any of it real?"

"Zo—" My throat was tight. "We signed a contract."

"Right." She let out a bitter laugh. "The contract."

I shook my head. "That damn contract." I wanted to rip it to shreds. "You have no idea, do you?" I let out a laugh. She had no idea how I felt about her. "Ask me."

"What?" Zofia looked confused.

"Ask me why I didn't sleep with any other women since you became my assistant. Why I haven't even looked twice at any of them."

"Nicolas—"

"My inheritance doesn't matter," I told her. Only she did. Didn't she know that?

Tears were streaming down her face now, and I so badly wanted to wipe them away. "It does if you *lied*. If you used me

—" My wife shook her head, slipping the ring off her finger. "I can't—"

"Don't do this," I said as she placed it in my hand. "Please."

I can't live without you. I don't want to.

"I'm going to spend the night somewhere else tonight." She pursed her lips. "I just need some space. Time to process."

I winced as she moved a step towards the elevator, stepping forward to close my hand around her wrist. "Stay." I wanted to beg her.

She shook her head. "I-I can't, Nicolas."

"You're my wife," I reminded her. "For better or worse."

"How much was I worth to you? How much was this marriage worth to you?"

My heart was breaking. "So that's it? We're over? Do you want a divorce?"

"I don't know what I want," she whispered. Her voice was so quiet, so broken. "Just let me go."

I dropped her hand—and she walked to the elevator, eyes full of tears, and I couldn't help but feel like I'd just broken us.

Because I hadn't been honest.

Because I hadn't told her.

I didn't need the damn money.

My dad dangling it over me, reminding me that I couldn't have it until I had a wife, a family, had felt so far away for so long.

Now, I wanted all of it. With Zofia.

Only with Zofia.

A child with her adorable nose, who scrunched it just like she did when she was deep in thought. One with her warm brown eyes that captivated me every second.

Why hadn't I told her?

Because I hadn't wanted to lose her.

And now… it felt like I was losing her anyway.

Fuck.

The house was empty. *Quiet.*

Exactly what it had been like, before she'd moved in.

Her stuff was everywhere.

Her blanket on my couch, her photos on my mantle. Her shampoo in my shower, her clothes in my closet. Her scent on my pillow.

I was surrounded by Zofia.

Even her cat, who meowed at me.

"I'm sorry," I told Duchess, smoothing my hand down her back. "Mommy's not coming home tonight, and it's my fault."

Even Cooper looked upset that Zofia wasn't home.

"She'll come back," I promised them.

Even though I didn't know if it was true.

"For better or worse," I muttered to myself, looking at my wedding band as it reflected the light.

What if she decided it was over?

That she wanted a divorce?

I'd given her that out, and I'd let her have it—if that was what she wanted.

Even though I only wanted her.

Even if I loved her more than I'd ever loved anyone else.

25
zofia

"Are you sure it's okay that I stay here?" I asked Angelina, holding a pair of pajamas I'd borrowed from her in my arms, standing in the middle of their guest room.

"For the fifth time, yes, Zo. It's okay." She patted me on the arm. "I'm here for you. And if you want me to fuck him up for you, I can do that, too. He's my friend, but I've got my girl's back first."

My eyes filled with tears. "I don't know what I'd do without you."

When I'd stumbled into her office—crying—after leaving Nic, she'd immediately bundled me up into her arms, pulling me into a hug, no questions asked.

It had been exactly what I needed.

"I'm here whenever you want to talk, too." She gave me a sad smile. "I know things are confusing right now, but I promise, they'll work out."

"I don't know if they will this time," I admitted.

"I mean… you love him, don't you?" Angelina asked, voice soft.

I froze. *Did I?* "It doesn't matter what I feel. This isn't some romance book where he's going to rush in and sweep me off my feet, both of us riding away on the back of a white horse. It's real life."

Angelina gave me a look. "Most people don't make contractual relationships in real life, Zo."

I sighed. "Maybe you're right. I just don't know what to do, Ang. I was going to tell him about the baby today. Had worked myself up. And then…" I blew out a breath. "Ugh. What do I do, Angelina?"

She sat me down on the bed. "I'm sure it feels worse than it is from the outside. Do you remember when I broke up with Ben?"

"Yeah," I nodded. "You found out he'd got the promotion, and thought he'd used you to get closer to Nicolas."

"And…"

I scrunched up my nose. "And he hadn't—not intentionally, anyway. But he loved you, and Nicolas is your friend, so it was natural that they'd become friends, too."

"But at the time, it felt like the most devastating betrayal. I worked from home for a week, hiding from him. Hiding from my feelings. And in the end, I was just being stubborn. I didn't know how to let myself be loved."

I flopped down at the bed, staring up at the ceiling. "This is bigger than that, though, Ang. He doesn't want kids."

"He said that?"

I nodded. "Yeah. Verbatim. *This is why I don't want to have kids. I don't want to fuck them up like you did.* His dad was shocked."

"Wow. That's…"

"A lot," I said, feeling glum. "I know. And I can't blame him, either. When we started this, I didn't think I wanted that, either. I'd given up on those dreams after what happened with my ex. I didn't think I'd ever be able to trust anyone again. But Nicolas…"

God, I did love him. I loved him so much, which was why it was breaking my heart that we didn't want the same things.

"I do," I whispered, an admission. "I love him."

That was why it had hurt so much, wasn't it? Finding out he didn't want kids.

Finding out about his inheritance.

I sat up, looking Angelina in the eye. "Did you know his grandfather left him an inheritance?"

She shook her head. "No, but it's not surprising, knowing how wealthy his family is."

"Apparently, there were two stipulations: that he gets married, and that he has a child." I saw her face morph into one of shock and surprise. "His dad dropped in for a visit today," I explained. "Wanted to convince me to get him to reconsider us *waiting* to have kids. Of course, he didn't know that I was already pregnant."

She winced. "And you think he married you just to get it?"

I sighed. "Maybe?" Though the more I thought about it, the more I knew how implausible that was. "No." I hung my head. "I think I was just scared."

"Been there, babe." Angelina patted my leg. "I think you should tell him how you feel. He might surprise you."

A knock sounded from the door, and I looked up to find Benjamin standing there, holding two steaming mugs. "Thought you two could use a pick me up. Hot chocolate," he explained.

"Thank you," I said, taking the mug and blowing on the hot liquid before taking a sip.

"You doing okay, Zo?" He asked, looking concerned. "Ang didn't tell me much, but..."

I looked at the swirling chocolate. "I will be. I just needed some space to figure some things out."

"That's what friends are for," Angelina said.

Her husband smiled at her. "Yeah, Angel." Benjamin pressed

a kiss to her forehead before looking at me. "If you need anything, let me know."

I bit my lip. "Can you tell Nic that I'm here? I don't want him to worry."

Benjamin looked guilty. "I might have already done that. He was panicking, and I didn't want him to freak out."

"Oh." My eyes watered. "God, I'm an awful wife, aren't I? I should have stayed to hear him out."

"No, babe." She took both of my hands in hers. "You're human."

"I was just worried that if we fought—if I told him how I felt and he didn't feel the same—that it would be over. And then I'd truly be alone. I can't…" My throat was dry, and I tried to swallow. "I don't think I'd survive it."

It was Benjamin who said, "Give him a chance, Zofia. I think he might surprise you."

I nodded, knowing I needed to talk to him tomorrow.

Before, I'd been too scared to go after what I wanted.

Was I still too scared now?

I didn't even know what I wanted, not really.

I wanted Nicolas.

Wanted our marriage to be *real*.

Wanted this baby, growing inside me, a tiny little unexpected miracle.

And maybe that was what terrified me most of all.

Because I wanted *everything*.

26
nicolas

BENJAMIN

Zo's here, with Ang, by the way.

I wasn't sure if I should tell you, but…

NICOLAS

I appreciate it. How's she doing?

Not great.

You fucked up.

Believe me, I know.

You need to tell her how you feel.

I was working on that.

Not hard enough.

She needs the grand gesture, alright? She deserves that. Because she's worth it.

Always has been.

How much was I worth to you? How much was this marriage worth to you?

Those words felt like a dagger to my heart, because all I wanted was to be there for her. To be the one to bring her comfort and joy.

I wasn't supposed to be the one causing her pain.

We'd agreed to share all of life's challenges together when we got married. I knew more than ever that I needed to prove to Zofia just how real this was to me.

After last night, I never wanted to sleep anywhere except beside her for the rest of my life.

I wanted her to be my wife in every way possible. For her to know that this was more than fake. That for me, it always had been.

The contract may have been the way we got together, but it wasn't our love story. I thought about all the nights we'd spent together, listening to her talk about her dreams for the future.

And yesterday, when she'd asked me about kids, I'd felt so confused. Because how long had I imagined us welcoming a child into the world, one that was half her and half me? And now I knew for sure—I wanted it more than anything.

It had been too much to ever expect from a contractual marriage.

A real one, though?

Yeah, I wanted nothing more than to have a baby with my wife.

To be a family. The family that I'd never had.

She believed in me. Believed I'd be a good father. And I wanted to prove her right.

But I also needed to show her how much I loved her—how much I cared for her.

I needed a grand gesture so she knew just how serious I was, how much she meant to me.

Was this big enough?

The proposal was spread out across my desk, and I'd already gotten a sign off from the board for the new position. Which meant all that was left was telling Zofia, and hoping she didn't hate it.

Hoping it was enough.

I was anxious, wondering if I'd made the right decision.

Over the last year, working side by side with her as my assistant had been more than I could ever expect, and I'd loved every minute. Every work dinner, every time I'd taken her out to lunch, just as an excuse to spend more time with her. It had all been worth it, because it had brought us here, married and living together.

NICOLAS

It's grand gesture time.

I'm going to do it. Going to tell her how much she means to me.

BENJAMIN

You got this, buddy.

HUNTER

Agreed. Don't let her go, Nic.

MATTHEW

If you need to punch her ex, I also vote for that.
It worked for me.

NICOLAS

No one's punching anyone.

Hopefully.

"You really ready to do this, Nic?" Benjamin asked, clearing his throat. He had his hands shoved in his pockets as he stood in the doorway of my office.

I nodded. "You think she'll be happy?" That was the most important part of this. I wanted her to *love* it. Needed it, actually.

"Angelina seems to think so." He dipped his head at the papers. "How are you going to tell her?"

"The girls have impressed on me the importance of the grand gesture. So I was thinking over dinner. With some flowers. And getting down on my knees, begging for forgiveness."

Benjamin chuckled. "I'll never forget how nervous I was confessing my feelings to Angelina. But you got this."

"My feelings?" I asked, staring at him, a disquieting feeling creeping down my back.

"My wife told me about your contract." He slid his hand up over his jaw, rubbing it.

I froze. "She… what?" If she was bringing it up to someone else, did that mean she wanted it to end, for real?

There was no way I could let that happen.

"Zofia told her and Gabs the other day at lunch. I know this isn't just about making her happy."

"You're right. I just…" I loosened my tie. "Fuck. We started this all wrong, but I don't want to risk losing her. Not ever."

"Because you love her."

I looked up at him. "Yeah. I do." It was so easy to say, now that I'd fully accepted my feelings. Only the person I wanted to say it to the most—my wife—wasn't here.

"So, what are you waiting for? Go get your girl."

"Thanks, Ben. I know we didn't start off on the right foot, but I'm damn lucky to have you as a friend, and as my CFO."

He grinned. "I know."

Leaving him in my office, I headed out, needing to finalize all of my plans so I could surprise my girl. Because by the end of the day, that was what I wanted her to be.

Contractually or not, she was mine.

Everything was in place. I'd gotten us reservations for tonight, and picked up a dozen roses on the way back from the restaurant. Angelina and Gabbi had even taken my info and made a slideshow for Zofia, though I wasn't really sure what that was supposed to accomplish, I had to admit it was better than I could have done myself.

Zo hadn't come into work yet today. I hoped she was feeling better, considering the bouts of nausea had still been plaguing her yesterday. If whatever was making her feel like this didn't stop soon, I was going to take her to the doctor's office.

Finally, in the late afternoon, there she was.

My wife.

Looking beautiful as ever, even in a pair of loose slacks with her hair down and a pair of flats. The opposite of her usual outfits, and yet she still looked stunning. I'd never told Zofia what she had to wear as my assistant, but over the last year, I'd observed just how much she loved her personal sense of style, whether it was traditional Tamil attire or her skirt suits and heels.

I waited for her to settle into her desk before deciding *fuck it.* I needed to see my wife. Needed to hold her. Needed the confirmation she was okay.

"Hey." I stood in front of her desk, feeling apprehensive. "I'm sorry again about yesterday."

Her eyes connected with mine, and I saw they were red. Had she been crying? "Me too." Her eyes darted around. "Can we talk in your office?"

I nodded. "Of course." I shoved my hands in my pockets, trying not to touch her. Trying to respect her space. It was a failing mission, of course.

"Gimme a second." She wiped her eyes.

I reached down, pressing my forehead to hers. "Take your time, baby."

She sucked in a breath, and I headed back into my office, trying not to pace nervously as I waited for my wife. *She was ending this.* I didn't know why I knew it, but I did. She was going to tell me she couldn't do this anymore. I respected her decision, but I couldn't let her go. Not when I knew how good we were together. Not when I loved her more than I'd ever loved someone.

Her soft voice brought me out of my spiral. "Hey," she murmured, sitting down in the chair across my desk.

"Hi. Are you feeling better?"

Zofia gave me a small smile. "A little. Thank you."

"Good." I nodded.

She lifted a paper, placing it on my desk before sliding it over to me wordlessly.

"What is this?" I frowned, staring down at it.

"My resignation," Zofia said. "I'm quitting."

I crossed my arms over my chest. "As my wife or my assistant?"

She furrowed her eyebrows in that adorable way she always did when she was frustrated with me. "*Nicolas.*"

"I don't understand what I'm looking at."

"My resignation," she repeated. Like that helped at all. "Effective whenever I can have my replacement trained and ready to go."

"Zo—" My palms were clammy. I couldn't lose her. Not when she was the best damn thing that had ever happened to me. And if she was quitting this, quitting us, quitting *me*, how would I survive that?

She just shook her head. "I can't be your assistant anymore, Nic. Not when…"

Standing up from my desk, I moved around to the other side to pull her into my arms.

My assistant—my *wife*. The woman I loved. My everything. "I don't care about you being my assistant," I said against her hair. "But I don't want to lose you, gorgeous. I can't." My throat wasn't working properly, and I swallowed roughly. "I know I should have told you about my inheritance, but the money doesn't mean anything to me, honestly. It wouldn't make a difference in my life. My dad's been taunting me with it for years." I sighed. "I didn't marry you because I wanted my inheritance. I didn't even marry you because I wanted the board to respect me. I..." My palms were sweaty, and I loosened my tie around my neck. "Don't leave me," I whispered, *begged*. "This is real to me. I want you in every way."

"I'm not," she promised, wrapping her arms around my middle as I buried my head in the crook of her neck. Inhaled her sweet smell that drove me wild and soothed my soul simultaneously. "I'm not leaving you, honey."

"You're not?" I pulled away, raising an eyebrow.

"No." Her face split into a hesitant smile. Damn, but she was beautiful. And *mine*. "But I think it might be hard to be your assistant, your wife, and have your baby."

I blinked. "What?" Sure, she'd asked me if I'd wanted kids yesterday, but we hadn't talked about *us* having them. *But what if things changed? What if I decided I wanted to have kids?* I realized exactly what she was saying. She'd heard what I told my dad—out of resentment and frustration—and thought I meant it.

Zo wiggled out of my arms, bending down to grab something out of her purse I hadn't even noticed she'd brought in—a white plastic stick.

A pregnancy test, I realized, as it was placed into my hands.

A *positive* pregnancy test.

"Really?" I blinked a few times, afraid I was going to wake up and find out this all was a dream. "You're *pregnant*?" This was not the news I thought I was going to get today.

"I'm pregnant." She confirmed, nodding. "I guess we weren't

as careful as we thought. But I hadn't been feeling well the last two weeks, and when I was talking to the girls and realized I'd missed my period, so I took a test." Zofia bit her lip. "I was going to tell you yesterday, before the whole thing with your dad happened. And then I was so freaked out about the whole thing, and how you'd said you didn't want kids, and I-I panicked. Angelina helped me realize the truth. I'm sorry if you're upset, or you didn't—"

A goofy smile spread over my face, cutting her off. "We're having a baby? You're really not leaving me?"

Zofia shook her head. "I thought you'd be upset. We used condoms religiously."

Our eyes connected, and I knew what she was thinking and didn't say. Except when I slid inside her bare, and it had felt so fucking perfect it had been hard not to come right then.

"I'm not upset," I told her, picking her up and twirling her around, nuzzling my face into her curly hair. "I'm ecstatic. The woman I love is having my baby. *Our* baby."

"The woman you love?" Her eyes were watery with unshed tears. "You love me?"

"How could I not?" I wiped under her eyes with my thumbs. "You're the best thing that ever happened to me. And I don't mean as my assistant. You reminded me what it was like to *love*. To put someone before myself. You made me want to be a better man for you." I tucked a curl behind her ear. "And I tried to be careful with the condoms because I knew you weren't on birth control, and I didn't want to take a decision away from you, or make you feel trapped."

"Oh."

"What I said yesterday was reckless. How do you feel about it?" I asked her, setting her back down on her feet. "It's your body."

More tears pooled in her eyes as she slid her hand over her stomach, still flat. "I was in shock at first. That's why I didn't tell you yesterday. But I want this. And not just because I realized I want to have a family—but because I want to have *your* baby," she told me. "Because I want a family with *you*."

"This baby is the biggest blessing I could have asked for," I told her, nuzzling my nose against hers. "You're the biggest blessing of my entire life, Zofia Larsen."

Zofia let out a giggle. "Either way, I really can't be your assistant now."

"That's okay," I told her, meaning it. "I was actually working on something for you. I was going to surprise you with it tonight."

"You were?" She frowned. "I thought—" Zofia shook her head. "It doesn't matter now, I guess."

I cupped her cheek, pressing a soft kiss to her lips. "No, it doesn't. And you're too good for this job," I told her, laughing. "Always have been. Honestly, the only position that matters to me is you being *mine*. My wife. My best friend. My partner in life." I rested my hand on her stomach. "The mother of my child."

"That being said, I've been working on something, and I hope you'll like it." I pressed a button, and the lights in my office dimmed, the presentation the girls put together coming up on the screen.

"*Company Event Planner?*" she asked, reading the words. "Nic, what did you do?"

"I don't want you to leave the company," I said. "I want you down the hall, where I can see you any time I want. But I want you to do something you love, too. You weren't born to be an assistant, and we both know it. Even if you're the best damn one I've ever had. And I realized, in this new era of the company, we needed someone to plan our events, just like the charity gala and work retreats. And I can't think of anyone better to do that than you."

"Nic…" Her hand was pressed over to her mouth. "Are you serious?"

"Yes." I nodded. "Sorry I was selfish and wanted to keep you," I told her, bringing my lips to hers. "You can tell me to fuck off if you want. I'll understand. But I want you to be happy. Because you're a great assistant, but I really prefer you being my wife." I grinned. "What do you think?"

She looked up at me, those warm eyes sparkling. "Can I see the rest of the presentation?"

I sat down on my chair, pulling her into my lap so her legs were across mine. "Of course, baby. Anything for you. You're the best fake wife I've ever had."

She rolled her eyes, her finger following the grain of the wood on my desk. "I better be your only fake wife, Nicolas."

"Forever and always," I promised her, peppering her face with soft kisses until she was laughing again. I pulled her rings out of my pocket, sliding them back onto her ring finger. "And I don't need a contract to tell me that."

27
zofia

*T*he last twenty-four hours had been the biggest emotional whirlwind of my life, but I didn't think there was anywhere else I'd rather be than right here. We were still in his office, him holding me on his lap, one hand rubbing up my back, the other draped over my legs.

"I can't believe you did all this for me," I murmured against his chest. My ring was back on my finger—where it belonged, because I'd felt naked without it the last day. You don't know what you've got til it's gone right?

Well, I knew one thing for sure—I never wanted to lose him.

"Of course," Nic said, giving me one of his signature smirks as he ran his thumb over my rings, over and over. "You're my wife. I'd do anything for you." He nuzzled his face into my neck. The tone in his voice made my heart soften. It was quiet, reverent.

"Nic…"

"I really do mean it, Zofia. I love you. I'm *in love* with you. This might have started out as a contract, but there's nothing fake about us, Gorgeous. There hasn't been for a long time."

My heart practically soared as I melted into him. I didn't

know how badly I'd needed to hear those words until I'd said them.

"I was so scared," I admitted. "When I took that test, and it said positive… All the fears came rushing in. That you wouldn't want this. That you'd decide you didn't want *me.*"

"Fuck. Zo." He pulled me into his arms, hugging me tight before pulling back to look me in the eye. "I could never not want you. Why would you think that?"

I gave a little shrug. There had been a million thoughts running through my head, and I hadn't shared any of them. "I didn't know if you'd want kids right now. You just took over as CEO. We got fake married, for goodness' sakes."

Plus, I was two years older than him. I might have been thirty, but he was only twenty-eight. There might have been a million things left he wanted to do before he had a kid.

He pushed the hair out of my face. "Zofia Larsen, even if our intentions were fake, that ring on your finger is real. Our marriage is *real.* I'm here for you, every step of the way. It's a surprise, yes, but the best one." He pressed a kiss to my forehead, then my cheek. "It's you. It's always been you. From the first time I met you in the elevator, I was intrigued by you. Watching you from afar as you grew with the company, I admired you. But when you became my assistant… I think that was when I started to fall in love with you."

My heart was pounding in my chest. I hadn't expected him to be so excited about me being pregnant. To be so on board, immediately.

Nicolas just stared at me, eyes sweeping over my face, like he was pondering something.

"What?" I asked him, furrowing my brows. "Say something, please."

He shook his head. "I told you I loved you."

I nodded. "You did." I wrapped my arms around his neck.

His hand was resting on my thigh. "You didn't say it back,"

he whispered. "And I hate to ask, but I need to know how you're feeling, gorgeous."

"Of course I love you, Nicolas," I said, curling my fingers into his blond hair. "Why do you think I was so terrified that you were going to end the relationship? I'd fallen in love with my husband, and all I knew was that we were supposed to be putting on an act, but it stopped feeling like we were just pretending a while ago. And then the way you took care of me made my heart practically explode in my chest, because you were so tender and I couldn't stand the thought of losing you."

His soft kiss on my lips made me melt into him. "You're everything I've ever wanted and everything I told myself I couldn't have. I figured if I could have you by my side as my assistant, it would be enough. But then I spent every day with you, and I knew how important you were to me. When you told me about your lie to your mom, I took advantage, and I shouldn't have." Nic shook his head. "I should have just told you how I felt without the stupid contract."

I laughed, my palm cupping his cheek. "I never would have said yes, and you know it."

He grumbled. "Maybe."

"Where's the contract now?" I asked, sitting up curiously.

Nic frowned. "Why?"

"Because it needs some amendments," I told him.

"I have a better idea," he said. "We rip it up, and then we make a new one."

He cupped my chin, pulling my face to his, kissing me deeply.

My husband—for real this time. No contract, no obligations.

"I can get on board with that," I told him, kissing him again. "We're still letting my mom plan a traditional wedding, though, right?"

He grinned. "Absolutely. I loved seeing you in that white dress, but I can't wait to see you in that saree. Whatever you want to do. Maybe we can have the ceremony on our anniversary, like a vow renewal? That day is important to us, and I want to celebrate our beginning."

"Yeah, maybe." I looked down at my stomach, knowing I'd be showing in a few months. "We'll have to wait until after the baby, anyway."

"Fuck." His eyes were reverent as they swept over my midsection. "A *baby*, Zo."

I let out a soft breath. "I know."

"When do you want to tell people?"

I bit my lip. "It's still really early. There's always a chance that I could… lose it." I winced, looked away. "I need to make a doctor's appointment. Maybe after then? Just so we can confirm first."

He brushed a piece of hair back behind my ear. "Whatever you want to do, Zo. I meant it when I said it's your body. I'll be here to support you every step of the way. To take care of you in any way I can. You're the one carrying our baby, and I'm yours for whatever you need."

I smiled. "Thank you. It seems so silly that I was ever worried now. About your inheritance—about all of it."

He grinned. "I hope you know you're stuck with me now."

"Promise?"

"Every day for the rest of my life." He stood up with me still in his arms, carrying me out of his office.

I buried my face in his chest. "Nic, set me down. People are going to talk."

"So what?" His voice was low against my ear. "If I want to carry my pregnant wife out of the office so I can take her home and make love to her, that's what I'm going to do."

I blushed. "You're too much."

"Nah. For you, there's no such thing."

"You can put me down now," I said as Nic carried me into the house, bridal carry over the threshold like we were newlyweds.

In a lot of ways, we sort of were.

My husband shook his head. "Nah. I enjoy carrying you." He grinned, making his way to our bedroom. *Ours,* because it was.

He sat me down on the floor, eyes sweeping mine like he was making sure I was okay. I wrapped my arms around his neck, appreciating how much taller than me he was as I stepped onto my tiptoes to kiss him. When I was wearing heels, the different wasn't as evident, but I liked how he made me feel tiny.

"I hated spending last night away from you," I admitted. "But I needed the space to figure out my feelings."

He gave me a sad smile. "I hated every moment of being apart. Sitting here, wondering if I was going to have to go back to being alone. All I wanted was you by my side. You in my bed."

"Our bed," I reminded him.

He brushed his nose over mine. "Our house isn't complete without you in it."

Nic's hands crept up my shirt as we continued kissing, and we finally pulled apart only for him to pull it off me. He unclasped my bra, dragging it off, before his hands found my breasts.

I gave a small whimper as he flicked my nipples.

"They're sensitive," I told him as he brought his lips to my breast, sucking one into his mouth as his hand massaged the other side. I couldn't hold back my voice as his tongue dragged over each stiff peak, making me moan.

"Fuck," he muttered as he switched to the other. "That's so hot."

We quickly helped each other undress, our clothes ending up

in a pile on the floor. As soon as we were both naked, Nic carried me onto the bed and sat me in the middle with my thighs spread wide for him.

He looked *hungry*, like he was ready to devour me.

"Let me make you feel good," he murmured against my lips.

I nodded as he kissed down my body, each press of his lips against my skin making me wet with anticipation. He rested between my thighs, hands gripping each of my legs to keep me spread, and then ran his tongue up my entrance. Nicolas let out a groan, the vibration going straight to my clit, before driving his tongue inside me, like he couldn't get enough of my taste.

"So sweet," he muttered, circling my clit.

I gripped the sheets when he slid a finger inside me, feeling just how wet I was for him while he continued to give my clit the attention I so desperately wanted.

He suctioned his lips to it, sucking hard as he added another finger inside, pumping them inside of me.

"Right there," I told him as his fingers rubbed against just the right spot. "Don't stop."

He didn't, fucking me with his fingers, bringing me closer to a climax with every stroke. "Soak my face," he murmured, alternating between suction and lazy strokes of his tongue, my clit hyper-sensitive from his ministrations.

I shook my head. "I-I can't."

"You can," he encouraged me, adding another finger and pressing them against my G-spot. "Let go for me." Nic's tongue fluttered against me, and I came, feeling my release rush out of me.

"Good girl." Nic pulled away, licking his lips, before slipping his fingers into his mouth and licking them clean.

He crawled back over me, his hips resting between the junction of my thighs, his hard cock pressed against my stomach as he cupped my breasts before kissing me softly. I could taste myself on him, and the kiss quickly became more intense, our actions filled with fervor. Nic tugged on my lower lip with his teeth, tongue swirling over mine. I moaned against his mouth as he repositioned his hips, allowing his cock to grind against me.

I'd never needed anyone the way I needed him, never *wanted* anyone the way I wanted him. Like he'd been made for me, the only man who could ever drive me wild like this. It was everything, and it still wasn't enough. I needed him in me.

Wanted to feel *all* of him.

No holding back. Not anymore.

I wrapped my arms around his back, fingernails digging into his shoulders as he kept rocking his hips against me, each motion bringing his tip in contact with my clit.

"Nic," I whined, dropping my head back against the pillows. "I need you inside me."

He dropped his head onto my shoulder. "I'm trying to go slow because I don't want to hurt you," he told me. "But fuck, Zo, I need you so bad."

I spread my thighs wider. "You have me. Now let me feel you. All of you."

"No condom?" He rasped, his voice dragging over my skin, making my nipples pebble.

I shook my head, giving him a small smile. "You already got me pregnant."

He groaned as his tip breached my entrance, sliding into my warmth. I was grateful for how wet I was when he slid in easily.

Nic made eye contact with me as he buried his hard cock inside me, never looking away.

"Good?" He murmured as his hands smoothed down my sides.

I nodded, tilting my hips to take more of him. I could feel every single inch, the stretch of taking all of him always incredible, but there was something even more intimate about having him inside me raw. No barriers. Just his warmth buried in me.

"Can't believe I'm bare inside your sweet pussy right now,

baby," he said with a grunt as he began to thrust. "Feels so fucking good, I'm not going to last. Fuck." He pulled out to the tip before plunging inside again, and I gasped from the sudden pleasure. Each snap of his hips drove him deeper inside, hitting my cervix with every stroke.

My hand stroked lightly over his spine. "It's okay," I told him. "Make love to me. Show your wife how you feel."

His eyes were burning as they met mine, and I knew exactly what he was thinking.

"I love you," he groaned as he pumped into me in a steady rhythm, my hips rising in time to meet his thrusts. Nic's lips met mine again, kissing me roughly as his hips bucked against mine.

"I love you, too," I murmured against his lips, wrapping my legs around his backside, keeping him pressed deeply inside me. My fingers tightened on his back, and I ran my nose up his neck, pressing soft kisses to the sensitive skin of his throat.

"Come inside me," I whispered. "Fill me with your cum, husband."

"Fuck. You want it, wife? You want my cum and my babies? Want me to bury it deep inside of you?"

I moaned as my second orgasm burst through me, this one feeling longer and more intense than before, somehow. "*Yesss.*"

"Can't believe I put a baby in you without even trying." Nicolas groaned again, fucking me through my climax, prolonging the pleasure. "I'm so close."

"Please," I begged.

He grunted, his cock growing even harder inside me, and I could feel the way his length pulsed as he spilled inside, warmth flooding my insides. Nicolas kissed me as he pumped every last drop into my womb.

His body pressed against mine when he finally relaxed, then rolled us onto our sides while keeping himself buried in me.

"That was perfect," he said, his voice deep.

I hummed in response, burying my face against his chest.

It was everything I'd wanted. A husband who loved me. A baby on the way. My dream job.

All because of a contractual relationship that had gone so terribly *right*.

"No more condoms," I said, wiggling myself to get him in deeper. He felt so good, and there was no going back.

He pulled out of me, and I let out an involuntary whine at the loss, already feeling his absence.

"Fuck, that's the hottest thing I've ever seen," Nic murmured, sitting back on his heels as he watched his cum drip out of me.

I smirked, widening my legs to give him a better view. "Now we just need a repeat on your desk, but this time, you can fill me up and keep my panties." Reaching down, I gathered his cum, pushing it back inside me. His eyes darkened as he watched me. "You'd like that, wouldn't you?"

"Zofia," he groaned. "I've made a monster."

"Maybe." I winked.

"Speaking of… there was more to my surprise," Nicolas admitted. "Tomorrow, I'll show you your new office."

"Office?" I asked, feeling surprised.

"Yeah. I wanted you to have your own place." He gave me a devious look as his hands gripped around my ankles. "With a door and a lock."

I fluttered my eyelashes. "Planning on doing naughty things to me, Mr. Larsen?"

Curling up at his side, I smiled when he wrapped an arm around me.

"Always, *Mrs. Larsen.*"

I wasn't sure I'd ever loved two words more.

28
zofia

lright, Mom and Dad. There's your baby," the ultrasound tech said, pointing at the little bean on the screen.

Nic squeezed my hand, and I looked over at him, finding his eyes filled with tears.

We finally had our first appointment after finding out I was pregnant, and part of me couldn't believe that this was real. That I was growing our baby inside me right now.

Somehow, they'd defied the odds, some of Nic's pre-cum clearly enough to knock me up. I'd teased him on more than one occasion about it, though it was clear all that did was make him want to do it again.

Any moment I wasn't throwing up, I was all over him.

I'd never had any doubts about him being the perfect husband, but the last month had been better than I'd ever imagined. Especially once he'd found out I was pregnant. Nicolas had doted on me, making sure I ate, even it was just crackers or the ginger candies he'd gotten me to help with my nausea. He'd held my hair back as I threw up, and we sat on the couch every night, curled up under a blanket, his hand resting on my stomach.

I never should have worried about him not wanting to have kids, not when he was so excited.

"You're not supposed to be the one crying," I told him, poking a finger at his cheek. My hormones were all over the place and I'd cried more in the last few weeks than ever, but today, all I felt was bone-deep happiness.

He pressed a kiss to the top of my head. "Can't help it, gorgeous." I smiled as he grinned down at me, blinking away the moisture.

Our tech smiled at both of us, clearly used to first-time parents being overly-affectionate. "Do you want to hear the heartbeat?"

"Oh." I nodded. "Yes."

She pressed some buttons, and then a fast, rhythmic thumping filled the room.

"It's really real," I said, throat tight.

Nic pressed his lips to my belly. "There's a baby in there."

"I just need to take a few measurements, and then the doctor will come in and go over the results. And I'll get a sonogram printed for you."

"Can we get two copies?" Nic asked.

She smiled. "Of course. Lots of dads want a copy, too."

He brushed my hair back behind my ear, both of us looking at each other as the tech finished her final examinations before pulling the ultrasound wand out of me, leaving us alone in the room. After sitting up and getting dressed, I rested my head on Nic's chest. "Did you hear that? She called me dad." He sounded like he was in awe. "I'm gonna hang the sonogram in my office," he said, grinning down at me. "I want everyone to know that you're having my baby."

"Caveman," I groaned. Though I liked how possessive he was over me, so I couldn't complain. Much.

"Only for you. Especially now that I can't see you from my office."

I rolled my eyes. "I see you more every day than I did when I was your assistant," I reminded him. "Every morning, every night, *plus* lunch…"

"And somehow, it's still not enough time with my wife." He leaned in, kissing my lips softly. "I love you. And I love our baby. Thank you for giving me this."

My eyes softened. "I should be the one to thank you," I told him.

"For knocking you up with my super-sperm? Noted." Nicolas gave me a sexy smirk. "Can't wait to do it again."

My stomach rested over my stomach. "Maybe let's wait until this one's here before we make plans for another."

He grinned. "Sure, baby. But that's not going to stop me from trying."

I hummed, loving the idea of him spilling his seed inside of me over and over again, like he was trying to knock me up, when the doctor came in the room.

I'd insisted on having my OB be a woman, and I was lucky enough to find one who was half Indian. It was comforting to see someone who looked like me on the other side of the table.

"Everything's looking great, Zofia. Baby's growing perfectly, and from everything you've told me, I'd estimate your due date is around May twenty-second. But don't get too attached to that, because most babies don't come on their due date."

I nodded. "Right."

"How are you feeling? Do you have any questions for me?"

I looked at Nic, who squeezed my hand.

"My wife made a list, if that's okay?" He'd known exactly what I needed last night when I was freaking out and spiraling over today's appointment, and had run his hand up and down my back as I rambled off my list, conveying every single one of my worries and concerns.

"Perfect. Let me have them."

And somehow, I knew everything was going to be okay. Because with Nicolas at my side, I had the best support system a girl could ever ask for.

The best husband I could have ever dreamed of.

"I'm so excited that we're doing this," I said for the tenth time as I wiggled my toes in the warm water, enjoying my pedicure.

Angelina and Gabbi had invited me out to celebrate my new job. I'd officially moved into my new office this week, and I was hard at work finishing the final prep for the charity gala later this month. It wasn't much different from when I was Nic's assistant, except now I got to do it all full time.

At least until our little one got here, and then I'd switch to working part time after my maternity leave. It was perfect because it meant I didn't have to give up doing what I loved, but I could also have the role I'd dreamed of: being a mom.

Everything was better than I'd ever imagined.

"I know," Angelina said, her head titled back against the headrest. "It's so nice."

"Agreed. I love girls' day," Gabbi sighed, a moan slipping from her lips from the massage setting on her chair.

We were getting manicures and pedicures, and I'd already picked my nail polish color to match my dress. It was a surprisingly decent day, despite it being November in Portland. The gray of winter had already descended, but even though there was a chill in the air, it wasn't raining, and that was a win in my book.

"How have you been feeling lately, Zo?" Ang asked.

"Honestly, awful." I laughed. "The nausea is constant, and I don't know why anyone decided to call it morning sickness when it happens all throughout the day. Nic started eating lunch with me in my office because any small scent can trigger me. And I'm so tired, all the time."

"But everything's good?" Gabbi asked, and I nodded.

"Everything's amazing." I curled a hand over my tiny bump. It wasn't visible yet, but I was pretty sure I could feel a difference now, the smallest curve to my stomach. "We had our first ultrasound this week, and I'll never forget hearing that heartbeat for the first time."

"How'd Nic do?"

I chuckled. "Oh, he cried."

"Yeah, that tracks," Gabbi agreed. "He's the biggest golden retriever I've ever met."

"I can't wait to see him as a dad," Angelina said. "I can't believe we're all at that age where people are having babies." She scrunched up her nose. I knew how Ang felt about having kids, and her apprehension, but I knew that one day, if she had kids, she was going to make an incredible mom.

Warmth filled my heart. "He's going to be such a good one. I know he worries, on account of losing his mother at a young age and his father not being around as much, but I can't imagine anyone more suited to being a dad."

"You got a great guy," they both agreed.

"We all did." And we were damn lucky to have men who loved us and doted on us.

"I can't believe we're all in relationships now," Gabbi said. "For the longest time, I was convinced it would never happen."

"How's everything with Hunter been?" I asked.

"Amazing." She giggled. "It's great. After we shared our feelings, it just felt like we unlocked this whole new side of our relationship. And now that we're moving in together..." Gabbi smiled to herself. "I'm excited to get to see him more."

"No way!" Angelina exclaimed. "Bitch, you didn't tell me! I'm so happy for you two!"

Gabbi nodded. "It just happened. But fuck, Ang, I'm so happy."

"One step closer to being my sister for real," she said, reaching over and squeezing her hand.

"But we'll always be best friends before sister-in-laws," Gabbi responded.

And I couldn't help but smile, because these were my girls.

This was the family I'd chosen.

I'd never trade it for the world.

"I thought we were going out to lunch next," I said, frowning as we drove down the highway in the opposite direction I'd expected. Angelina pulled off at the exit for Washington Park, and I frowned. "Where exactly are we going?"

"Shhhhh, babe. It's a girls day surprise."

I furrowed my brows. The only things up there were the Rose Garden and the Zoo, neither of which seemed like a location we'd be heading to.

After getting our nails done, I'd thought we were going directly to the restaurant, but then they'd dragged me to a salon, where we'd had our makeup done. My curls were down naturally around my shoulders, and everyone agreed they were all too pretty to touch.

"I didn't even get this pampered before my wedding," I admitted to my stylist.

She offered me a small smile, continuing to put the finishing touches on my eyes. "You're gorgeous," she said, squeezing my shoulder. "And every woman deserves to feel good—no matter what day it is."

"Thank you," I said, feeling a little choked up. "Damn pregnancy hormones," I muttered to myself.

But I felt even more beautiful than I had in weeks, and maybe it was because my friends had pampered me all morning.

The car stopped, and I looked up at the rose garden. "This is still open?" I asked, frowning at the sight. I'd been here during the summer as a girl because my parents loved bringing our family here. It was probably why I loved flowers as much as I did, used to seeing the hundreds of colors and types of roses scattered along the hillside.

I followed the other two girls inside, surprised that no one else seemed to be around. They led me to a spot that overlooked the city. Since it was a sunny day, you could actually see Downtown Portland. I smiled, finding our office building easily.

Thought it was November, and most of the flowers had already bloomed, there were still some holding on. It might not have been as colorful as the summer, but it was still gorgeous.

"So what are we—" I turned back to Angelina and Gabbi, but they'd both disappeared. "Hello?" I turned around completely, and there was my husband.

Nicolas.

I couldn't move.

There he was, in the middle of the rose garden, hand outstretched towards mine. He was dressed more casually today, in a maroon polo and slacks, and my heart fluttered at the sight of him.

"Nic." I could hardly breathe. I placed a hand over my mouth as I stared at the gorgeous man who was undoubtedly mine.

"Hi, gorgeous." Words that made me melt.

I took a step towards him. Then another.

And then he sank down.

Down on one knee.

A thousand thoughts flew through my mind.

"What are you doing?" I took the final steps towards him, taking his hand as I came to a stop in front of him.

"What I should have done from the beginning," he said,

those deep blue eyes that reminded me of the ocean staring up at me.

"Zofia Avanthika Narayan Larsen, you know I love you. You know I have for a long time." I nodded, tears pooling in my eyes, and I tried to blink them away so he didn't grow blurry. "Being your husband has been the single greatest thing I've ever done in my life, and it's all I want to be for the rest of my life. Before, you were contractually mine. But now, I'm giving you the story that you deserve. So, I wanted to ask you..." His hand held mine, finger rubbing over my wedding ring. "Will you marry me?"

I quirked an eyebrow, flashing my ring at him. "We're already married, Nicolas." Like he needed the reminder.

He gave me a small pout. "Let me have this, why don't you? I had an entire speech planned."

"Sorry. Continue, husband."

"Be my best friend. Be my partner. Be my wife. Be everything, because you're already the best thing that's ever happened to me." Nicolas grinned. "Marry me again. Because I love you, and I want to do it right this time. The big wedding that you deserve. All of your family there, and all of mine. Surrounded by our friends and loved ones as we reaffirm our love for each other. What do you say?"

I shook my head, loving how ridiculous this was that he'd clearly had the girls go through some elaborate scheme just so he could propose to me. "I don't need any of that." The corners of my lips turned up in a smile. "I just need you."

He pulled me up into his arms, kissing me softly. "That's all I need too, gorgeous. You and our baby."

My eyes fluttered shut as he kissed me again.

"But, for the record, we're still having the ceremony next year, right? Because I kinda already told your mom about my plan, and she threatened to disown me as a son-in-law if I didn't let her plan this wedding."

"Yes," I laughed. "I will marry you again, Nicolas Alexander

Larsen." We both rested our hands on my belly. "And our little one will get to be there, too."

He was beaming. "You know the grandparents are going to eat that up."

I interlaced my fingers with his. "I love you for doing this for me, Nicolas, but you really didn't have to."

"Oh, no. I did. It's part of the grand gesture. The girls explained it all to me." He turned, cupping his hands over his mouth. "She said yes!" he shouted the words, and all our friends flooded out of the trees—and our parents.

"Oh, Nicolas." My eyes filled with tears. I noticed Gabbi had a camera strapped around her neck, and I realized she'd taken photos of Nic's proposal. He'd planned this all along—for me.

"Baby, don't cry," he told me, cupping my cheek.

I shook my head, laughing. "Happy ones, I promise."

"Come on. We're celebrating. It's our re-engagement party." Nicolas laughed. "Everyone wanted to come when I told them my plans, and I couldn't say no, so here we are."

He tugged me towards our families, and I let him, knowing that there was nowhere else I'd rather be—and no one else I'd rather be with.

Everything was better than I could have ever imagined it.

The best part? It was real.

No contract—just us.

29
nicolas

My leg bounced as we sat in the waiting room chairs. Zofia reached over, placing her hand on my knee. "Are you alright?"

I pulled my eyes away from the closed door, turning to look at her. "Sorry. Just nervous and excited. I can't believe we're gonna find out what our little one is today." My wife just smiled, leaning her head against my shoulder. I pressed my lips to her forehead.

"I know." She smoothed a hand over her belly.

Over the last few weeks, she'd really popped, and there was no hiding anymore that she was pregnant. I still couldn't believe my little swimmers had done the job in Vegas, but I was so grateful they did. Otherwise, we wouldn't be here right now, about to find out if we were having a little boy or a girl.

They called us back, and I held her hand the whole way into the ultrasound room, holding onto her like she was my lifeline. We were in this together, and I'd never been so damn grateful. After everything we'd been through to get here, I never wanted to let her go.

We settled into the examination room, the nurse asking Zofia her routine questions and chatting about how the last few weeks had been.

"Better," my wife answered. "The nausea's lessened, thank goodness. But the heartburn has been awful." She rubbed her breastbone, wincing. "And my breasts are really tender."

I knew she was self-conscious about how much they'd grown, but she looked incredible. I was more attracted to her now than ever, knowing she was growing our baby inside her.

"All normal," she agreed. "Now let's get the tech in here so you can see your sweet little baby."

Zofia nodded, and I dragged my chair towards her, picking up her hand and dropping a kiss on the top of it.

"You ready?" I asked, staring into her big brown eyes. I brushed a curl off her forehead, twirling it around my finger.

She let out a breath. "Yes. Mostly because my bladder is way too full and I have to pee so bad." Zo scrunched up her nose. "But you know how I feel. I don't care either way, as long as they're healthy."

I pressed my lips between her eyebrows. "I still hope we have a little girl just like you one day." I grinned. "Even if this one's a boy."

We'd had this conversation before, but I had a feeling it was a boy. The Larsen genes were strong, and there were a lot of boys in our lineage. Still, I loved the idea of a daughter to dote on just as much as a son.

"Slow down there, honey. One at a time is all I can handle."

"No matter what, they'll be so loved," I told her.

She rested her hand on her rounded belly. "Yeah. They will."

I pressed a soft kiss to her lips just as the door opened, the ultrasound tech sliding in.

"Hi, Mom," the tech said, giving us a warm smile. "Ready?"

Zo nodded. "Please. I know they said to drink lots of fluids, and I desperately need to empty my bladder." My wife lifted the top of her blouse, exposing the bump.

She laughed as she squirted out the ultrasound jelly onto Zofia's belly. "Don't worry, I hear that all the time. You know the drill—I'll get some measurements for the doc, and hopefully we can see the gender today." She looked at both of us. "You want to find out, right?"

We both nodded. "Please," Zofia answered. We'd talked about going the envelope route, taking it home and planning a surprise, but neither of us wanted to wait any longer.

"Perfect." She placed the wand down, moving it around until the baby came up on the screen.

Zo squeezed my hand as we waited. "Hi, little one," she murmured, so softly I barely caught it. I smiled.

"Look how much our baby's grown, Gorgeous." I couldn't take my eyes off the screen.

The tech pointed at the screen. "Look at that little nose. So cute." She moved around the wand, taking measurements and making notations, before looking up at us. "He's going to be one handsome little boy."

"*Boy?*" Zofia whispered, and I grinned.

"A boy," I said against her ear. I was elated.

We were having a son.

The tech smiled at us. "Congratulations. I'm just going to finish up, and then the doc will review the scans and follow up with you."

"Thank you," I choked out, my hands still clutched in Zofia's.

After the doctor confirmed the gender—yes, we were having a baby boy—she went over everything with Zo, but I barely heard anything, still staring at the sonogram they'd printed out for us, tracing my finger over his little cheeks and nose.

Our miracle.

We hadn't planned for this—hadn't planned to have a baby during our contract marriage, period—but I was so grateful for it, because it meant we were starting our family that much sooner.

I couldn't wipe the smile off my face as we headed outside after our appointment was finished and Zofia scheduled the next one. We both bundled up, and I helped her into her coat. Portland in January was cold, and even though it rarely snowed in the city, we were more than prepared for the bad weather.

"Back to the office?" I asked her after getting her settled into her seat and buckling her in, making sure the seatbelt was laying the right way over her belly.

She pouted. "Do we have to?"

I laughed. "No. Do you want to play hooky today? We could go to that big baby store you've been talking about."

Being the first in our immediate friend group to have a baby meant we didn't have a bunch of friends giving us advice, but it also meant that I spent a lot of time reading baby books. Zofia had joined a first time mom group on social media, and I always loved catching her browsing it when she thought I wasn't watching.

We were truly two peas in a pod.

"Really?" She perked up. "And lunch?"

"Yes." I reached over, popping my thumb under her chin. "Gotta feed my wife so she can grow our baby boy all nice and strong."

"I can't believe we're having a boy," she murmured, stroking her belly. "I grew up with two brothers, and I still feel like I don't know the first thing about boys," Zofia admitted.

"It's okay, because you've got me. We're in this together. I'd never throw you into the deep end and walk away."

Her eyes filled with tears. "Really, Nic. I know there will be times where your job has to come first—and that's okay."

"Fuck the job," I told her. "You and the little one are the most important thing to me." I reached over, placing my hand on her belly. "I'll do whatever I can to never let you feel abandoned, the way I know my mom felt."

"You're a good man, Nicolas Larsen."

"And you're the most amazing woman, Zofia Larsen."

"Mmmm," she hummed, leaning in towards me. "I think you should kiss me, husband. And then take me shopping and feed me Chinese food."

I leaned in to drop a soft kiss on her lips, which quickly deepened when she wrapped her arms around my neck, pulling me in deeper. Her tongue pushed against my lips, seeking entrance, and she swept it over mine. Groaning, I let myself get lost in the kiss.

Lost in this moment, because it was everything I'd never hoped I could have—and more.

a few weeks later...

"What are you doing here?" Zofia asked, looking up from her desk. "Lunch isn't for another two hours."

I shrugged. "Do I need an excuse to visit my wife?"

She shrugged. "No... But you're supposed in a meeting right now, aren't you?"

Grinning, I pulled the bag out from behind my chest. "Guilty. I brought the pistachio burfi that you were craving. I had to go to like five different stores, but I finally found it." The treat was fudge-like, dense and rich, and had been one of Zo's favorite Indian desserts growing up.

My meeting this afternoon had been rescheduled because of an emergency, and I'd taken that excuse to go find her the treat she'd cried over wanting last night. It had been too late at that point, since the stores had all been closed, but I knew she was probably hyper fixating on it and would until she got some.

"Ohmygod." She extended her hands. "Gimme." I handed her the box, and she tore into it. Zofia let out a moan after she took a bite. "This is the best thing I've ever put in my mouth." She devoured another square, looking like she was in heaven.

"Nicolas." Her eyes filled with tears as she grabbed them, holding them possessively. "You didn't have to do that."

I pulled her into my arms, frowning as tears dripped from her eyes. "Why are you crying, baby?"

She shook her head. "Hormones." The word was a groan. "I don't know. I just really love you. And you're way too good to me."

Kneeling down, I cupped her belly with both hands. God, I was obsessed with her bump. "Anything for my wife who's growing *eyelashes* right now."

She rolled her eyes, setting the snack bag on her desk. "I can't believe you know that."

"I've been very diligent about keeping up with my reading, Mrs. Larsen. It's important to me I know what's happening every step of the way with this pregnancy. Did you know our baby is currently the size of a mango?"

She shook away a few tears.

"My dad might not have been that involved with my mom's pregnancy when they had me, but I'm not going to be like him," I told her, winding my arms around her waist and pulling her body into mine. "I'm here for you. *With* you." I nodded towards the bag. "Anything you need, I've got you."

"I know." Tears pricked her eyes again, and she looked up at the ceiling. "Now I need you to stop being so sweet so I can stop crying and do my job."

"Your main job is growing our baby, Gorgeous." I pressed a kiss to her cheek. "That's all I care about."

She closed her eyes, burying her face into my shirt and taking a deep inhale. I rubbed her back, doing whatever I could to comfort her.

I'd do whatever I could to make her feel taken care of—and loved.

I came home to find Cooper with his head in Zofia's lap, his nose pressed against her baby bump. She was wearing leggings and an oversized t-shirt, looking comfortable and adorable all curled up with our animals.

"Hi, gorgeous." I leaned down, dropping a kiss on her lips.

"Hey, honey." She smiled, setting down the book she'd been reading. "How was your day?"

I shrugged. "It was fine. Better now." She'd stayed home today since we were expecting a few deliveries, and I'd missed her. There were a few times I'd almost walked into her office, forgetting she wasn't there. It would take some getting used to when she was on maternity leave—just like I'd gotten used to her no longer being right outside my door. My new assistant wasn't as incredible as my wife, but he'd gotten the hang of things quickly, which I appreciated. He was eager and a quick learner, some of the most important skills to have.

Plus, much to Zofia's delight, he wasn't a beautiful woman. Even though I liked it when Zo got a little jealous, I definitely had no desire to spend all of my time with any woman other than my wife.

Sliding onto the couch next to her, I wrapped my arms around her, letting my hands rest on her belly.

Cooper, annoyed, jumped off the couch, going over to his bed in the corner.

"Hi, little one," I murmured to her belly. "Daddy missed you today." I kissed the bump before sitting up straight and giving my beautiful wife a wicked grin. "Did you get everything done that you needed to?"

She tilted her head to the side. "Yes… why?"

I smirked. "Because I have plans for you, my darling wife.

And after not seeing you all day, I don't want to keep my hands to myself.

A hum slipped from her lips. "Mmm. I like the sound of that, my handsome husband."

"Fuck, I love you," I said against her lips before pulling her shirt off, exposing her bare breasts. I let out a groan, cupping them both in my hands. They'd grown bigger since she'd gotten pregnant, her nipples darkening, and I couldn't get enough. I squeezed them both lightly, watching her reaction.

When she titled back her head, letting out a moan, I dropped my mouth to one, sucking her nipple in between my teeth.

Wrapping my hands around her hips, I pulled her into my lap so she was straddling me, her core pressed over my erection. She rocked her hips, letting out a small whine at the sensation.

"Nicolas, ohmy—*fuck,*" she cried. "That feels so good."

"I love how sensitive they are now," I told her, circling my tongue around her peaked nipple. "I can't wait till they're full of milk."

My cock jumped in my slacks at the thought, pressing against the zipper, eager to be inside of her.

She gasped. "Nic. My God." Her cheeks had darkened the slightest bit, a rosy hue, and I loved it.

"Can you blame me? I'm obsessed." I chuckled. "You're so beautiful carrying our baby, Zofia."

Zofia ground down on my hardened length, letting out a small moan. She was so much more sensitive while pregnant, and I loved how easy it was to drive her wild.

Slipped her hand inside my pants, my wife wrapped a hand around my cock.

She squeezed my length, and I sucked in a breath, trying to hold back so I didn't come in my pants. "Stop teasing me and get inside me," she told me, nipping at my neck.

"Your wish is my command, baby." I slid my hand inside her panties. "Now, be a good girl and sit back for me." I lazily circled her clit, enjoying her small gasp when I slipped a flinger inside her.

We both worked at getting her leggings off, Zofia raising her hips as I rolled them and her panties down. I plunged my fingers inside her, confirming that she was soaking for me.

"Fuck, did you get this wet from me sucking your tits?" I groaned.

"Yes," she nodded, fingers scrambling with my zipper and to push my underwear down. "Now fuck me, husband."

I kissed her as I plunged her down onto my length, slamming to the hilt. We both groaned as I filled her. Keeping still, I waited until she squirmed on top of me before fucking her in earnest, eager to feel her sweet pussy spasming around me. It wouldn't take much, especially with the extra sensitivity. One stroke of my thumb against her clit, and she'd be coming all over my cock.

Picking her up, I kept my cock buried deep inside her as I carried her towards our bedroom, ready to make love to her all night long.

I never wanted to stop.

30
zofia

may

*H*ow are you feeling?" Angelina asked me, folding another tiny onesie. "God, this is *tiny*. I can't believe how small newborn clothes are."

Considering the little one had been consistently tracking off the charts for his size, he wouldn't be tiny at all. "Yeah, until you consider the fact that I have to push a baby that size out of me," I said, quirking an eyebrow. Between his genetics and mine, there was no way our kids would be small.

"Another reason Ben and I aren't having kids any time soon," Angelina insisted, nodding to herself. "I'm extremely happy with the DINK lifestyle. Just us and the cats." They'd adopted two black kittens soon after their honeymoon, naming them after Batman and Catwoman—Bruce and Selina, respectively.

I chuckled as Gabbi grabbed a finished pile of folded clothes, putting them into the dresser. The girls had insisted on coming and helping me when I told them I had to finish the nursery today, and I was honestly grateful for the companionship.

"I never really knew how I felt about having kids, but being with Hunter, I just... I really want to see him be a dad," Gabbi admitted as she spun her engagement ring around her finger. Hunter had just proposed to her last week, and I knew everything was still new and exciting for her.

Part of me wondered what it would be like if Nic and I had that experience—an actual, genuine proposal from the start—but no matter how strange our start was, I didn't regret one piece of Nic and I's story.

That contract changed my life for the better. It made me realize how the right guy had been standing in front of me all along, but I'd been too stubborn to see it.

And now, well... we were married, happier than ever, and expecting our first baby at the end of the month. Life couldn't be any better.

"The way he dotes on you... I can guarantee, if Hunter's anything like Nic, he'll spoil you rotten when you choose to go down that path." From watching them interact, I knew he was. We'd gotten lucky, and I knew there were a lot of women who couldn't say that. I looked down at my bump, feeling him moving around inside. "This baby wasn't exactly part of the plan—you both know that—but Nic has shown me how supportive and caring he is every single day. I'm feeling... ready, I guess?" I said, going back to Angelina's earlier question. "I mean, maybe not right this minute. Little man can stay in there till his due date—" He kicked, and I patted my belly, like I was telling him to stay right where he was. "But I'm excited. For the longest time, I didn't think this would ever happen to me. After I broke off my engagement with my ex, I wasn't sure I'd have a family of my own. Now I'm about to be a mom."

I couldn't believe that in just a few short weeks, Nic and I would be bringing him home from the hospital. Shifting in the rocking chair, I attempted to get comfortable—a feat made harder since that I was currently *huge*, carrying low. When was the last time I'd been able to see my feet? I didn't know.

"You good?"

Sighing, I slumped back. "Yes. I just need to pee. He's sitting on my bladder." Wincing, I rubbed my bump.

Angelina quirked an eyebrow. "You're really selling this whole pregnancy, babe."

"It's not that bad," I told her. "And the sex is *incredible*. Oh my god."

"Really?"

I nodded. "There's more blood flow down there, which makes you so much more sensitive. And then with the hormones…" I fanned myself. "Nic is so obsessed, we have a hard time keeping our hands *off* each other."

Angelina made a noise of appreciation.

"Just wait until you hold your niece or nephew in your arms," I said, remembering the first time I'd held my brother's son after his wife had delivered their first. How surreal it had been, cradling that tiny little bundle. "Then you'll be changing your tune."

Charlotte and Daniel had just told all of us they were pregnant, after a whirlwind engagement and marriage this winter. Apparently, they were eager to start a family, and I'd never seen her so happy. She was already glowing.

She shrugged. "*Babies* aren't the problem, Zo. They're plenty cute. It's just pregnancy that freaks me out. And the thought of losing who I am to motherhood." Angelina looked down at her lap, her pile of onesies completely folded. She stole part of my stack and continued. "I mean, Ben said he'd be willing to be a stay at home dad when the time came, so I'm not *completely* opposed to it." She looked up, her eyes meeting mine. "After we've had a few years to ourselves." She was a few years younger than me, so I understood.

I laughed. "Fair enough. Now, help me out of this chair so I can go evacuate my bladder before I wet myself in this beautiful new chair Nic bought for me."

We'd found it during one of our shopping trips while playing hooky from work, and I'd fallen in love with it immediately. Little did I know Nic was going to buy it as a surprise for my baby shower last month.

The nursery was pretty much completely put together. We'd gone with a baby blue color scheme with a slight ocean theme, and it might have been my new favorite room in the house.

Angelina and Gabbi helped me off the chair, and then I waddled towards the restroom, rubbing my back as I went.

"Are you sure everything's fine?" They asked as I let out a small groan.

"Yeah. Just my back bothering me with all the weight. I'll be fine."

Over the last few days, the pain had come and gone, but I was trying not to worry about it. I'd had some Braxton Hicks contractions a few weeks ago, and these pains were nothing compared to that.

I planned to spend the rest of the day curled up with Duchess and Cooper in bed, watching TV or reading a book until Nic got home from work. Technically, I wasn't on maternity leave *yet*, but Nic was too worried about me over-exerting myself in the office, and I'd already switched to working part-time hours. After the baby was here, I'd be off for the first few months entirely.

So instead, I'd been nesting. The entire house was cleaned, and organizing the freshly laundered baby clothes was the last thing on my to-do list. I'd even packed my hospital bag yesterday.

Another wave of pain hit me as I headed back into the room, causing me to grip the back of my chair as I exhaled deeply through my nose.

"Zofia." Angelina frowned. "Are you having contractions?"

I shook my head. "No. Well, uh… maybe? But just small ones. We're still two weeks early though, and my water hasn't broken yet."

"Still, I think we should call Nic."

Even though I knew it was the right call—I probably *should* call my husband and tell him I'd been having small contractions since last night—there was nothing to do yet.

Which meant all it would do was to cause him to hover and dote on me. Though I liked the latter, the former would drive me crazy. I knew how powerless he felt when he didn't have full control of a situation—it was why he'd begged me to be his assistant, after all—and there was no controlling this.

"Do we have to?" I pouted.

"Zofia."

I sighed. "*Fine.* But can we finish putting these clothes away first? I really want to get this room done before I go to the hospital."

"Zofia?" Nic's worried voice shouted, echoing through the house.

"Up here," I shouted, bent over the bed, my elbows resting on the mattress as I breathed through another contraction. The girls had left a few minutes ago, once Nic had reassured them he was on their way home, and I could tell the contractions were already coming closer together.

My fists clutched the blanket, clutching on for dear life as the pain started to subside.

Then Nic was standing there, staring at me with concern. "Baby. Why didn't you tell me this morning?"

I gave him a weak smile. "I didn't know if they were just false contractions again. I didn't want to get our hopes up." The doctor had told me she wouldn't be surprised if I delivered early, since our son was running out of room, but I'd been determined to go full term.

Nic pulled me into his arms, cupping my bump. "I don't think they're fake contractions, baby." Nodding, I buried my face in his chest. He held me, hands stroking my back, and I sank into the comfort, letting him hold me up.

My husband swayed me back and forth, the two of us standing there until I felt a small gush of water between my legs.

"*Nicolas.*" I gasped, looking down at my feet. I was wearing a sundress since the weather was finally nice outside again, but I *knew* what had just happened.

He frowned. "What?"

I squeezed my eyes shut. "My water just broke."

Nic smoothed his hand over my forehead as he helped me to the bathroom. "You're in labor, gorgeous. The *real* kind."

I bit my lip. "Yeah."

"You're still only thirty-eight weeks," he whispered, shaking his head as he rushed to the closet. "I thought we had more time."

Another contraction hit, this one more painful than the last. I tried to breathe through it, but let out a groan. "*Tell that to your son,*" I bit out as he came back. "Because he seems really eager to come out *now.*" I slumped as the pain subsided.

"We need to get to the hospital," he told me, pressing his lips to my forehead. "Your bag is all ready to go?"

I nodded. "It's in the closet."

"I'll grab it, and then we can head to the car. Do you want to change before we go?" He held up a pair of clean clothes.

"Mmm, yes. Good call."

"Come on, then, baby momma. Let's get you dry and comfy, and then let's go have a baby."

He held out his hand to me, and I slipped my fingers through his, knowing there was no one in the world I'd rather be doing this with.

31
nicolas

"Y ou're doing so good," I told my wife, pressing my lips against her sweaty forehead. "Just a little more, and he'll be here."

The nurses nodded as I put another ice chip up to her lips, encouraging her to suck on it.

"I can't do it," Zofia cried. "I'm so tired, Nic. I just want to rest."

Her labor had hit her hard and fast, surprising all of us. By the time we'd gotten to the hospital, there had been no time for an epidural, much to Zo's disappointment.

She was a fucking superwoman, going through all of this. I suddenly understood the concept of push presents, and didn't understand why any man didn't praise his woman for giving birth. She deserved to be doted on, hand and foot.

Which was why I was currently behind her, letting her rest her back against me, supporting her every step of the way. Her hand gripped mine tighter as another contraction hit, and I didn't even care if she broke it. I was here for her in any way she needed me.

"Just a few more pushes, Zofia. You're doing great, love. Give us another big one."

"You can do it," I murmured in her ear. "You heard her. Just a few more, and our son will be in your arms, and then you can rest."

Zo let out a strangled cry as she pushed. She shook her head, tears streaming from her eyes. "I can't *believe* you did this to me," she said, exasperated.

"I'm sorry," I told her as she squeezed my hands. "If I could take your pain away, you know I would."

"This is all your fault," she groaned. "*Fuck*, it hurts so bad."

The nurse smiled. "The head's almost out. Take a breath, and then on the next contraction, I want you to give one more big push for us."

She nodded, my perfect, brave wife, and when the next one hit, bore down, squeezing my hands until my skin was practically white with her effort.

"Breathe," I reminded her as she grunted. "Just like we practiced."

She let out a whimper, a strangled cry that made me want nothing more than to wrap her up and do whatever I could for her, but I knew that being here, right now, was what she needed more than anything.

"That's it," the nurse said. "Last push, and he'll be out."

Zofia slumped against me, her head resting on my shoulder, as a cry broke free in the room.

"It's a boy," the doctor said, smiling at both of us.

Then, he was placed on Zofia's chest, where he immediately quieted, lulled by the allure of his mother's arms. I knew the feeling well.

Tears streamed down her eyes as she looked at our son.

"You were so perfect," I told her. "Look at what you did, bringing our son into the world." She looked back at me, and I pressed a soft kiss to her lips. "Our little miracle. Fuck, I'm so proud of you."

She smiled, brushing a finger over his cheek. "He's ours."

I felt choked up. "Yeah, he is, baby."

The nurses and doctor let us have our little moment as a family before turning to me.

"Dad, do you want to cut the cord, and then we can clean baby up before we do some skin to skin?"

I nodded. "Yes. Absolutely."

I knew in my heart, for the rest of my life, that I'd do whatever I could for the little man in front of me. His mom was already my everything, and I knew without a doubt that he was going to be my entire world.

"He's perfect," I murmured, running a finger over our newborn son's perfectly chubby cheek. He was eight pounds, nine ounces, and twenty-one inches long—already a big boy, though that wasn't surprising, since neither Zofia nor I were short. I swept the hair off her forehead to press my lips against it. "And so are you, gorgeous." She closed her eyes as I rested my forehead against hers. "Thank you."

My wife had him cradled in her arms, already suckling from her breast like a pro. The lactation consultant had dropped by soon after delivery, helping Zofia and showing her how to get the baby to latch.

"For pushing your giant baby out of my vagina? You're welcome," Zofia snorted.

"No," I told her, looking down at her in awe. "For marrying me. For *loving* me. For this. Our son, our family." My voice was choked up, and I blinked back the tears. "I'm in awe of you every day, but especially today."

"Just as long as you don't expect me to do this again any time soon."

I laughed. "I'm happy with our family, even if he's our only. You and our son are all I need, Zofia." I meant it, too.

I loved the idea of a daughter, of a little girl that was just like Zo, but she was in the driver's seat. There was no way I'd ever force her to go through that again if she didn't want to.

"What should we name him?" I asked, both of us staring down at his chubby little face. "I know we were back and forth between a few names, but…"

She looked up at me, her brown eyes holding mine. "He looks like a Xander, doesn't he?"

I swallowed roughly. "You want to name him after *me?*" Alexander was my middle name—and my father's before that.

"Yeah." Zo bit her lip. "Do you hate it? Because if you do…"

I shook my head. "I love it. I… are you sure?"

"I can think of nothing better than our son being named after the father who's going to show him just how loved he is, every single day."

"Alexander," I whispered, letting his tiny hand wrap round my finger as he looked up at me with his big eyes.

"Alexander Saran Larsen," she murmured.

I grinned. "My dad's going to lose his mind," I told her.

She gave me a sad smile. "Maybe he'll be a better grandparent than he ever was a dad."

"One can hope."

But none of that mattered to me. Not when I had her—had the family I'd never thought to dream of but had always craved. The life I'd desperately wanted, ever since we'd said *I do*.

"Can you take him?" She asked, yawning sleepily after Xander detached from her breast, looking a little milk drunk.

Carefully, I cradled him in my arms, unable to look away from him. He was like the perfect blend of both of us—Zo's nose, and an entire head of hair, just like I'd had when I was born.

"Sleep," I whispered. "You deserve it."

After burping him, just like we'd been shown, I set a sleeping Xander down in the little bassinet, watching as Zo's eyes slowly drifted shut.

I smiled, watching the two most important people in my life sleep, and wondered how I'd ever thought I didn't want this life.

After a visit from Zo's parents, who were ecstatic to meet their new grandson, we were officially being discharged. As I packed up the last of our things into the bags, I zipped them shut, turning to my wife. "Ready to go home, gorgeous?"

Her eyelashes fluttered as she looked down at our baby in her arms. "They're really going to let us take him, aren't they?"

I chuckled. "Yes."

"But we have no idea what we're doing."

"I read the books," I reminded her.

She blinked. "We have no idea what we're doing," she repeated.

I laughed. "We'll be fine, Zo. You kept him safe for nine months inside you. I think we can manage a brief car ride before we show him his new home."

Zofia cradled him against her. "I'm terrified," she admitted.

"Me too." I knew she needed to be vulnerable right now—for me to be vulnerable too. "We made a whole little person, Zo, and now we have to take care of him. Love him. Mold him into a good man. But as scary as it is, it's going to be the best adventure, too. You know why?"

She shook her head. "Why?"

"Because we're in it together," I told her. "Every step of the way."

Every last one of them.
And I didn't need a contract to tell me that.

nicolas

Z o?" I asked, straightening my tie as I cleaned up a bin of our toddler's toys off the living room floor, just getting home from my day at the office.

"In here!"

I poked my head into her office, which also functioned as her library and reading room, finding her sitting in front of her computer, face furrowed in concentration.

"Hi." I pressed a kiss to her lips. "What are you working on?"

"Finalizing the contract for the venue for this fundraiser. It needs to get done before end of day."

While some days I missed Zofia being my assistant, I had to admit she'd thrived in her position planning events for our company, and our community outreach had greatly improved since she'd started it. Even better was that she got to be home with our son, making her own schedule and working part-time hours. Of course, she still came in to the office when she wanted to—or for any important meetings—and her parents were more than happy to babysit Alexander when that happened. In fact, I think they wished Zo would come back full time, if only so they could have more time with their grandson.

Though as much as she loved planning events, I'd never seen a role that made her smile more than being a mother.

I watched her as she finished up, a look of concentration as she finished typing, and then slid her chair back, looking up at me. "All done."

"Perfect. Where's Xander?" Our house was too quiet.

She chuckled. "My mom came and picked him up to take him to the park. Before they left, he asked if you would read to him tonight."

I smiled. "He takes after you more and more every day." I loved that our son was already a little bookworm, three years old and adoring when we'd read to him.

"Good. We don't need to have a little heartbreaker on our hands if he takes after you."

Crossing my arms, I pouted at her. "Hey. Not fair. You love me."

"Of course I do, honey." Standing up, she wrapped her arms around my neck. "But that doesn't change the past."

I kissed her again, deeper this time. "I happen to love our past."

She hummed against my lips. "Me too."

"Smartest thing I ever did was asking you to marry me."

It was our fourth wedding anniversary next week. Four years since we'd eloped in Vegas, and though we'd had a ceremony on the same day, a year later, we both preferred our private, intimate ceremony, because it was when we'd began.

Even after all this time, I'd never gotten over how much I loved calling her my wife.

She laughed. "Is that how it happened? You'll have to remind me."

"Oh, you love being reminded, do you?" I slid my hands

under her thighs, lifting her up into my arms. "Do you want me to remind you how you're mine?"

Her eyes fluttered. "Yes, *boss.*"

Fuck me. Even after all this time, something about that still drove me wild. "You're the best thing that ever happened to me," I told her as I carried her to our bedroom. "Thank God you agreed to being my assistant."

"It had its perks. Mainly, I got to work with the most hand-some man every day. And he was constantly reminding me just how much he needed me." She smoothed a strand of hair back off my forehead as I set her on our bed. Carefully, delicately—she was carrying precious cargo.

"I followed you around like a puppy back then," I admitted, pressing kisses to her cheeks. "It was so hard to stay away from you even before Napa."

She smiled, no doubt thinking of our trip this spring. We took a long weekend off work to explore, leaving Xander with his grandparents. It was our first non-work trip away from him since he'd been born, and they'd insisted we needed some alone time for just us.

I was pretty sure it was all just an ulterior motive for them to get another grandchild, but neither of us had complained.

And somehow, neither of us had been surprised when the pregnancy test was positive the next month.

I slid my hand up her leg, resting it on her thigh. "So we're completely alone for the rest of the afternoon?"

Zofia bit her lip. "Yes."

"Mmm." I pressed my forehead to hers. "Good."

Tugging her blouse off, I exposed her pretty lace bra. She'd long since stopped nursing, but I swore her tits were already huge again.

I cupped her bump, pressing my lips to the swell of her belly, loving that she was already showing. "How did our girl treat you today?"

"You don't know that it's a girl yet," she said, furrowing her brow at me. "It could be a boy again."

I grinned. We'd had this conversation ever since she'd gotten pregnant. "I just have a feeling, Gorgeous. She's a girl." And even if it was another boy, I'd love him just as fiercely. "So fucking pretty, carrying my baby again."

Her eyes heated, and I knew what she needed. I stripped out of my top, loving the feeling as her eyes roved down my torso. Even as a dad, I stayed in shape, if only because I loved the way Zo ran her fingers over my abs, practically drooling over my naked body.

She lifted her hips, helping me remove her pants, and I dropped to my knees in front of her. Pressing my face against her entrance, I nuzzled against her inner thigh, pressing soft kisses to the sensitive skin.

"Nicolas," she whimpered as I delved my tongue through her entrance, lapping up her arousal.

"Shhh, baby," I said, spreading her legs wider for me. "You deserve a reward for working so hard all day. And I'm going to give it to you." I gave her a wicked grin before I sucked her clit into my mouth, giving her the stimulation I knew drove her wild.

After all the years together, I loved how I knew every inch of her body, how I could make her climax hit fast or drag it out, bringing her to the edge over and over before finally letting her come.

Today, though, I wanted to feel her fall apart as I was buried deep inside of her. I slid a finger inside, feeling her warmth surround me. "So fucking wet for me."

She groaned as I thrust my finger into her, sliding a second one in as I twirled my tongue around her clit. Zofia let out a cry, and I unzipped my pants, pulling out my cock before plunging inside her. She spasmed around my length, both of us letting out a groan as I filled her.

"Feels so good," she said, wrapping her legs around me, forcing me in deeper. "Don't stop."

"Never," I promised her.

Zo's head fell back as I started fucking her in earnest, both of us needing it fast, hard. With a toddler, alone time was practically its own form of currency in our household, and I was not going to waste a single moment.

"Come for me, Gorgeous," I groaned against her ear, feeling her tighten around me. "Come all over my cock, and I'll fill you up."

"Ohmygod," she cried as I pressed my thumb against her clit, rubbing it in a circle as I gave her the pressure she needed.

As if it was the catalyst she needed to finish, she came, clenching around my length. It set off my own, releasing every spurt inside her. When we both came down, breathing roughly, we were still holding on to each other. Pulling out, I watched as my cum dripped out of her before scooping it up with my fingers and pressing it back inside her. "Where it belongs."

She gave me a heated look that had me wanting to take her again. "I should ask my mom to watch Xander more often if that's the result," she said, letting out a small giggle.

I nipped at her ear. "It's only going to get harder once we have two."

"Bring it on," she smiled. "More chaos, maybe. But also, more love."

Brushing her hair back from her face, I pressed my lips to her forehead. "More happiness."

"I can't imagine being any happier than I am now," she admitted. "You've given me everything I've ever wanted, Nicolas. A job I love, that brings me so much fulfillment. A family to cherish. A husband who dotes on me and treats me like a queen."

"Because you are." I picked her up, carrying her towards our bathroom.

She gave me a look. "We don't have time to go again before mom brings Xander back."

I smirked. "Wanna bet?"

zofia

"There's my big boy," I said as Xander ran straight towards us, his dark brown hair flopping in the wind. "I missed you so much."

"Amma!" He wrapped his arms around me, and I hugged my son, before he attacked Nic. "Appa!"

My heart was so full as my husband lifted him up into his arms, tickling his stomach.

"Did you have fun today, buddy?" Nicolas asked our son as he pulled tugged on his Star Wars t-shirt. It was his favorite, and we practically had to fight him to get him to wear anything else.

I looked up at my mom, who was carrying his backpack. "Thank you again for watching him."

"Of course, Kutti. You know how much I love spending time with Xander." She stepped forward, ruffling my son's hair. "Anytime."

I hugged her, and we chatted a bit before heading back inside. Nic headed to the kitchen, and I got Xander cleaned up before getting him set at the table with a coloring book and some crayons.

Then, I slid into the kitchen, wrapping my arms around my husband's waist.

"Smells good."

He grinned. "Thought I'd make your favorite." Over the years, he'd had my mom teach him how to make more traditional Tamil and Indian recipes, and I loved how much he wanted to bring my heritage into our home—and to ensure Alexander learned it too.

"You're the best." I kissed his cheek. "Thank you."

"Anything for you." He turned around, giving me a soft pat on the ass. "Now go sit down and let me cook. You deserve to rest."

I grumbled. "It's not like you weren't also working all day."

He glared at me. "I'm not three months pregnant, either."

Crossing my arms over my chest, I pouted at him. "I'm *barely* pregnant. And besides, the first trimester nausea has finally gone away. I feel better than I have in weeks."

He poked my forehead, softly pushing me out of the kitchen. "Sit down. I want to take care of my family. Let me."

With a sigh, I finally relented, sliding onto a barstool at the island, watching Nic's back as he stood at the stove, the familiar scents of beloved spices filling the room.

Duchess jumped up on the chair next to me, letting out a soft purr as I ran my hands over her spine. "Such a sweet girl," I whispered to my cat—the cat who had been through everything with me. "My pretty princess kitty, huh?" I scratched under her chin.

Nic chuckled. "She's so spoiled."

I raised an eyebrow, looking at Cooper, curled up under Nic's feet—waiting for him to drop any morsel of food. "You were saying?"

He shrugged. "No comment."

I shook my head, laughing. "You're going to spoil our little girl just as much, aren't you?"

My husband's face transformed. "So you admit you think it's a girl?"

"I didn't say *that*." But I loved the idea of a little girl running around our house—especially since I'd no longer be outnumbered. "I'm just saying, it's too early to *know*."

"Not if we do one of those blood tests." He leaned against the counter. "Didn't Matthew and Noelle do one when they were pregnant with Penelope?"

I furrowed my eyebrows. "Well, yeah. But sometimes they're wrong. And I kind of liked how we found out before at the ultrasound." Turning to look at Xander, who was quiet as he focused on the coloring page, I turned back to Nic. "But if you want to… let's do it."

"Really?" He raised an eyebrow. "What's changed your mind?"

"Honestly, the idea of proving you wrong," I laughed. "If it's a boy, I'm holding it over your head *forever*."

"And if it's a girl?" He raised an eyebrow.

I bit my lip, thinking. "Then… you can pick her name."

"Deal." He grinned. "But I'm right, Gorgeous. Just you wait and see." He pulled me out of my chair, twirling me into his arms and swaying me slightly in the kitchen. "And you're right. She's going to be so spoiled."

"What if it is another boy?" I asked. "Do you want to keep trying until we have a girl?" I knew how badly he wanted one, but as much as I loved our family, I wasn't sure I wanted more than two.

He shook his head, cupping my bump. "We got pretty damn lucky with the first one. Two boys or a boy and a girl, I'm happy. But if you want to, you just say the word."

I shook my head. "Two kids is perfect."

Nicolas laughed. "Good. Because I'm not sure I could keep up with three."

"You're still young," I teased him, patting his six-pack. "You should have more energy."

My husband rolled his eyes. "I'm only two years younger than you," he grumbled. "And you never let me forget that."

I stepped up onto my toes, kissing his cheek. "Who would have thought I'd fall in love with my younger, attractive boss?"

He just rubbed his nose against mine. "Everyone, Zo. Because contract or not, we were *meant to be.*"

"I love you," I whispered against his mouth.

"I love you more, gorgeous."

Contractually mine, and I never once regretted it. Because all of that brought us here.

Right to this moment, in the kitchen with our son—and, as it turned out—our daughter in my belly.

Because of course he was right.

He always had been.

I'd just had to give him a chance.

extended epilogue

zofia

"We're going to be late!" I shouted, standing at the garage door, waiting for the rest of my family to come down the stairs so we could head out. "Everyone almost ready to go?"

The bags were already packed in the car, including the presents we'd bought and wrapped last week.

Today was the twins' eighth birthday party. Angelina and Benjamin were throwing it at their house, and I was excited to see my girls. We still hung out all the time—but nowadays, it was normally while our kids played together. While our book club had changed, I didn't think I would have made it through either of my pregnancies or parenthood without them.

It was nice knowing I had such a strong support system in all of them.

"Sorry, Mommy," Bianca said, traipsing down the stairs as she smoothed her hand over her dark brown curls. Her turquoise eyes—her dad's color—were big as they met mine.

"Daddy was helping me look for my goggles." She was wearing a ruffly sage green sundress, one we'd picked out together the night before.

Our daughter was six, and some days it still amazed me how Nic had been right all along about her being a girl. He loved our son, but watching him dote on our daughter was something else entirely. He was the best partner I could have ever asked for, and the best father to our two kids.

My husband followed behind her, holding up said swimming goggles. The Sullivans had put in a pool, and the kids loved swimming in it during the summer.

I sighed, knowing we'd told them to pack everything last night. "Where's Xander?"

"Right here." My nine year old was next, wearing a blue button up and jeans. He was already well over five feet tall, and I wouldn't be surprised if he ended up taller than his dad when he finished growing. "Sorry, Amma. I told Zach I'd bring over my game to show him next time." He had a handheld console in his hand.

"Alright, in the car, everyone. Let's go."

"You're excited," Nic said, pressing his lips to my cheek before he headed into the garage.

"More like cooped up," I muttered. Summer vacation with two kids who were way too smart for their own good was a constant challenge, especially when I had my own work to get done.

Nic helped Bee into the car before opening my door for me—same as he'd always done. Chivalry was alive and well in the Larsen household. He was even teaching Alexander to always hold the door open for us—with varying levels of success, depending on his level of attentiveness. Our son was a good kid, but he was still only nine, and sometimes was more involved in his Pokémon game than in his mom or sister.

I cut him slack, considering he helped with the dishes and

kept his room clean, and I never had to ask him to do his homework.

Our drive to the Sullivan's house wasn't too long, thankfully not running into too much traffic as we drove across town.

When we piled out of the car, the kids immediately took off towards the backyard as Nic and I grabbed the bags from the trunk.

Nic wrapped an arm around me, tugging me into his side as we walked in the front door, finding our friends all congregated in the kitchen.

"Hey." I grinned. "Sorry we're a little late."

"Bianca couldn't find her goggles," Nicolas said, chuckling.

Hunter shook his head. "I know the feeling." Their daughter, Quinlan, was almost a year older than ours, and she *loved* the outdoors. Maybe because her parents also loved adventures and hiking, but I'd never seen a kid so at home in the wilderness.

"It's no biggie," Angelina said, coming over to give me a hug. "We figured we'd let the kids all play outside for awhile before we do cake and presents."

There was a hoard of kids running around the backyard, including a few I could see in the bounce house. Bianca was gathered with Ellie, Penelope and Quinlan. As the youngest girls, they were often all together, and it made me smile, feeling like we were growing a second generation of best friends.

This was our second family, and I never took for granted how they'd included me, or how loved I felt being a member of the group.

"So, they talked you into the bounce house, did they?" Nic asked Benjamin, who let out a long sigh.

Angelina smirked. "They knew they had him when they showed him the Batman one." He was Benjamin's favorite superhero, and they'd gone all out with the theme of the party, decorating it like Batman and Robin.

"Yup," he agreed, kissing his wife's cheek. "They love to

gang up on me. That's why this one has to play bad cop." Angelina rolled her eyes, pulling out of his arms and going over to the fridge.

Because my husband was a total golden retriever, I totally understood it. I laughed.

"Everyone grab a drink, and we can hang outside," Angelina said. "Then Hunt's going to grill in a bit. The boys requested it."

Gabbi patted him on the shoulder. "Uncle duties."

He shrugged. "I'm better at it than Ben, so honestly, valid."

"*Hey.*" His brother frowned.

Our gatherings were always like this—full of good natured teasing and riffing on each other. It was crazy to think I'd known them all for twelve years. Nic and I were celebrating our eleventh wedding anniversary in August, and I couldn't believe how fast the time had gone.

We followed everyone outside, each grabbing a beverage from the fridge.

"How are we going to top this?" I muttered to my husband, looking around the yard as I sipped my drink.

Nic bent his head. "Yeah, especially since this is the big *one-zero.*"

"I can't believe he's almost ten," I said, watching as Xander crossed the yard towards Abigail, Charlotte and Daniel's oldest daughter. "It feels like I blinked. He's so grown up."

Charlotte, who was standing nearby, nodded. "I know. I miss when they were tiny." They'd had three of their own—Abigail, followed by their son, Beau, and then their daughter, Ellie. "Now we're dealing with three different schedules, and I feel like I'm losing my mind."

I laughed. "Yeah. It's only going to get worse, I think." Alexander was more into academics than sports, but Bianca loved singing and spent a lot of hours in vocal lessons."

We both watched as my son handed her oldest daughter a

flower—where he'd found it, I wasn't sure, but Abigail smiled, tucking it behind her ear.

We were too far away to hear their conversation, but it seemed sweet. They'd always been friends—especially since they were the two oldest.

"Aww." Charlotte placed her hand over her heart. "They're adorable."

"They really are."

Our kids were all staples in each other's lives, thanks to our strong friendships. We all helped each other with the kids, from hosting sleepovers and letting them hang out after school if one of us needed it. It made this parenting thing a lot easier. Plus, how many people could say that their friends' parents were also friends?

If it hadn't been for Nic being friends with Angelina since college, and me befriending the girls, I doubted we'd have this group of friends that felt more like a family.

Of course, my kids were close to their cousins, too. We spent a ton of time with both of my brothers and their kids, and I loved teaching them more about their background at their grandparents' house.

Bianca came up to me, her hair already wild from being in the bounce house. "Amma, can I give Wesley his present now?"

I looked at Angelina, who nodded. "Sure, sweetie. It's just inside in my bag, if you want to go grab it."

She'd picked out Wes's gift herself. Anytime the twins were together, they were troublemakers, but individually, Zachary was the jokester and the mastermind of pranks, while Wesley was the quieter one.

I'd often find Wes and Bianca in a quiet corner, reading books or playing on their handheld consoles.

My daughter went inside, coming back out holding the wrapped present.

"Hi," Bianca said, holding out the present to Wesley. "This is for you. Happy Birthday." She smiled at him, so shy and sweet, and my heart clenched.

"Thank you," he said, a small blush blooming on his cheekbones. He looked at his mom. "Should I open it now?"

Angelina nodded. "If you want to, I'm okay with it."

He gave an eager nod before turning back to my daughter, tearing into the wrapping paper.

"It's a music player," she said, beaming. "Since I know you love mine so much."

"Oh, wow. This is so cool."

"I picked it out," Bianca admitted, looking a little shy. "Xander found the gift for Zach, so I got to choose yours."

"Thanks, Bee," Wesley said, grinning. "I can't wait to play with it." He handed it to Angelina. "Mom, can you keep it safe? I don't want someone to break it out here."

"Of course, bud. You go play now, and then we'll bring out the cake, okay?"

She took it from him, and he hugged her, grinning. "Thanks, Mom. You're the best."

Angelina patted him on the back. "Glad someone thinks so," she muttered, glaring at her husband.

He held up his hands in surrender.

There was a gaggle of kids gathered around the table that held the Batman themed cake, excited for Angelina to cut it. Though I loved cake, I wasn't looking forward to the stains that would come from the black frosting.

I leaned on my husband's shoulder, happy to just watch all the kids having a good time. Twisting my wedding ring on my finger, I looked up at him. "Do you ever think about how different our lives would be if we'd never signed that contract?"

"All the time," he admitted, watching our two kids dive into their cake.

"Really?"

"Uh-huh. But not in the way you're thinking." I frowned, and he kissed my forehead. "I think that even if we hadn't, I still would have found a way to make you mine. We were inevitable, Zo. One way or another, those two little ones would have come into our lives, changing everything for the better." He wrapped an arm around me, hugging me tight. "You showed me I could have everything I wanted; I just needed to fight for it. That it didn't have to be the way I always imagined it to have the life I'd always dreamed of." Nic tucked a strand of hair behind my ear. "Losing my mom when I was younger and having my dad always working made me worry if I could be a good father, but from the moment I held Xander in my arms, I knew I'd do anything for him."

"You are," I told him, wrapping my arms around his neck. "You're the best dad."

He grinned, his hands resting on my waist. "And you're an amazing mother. Just like I knew you'd be." He flicked my nose, and I wiggled it at him.

"I love you. Thank you for asking me to marry you." I pressed my finger into the spot between his eyebrows, smoothing out the creases. "I've never regretted that, honey. Not for one moment."

"Not even when you found out I'd gotten you pregnant, and you thought I didn't want to have kids with you?"

Poking at his chest, I frowned. "Don't remind me of that, husband."

He just smiled. "I've loved you for a long time, wife, and I plan to love you for the rest of our lives."

"You better," I said, chuckling as he pressed a soft kiss to my lips.

He wagged his eyebrows. "Tonight, I'll remind you just how much."

Another promise—a lifetime full of ones he'd always kept.

"*Ewww*, Dad," Xander said, catching us sharing another kiss. "Gross."

Nicolas laughed. "It's my job to remind your mom just how much I love her. Every single day."

My heart filled with warmth as his eyes met mine, full of so much love.

"For better or for worse."

I smiled. "But somehow, it's always *for better* when we're together."

And that was why I'd fallen in love with him in the first place.

My coworker, who became my boss.

The boss who became my friend.

And the friend who became my husband.

My everything.

"Forever," he promised me.

And I knew it was one he'd never break.

The End.

acknowledgments

Four years ago, when I was just starting to write the Best Friends Book Club series, I had no idea how my life would change over the next few years. Now, I'm publishing my fifteenth novel, and when I tell you I struggled a lot with this one. Zofia and Nic have always been two characters I loved, ever since they first came on the page in Disrespectfully Yours. Which was why I knew if I was going to give them a book, I wanted it to be *good*. They deserved a great plot, a great story, and for a long time, I struggled with what that would be. Revisiting the BFBC universe these last few releases meant I got to spend more time with the first characters I ever fell in love with, and I truly felt like home being back with them.

This one was one of the hardest books I've ever written, and I'm so proud of myself for finishing it and bringing Nic and Zo to life.

To Joni, who sensitivity read for this novel, I cannot thank you enough!! For answering all of my questions to giving me such helpful answers with such thoughtful care. I'm so glad to have you on my team and even more grateful that you said yes to helping me bring Zofia to light in a way that brought love and respect to her heritage—and yours.

To Cat, Hannah, and Olivia: thank you for putting up with endless texts, questions, and all of my worries that this book was going to suck. I love you and am so glad to call you all my best friends. I don't know what I would do without you.

To Meagan, my girl: thank you for always being in my corner— you know I'm always in yours. I love you so much and don't know what I'd do without our daily texts, phone calls, and I wish you were closer so I could hug you on a daily basis.

To my agent, Valentine: thank you thank you thank you for literally being the best. Don't know what I would do without you!! I'm so excited for everything we have planned.

To my family, and especially my mom: thank you for always supporting me, loving me, and bragging about me to everyone you know (even when it embarrasses me and I beg you not to). I truly think I got so lucky to have a family that is willing to travel just about anywhere to come with me to book events.

To my readers, always: thank you. I love you. I am so glad you're here with me on this crazy ride.

also by jennifer chipman

paranormal romance

Witches of Pleasant Grove

Spookily Yours - Willow & Damien

Wickedly Yours - Luna & Zain

Bewitchingly Hers - Eryne & Barrett

Eternally His - Rina & Ezra (coming fall 2026)

Hauntingly Hers - Wendy & Cassius (coming winter 2026)

contemporary romance

Best Friends Book Club

Academically Yours - Noelle & Matthew

Disrespectfully Yours - Angelina & Benjamin

Fearlessly Yours - Gabrielle & Hunter

Gracefully Yours - Charlotte & Daniel

Contractually Mine - Zofia & Nicolas

Famously Mine - Tessa & Oliver

Merrily Mine - Emily & Mason

Cousins Coffee Club

(Best Friends Book Club Second Generation)

Uniquely in Love - Ellie & Owen

A North Pole Christmas

Elfemies to Lovers - Ivy & Teddy

about the author

Originally from the Portland area, Jennifer now lives in Orlando with her dog, Walter and cat, Max. In her free time, you can find her with her nose in a book or going to the Disney Parks. She loves writing romance heroes who fall first and hard for their women. Jennifer writes Contemporary Romance, Paranormal Romance, and Sci-Fi Romance.

Website: www.jennchipman.com

amazon.com/author/jenniferchipman
goodreads.com/jennchipman
instagram.com/jennchipmanauthor
facebook.com/jennchipmanauthor
x.com/jennchipman
tiktok.com/@jennchipman
pinterest.com/jennchipmanauthor

www.ingramcontent.com/pod-product-compliance
Lightning Source LLC
Chambersburg PA
CBHW051501030726
47592CB00006B/2042